RAVES FOR THE NOVELS
OF PETE HAUTMAN

Mrs. Million

"*MRS. MILLION* is a hot-dog-at-the-ballgame book: You can't believe you ate it; you can't believe you ate it so fast; you probably could eat another one."

—*San Diego Union-Tribune*

"Fun and engaging. Read it for the heroine who is tough, sensitive, and entangled in a family she both loves and hates."

—*Newsday* (New York)

"*MRS. MILLION* is a heck of a fun novel and deliciously written, too."

—*Omaha World-Herald* (NE)

"A winding and surprisingly satisfying story. . . . This book is a sweet-dizzy ride that shows Hautman is one of those rare authors who can love his characters while laughing at them."

—*Detroit Free Press*

"A fabulous tale that will thrill readers who relish an offbeat novel. The story line never lets up, but as in all of Hautman's delicious books, the eccentric characters control the plot . . . and bring a brilliant mystery to life."

—*Midwest Book Review*

"The tale is outrageous and decidedly funny with a tightly drawn plot, suspense and even violence. . . . The whole thing has a wonderful lunatic tinge that brings crime fiction to a near hysterical level."

—*Baton Rouge Magazine* (LA)

SHORT MONEY

"Exhilarating. . . . By turns funny and soulful and always unpredictable. . . . Hautman's dialogue sparkles, his plot hums, he's got a nicely complex sense of morality and he's a virtuoso when it comes to describing what it feels like to get punched."

—Publishers Weekly

"Hautman reminds me most of Carl Hiaasen, the Florida author who combines action, comedy, and mystery in outrageous ways."

—Albuquerque Journal (NM)

DRAWING DEAD

"A rollicking crime caper. . . . Brilliant enough to dazzle the likes of Joe Gores and Elmore Leonard."

—The New York Times Book Review

"Hautman keeps the plot moving at an exhilarating pace. The people are unexpected, the dialogue is terrific, and the descriptions are laugh-out-loud funny. Bawdy, gritty, and unpredictable, *Drawing Dead* is a sparkling debut."

—The Wall Street Journal

"The year's best American debut was this rambunctious tale of hoodlums, gamblers, con artists, real-estate hustlers, gold-digging bimbos, and crooked stockbrokers."

—Atlanta Journal-Constitution

Books by Pete Hautman

Drawing Dead*
Short Money*
The Mortal Nuts*
Mr. Was
Ring Game*
Mrs. Million*

*Published by POCKET BOOKS

PETE HAUTMAN

Mrs. Million

A NOVEL

POCKET BOOKS

NEW YORK   LONDON   TORONTO   SYDNEY   SINGAPORE

This book is a work of fiction. Names, characters, places and incidents
are products of the author's imagination or are used fictitiously. Any
resemblance to actual events or locales or persons, living or dead, is entirely
coincidental.

POCKET BOOKS, a division of Simon & Schuster Inc.
1230 Avenue of the Americas, New York, NY 10020

Copyright © 1999 by Pete Hautman
Originally published in hardcover in 1999 by Simon & Schuster Inc.

Library of Congress Cataloging-in-Publication Data

Hautman, Pete, 1952–
   Mrs. Million / Pete Hautman.
     p. cm.
   ISBN 0-671-03865-6
   1. Lottery winners–Fiction. 2. Runaway husbands–Fiction. I. Title.

   PS3558.A766 M77 2000
   813'.54–dc21   99-052911

First Pocket Books trade paperback printing March 2000

10 9 8 7 6 5 4 3 2 1

POCKET and colophon are registered trademarks of
Simon & Schuster Inc.

Cover design by Tom McKeveny

Printed in the U.S.A.

FOR MARYLOUISE

Dear Mr. King,

I recently read your book MISERY and it changed my life.

Previous to reading MISERY I was deep in a Clinical Depression. My doctor prescribed Prozac but it made me sick. Also it was expensive. But the fact that I still have the use of my arms after the motorcycle accident where I ran off the road to avoid hitting a bus filled with innocent schoolchildren is a good thing. Life was very hard, for me after they amputated my legs, but all the innocent children survived!!!

After my accident I struggled hard to find a purpose in life to go on living. The Clinical Depression made me extremely suicidal so I decided to take an overdose of drugs. But then I read your excellent and profound book, MISERY. Once I read MISERY I knew that life was worth living if only to read your other books. You are not merely Talented, you are a Great Writer!!! Maybe you know that already. I am inspired to read your other books. Unfortunatly, I am on an extremely limited budget. No one will hire me as I am a cripple now and the amount of money I get from also getting wounded fighting Saddam in the Gulf War is very poor. I hardly get enough for food and rent.

Do you have any extra copies of any of your inspiring books? Preferably with your signature? I would be extremely grateful if you could spare some. Or if not, if you would send a donation in any amount, I could afford to buy them myself.

> Admiringly,
> Your biggest fan!!!
> Jonathan James Morrow

Mrs. Million

1

When Barbaraannette Quinn heard the Powerball numbers come over the radio she was busy decorating a Cowboy Cake for her niece, spelling out "Brittany" in pink script beneath a peanut-butter-frosting rendering of a cowboy hat.

She was giving this cake her all because she could still remember her own seventh birthday party. Her mother had served Hostess chocolate cupcakes with the little corkscrew of icing on top. No candles. Her birthday present that year had been a *Star Trek* metal lunchbox. She still had it. According to *Schroeder's Antiques Price Guide*, it was worth more than five hundred dollars, but what she remembered most was that she had not gotten a real birthday cake.

Barbaraannette did not know how her niece had become interested in cowboys. Possibly some old *Bonanza* rerun off the satellite dish. She hoped the girl would outgrow them. Cowboys were trouble.

But this year Britty would get her cake, a three-layer devil's food covered with dark brown chocolate frosting and topped with a peanut butter cowboy hat and her name in pink frosting, all surrounded by a peanut butter frosting lasso. Barbaraannette would have drawn a horse, too, but she did not think her artistic skills were up to it.

When she heard the Powerball numbers coming over the radio—2, 4, 10, 19, 29, and 16—she stopped moving for several seconds, then took a breath and fitted a fluted nozzle onto her cake decorator and applied a pink scalloped ridge around the base of the cake. It wasn't an authentic cowboy touch, but she had a lot of frosting left and besides, in addition to cowboys, Brittany adored all things pink.

The lottery numbers were interesting because 10-29, 2-19, and 4-16 were the birthdays of relatives, specifically, those of her sister Toagie, their mother, Hilde, and Toagie's daughter, Brittany. They were *especially* interesting because Barbaraannette always based her weekly Powerball numbers on family birthdays. But with two sisters, two nieces, and a nephew, she could not for the life of her remember whose birthdays she had chosen for her most recent ticket.

Barbaraannette set aside the cake decorator and regarded her work. Using the handle of a teaspoon, she touched up a stray glob of pink frosting. Brittany probably would not have noticed the tiny flaw, but there was no point in doing half a job.

The Powerball ticket she had purchased last Sunday at the Pump-n-Munch waited in the purse hanging from the knob on the kitchen door, not six feet from her elbow. Barbaraannette was powerfully curious to have a look at that ticket, but she took a few more minutes to press seventeen tiny cinnamon hearts into the band of the peanut butter cowboy hat. She knew that if she looked at that ticket now, and it was a winner, her hands would be shaking so hard she would never be able to finish decorating that cake. She placed the hearts carefully, spreading them out nice and even. Britty loved little cinnamon hearts.

After positioning the final heart, Barbaraannette washed her hands, then placed a clear plastic cake protector over her creation. She lifted her purse from the doorknob and fished the lottery ticket from the inside pocket. Before reading the numbers, she took one last look at the Cowboy Cake. Britty was going to love it.

2

Toagie Carlson stood in her sister's kitchen staring wordlessly at the Cowboy Cake beneath the sparkling plastic dome. Barbaraannette had outdone herself.

"Barbaraannette?" Toagie called. Her thin, ragged voice echoed through the house. No response. Strange. Toagie lifted the pack of Salems from the elastic waistband of her purple sweatpants and shook out a cigarette.

Barbaraannette, the cake, and Britty's birthday present from her mom and dad—this year a two-foot-tall barn Bill had built to house her plastic horse collection—were due at Britty's party in less than ten minutes. The toy horse barn was in Barbaraannette's garage, wrapped and ready to go, and so was the cake—but where was Barbaraannette? It wasn't like her to be anywhere other than where she was supposed to be. Toagie walked down the hall to her sister's bedroom and called out, "Barbaraannette? You in there?"

No reply. Very strange indeed, and a little frightening. Toagie fixed the unlit cigarette between her lips, stabbed her long fingers into her sprawling mop and clawed at her scalp. Her hair this week was the exact color of a not-quite-ripe banana, right down to the faint green highlights. Had Barbaraannette forgotten Britty's party? Not likely, what with that cake sitting so pretty on her kitchen counter. Had she forgotten that Toagie had planned to stop by and help her carry the cake and the toy barn to her house, one and one half blocks up the street, where Britty and her friends were waiting? Not Barbaraannette. Toagie returned to the kitchen, turned on one of the gas burners, lit her Salem, took a huge calming lungful of smoke. She raised her voice loud enough to penetrate every wall of the house.

"Barbaraannette!"

She listened, then heard a sound something like the peeping of a baby robin. But it was too early in the season for baby robins. Piles of dirty snow still dotted the street corners and the earth too frozen for worm-picking. Also, the sound seemed to be coming from the basement door, which she now noticed was cocked open. Toagie gripped her necklace, a collection of brightly colored exotic seeds strung on a nylon cord. Leaning into the stairwell she called out, "Barbaraannette, is that you down there?"

"I'm here," came Barbaraannette's quiet voice.

Toagie clomped down the stairs, necklace rattling, Salem clenched in her teeth. She found her sister sitting on an upended five-gallon bucket that had once contained Amway laundry detergent, her posture excellent as usual, blinking her eyes, staring at the chest freezer.

"Are you okay?" Toagie demanded.

Barbaraannette nodded, then said, "No."

Toagie knelt and looked up into her sister's face. Where Toagie's features were large, mobile, asymmetrical, and rather out of her control, Barbaraannette's were neatly arrayed and centered on her broad, Irish-looking face. Her mouth was small, but perfectly shaped. Her slightly upturned, almond-shaped eyes were an unusually deep shade of blue—they reminded Toagie of Tidy-Bowl. During the summer Barbaraannette would display a galaxy of freckles, but now, after a long winter, her ivory skin was smooth and unmarked but for a single lozenge-shaped mole high on her left cheek. Toagie thought her sister to be quite beautiful.

"B.A.? What's a matter, hon?" She felt scared. Barbaraannette was one of the cornerstones of Toagie's universe.

"What are you doing here?" asked Barbaraannette, blinking at the cloud of mentholated smoke that had accompanied Toagie down the steps.

"I came to help you carry the cake and horse barn, hon."

"Oh." Barbaraannette looked at Toagie and smiled. "Toag, I think I won it. Will you look and see if I really won it?"

"I don't know what you're talking about."

"I think I won the Powerball, Toag. I think I won it. I think I won the thing."

Toagie's mouth went slack and the cigarette dropped to the floor. She stood up and staggered back, catching herself on the freezer.

Barbaraannette's right foot ground out the burning cigarette. She said, "Look at the ticket for me, would you, Toag?"

Toagie said, "Ticket?" Numbness descended upon her.

"Just take one good look at it and tell me if the numbers are your birthday, Mama's, and Britty's."

Toagie blanked for a moment, then recalled her sister's custom of basing her lottery picks on family birthdays. "Where is it?" Toagie asked.

"I put it in the freezer."

"You froze it?" She turned and looked down at the white top of the chest freezer.

"After I looked at and saw the numbers I got scared. I didn't know what else to do, Toag. It's in a Tupperware marked 'hot dish.' "

"You put it in Tupperware? You *froze* it? Criminentlies, Barbaraannette, why'd you go and do that?"

Barbaraannette shook her head and smiled, her usually small mouth stretching across a third of her face. "I kept thinking, what if the house burns down? Then it came in my head to put it in the freezer to keep it safe, so that's what I did."

Toagie put her hand on the freezer handle. She looked back at her sister and said, "You know I think you're out of your fleeping mind, doncha?"

Barbaraannette's smile grew impossibly wider. "Toag, if those numbers are what I read them to be, I don't believe I give a damn what anybody thinks."

3

The longest hours of her life, Barbaraannette thought, were those spent at her niece's birthday party—seven shrieking sugar-charged kids—all the while feeling that Powerball ticket wrapped in Saran Wrap and stuck to her right buttock. Toagie had laughed at her when she'd stashed the ticket in her undies, but Barbaraannette had said, "It's nine million dollars, Toag. Shut up."

It took the girls two hours to play their games and open presents and eat their cake. Barbaraannette was too keyed up to eat any herself. She sat in a chair with the ticket stuck to her butt hoping her body heat wouldn't fade the numbers. She did her best to act interested when Britty showed off her presents but all she could think about was the time.

When she'd called the phone number on the ticket, the woman at the Minnesota State Lottery Headquarters in the Twin Cities, seventy miles from Cold Rock, told her she could bring it in anytime before 6:00 P.M. Otherwise she'd have to wait till Monday. Barbaraannette didn't think she could wait till Monday. She was afraid the ticket would somehow change, or be stolen, or that she would wake up. She was too nervous to drive herself, and she wasn't ready to share the news with anyone else, so she'd had to sit through Britty's party, waiting for Toagie. In that time she imagined several hundred things that might prevent her from realizing her good fortune.

They were now headed south on I-35 in Toagie's battered and sputtering minivan, twenty miles to go. Brittany curled up in the back, sleeping off her sugar buzz. Barbaraannette kept herself busy imagining a variety of fatal highway accidents. The way her sister drove, it was easy.

"What's the first thing you're gonna do?" Toagie asked, passing a Green Giant semi on the right.

Barbaraannette cringed, envisioning death beneath ten tons of frozen broccoli.

Toagie laughed. "You want to get there by six, right?" She swerved onto the shoulder to miss a dead skunk, then back into the right lane. "So what are you gonna do with the money?"

Barbaraannette willed her fingers to unclench. "I don't know, Toag." Her leg was cramping from stomping on a brake pedal that was not there.

"You gonna buy a new car?"

"My car's not that old."

"Well you have to buy *something*. I mean, jeez. All that money? Nine million? You know what I'd do? I'd buy a horse." A red car pulled out onto the freeway a quarter mile ahead. Barbaraannette pumped her imaginary brake pedal; Toagie sped up and switched lanes.

"I might invest it in something," Barbaraannette said. "Maybe buy some stocks. Buy some stock in Green Giant. Everybody eats broccoli."

"Bill doesn't," Toagie said, referring to her occasionally employed husband.

"Maybe I'll invest in a beer company, then."

Toagie laughed, but it sounded forced. Barbaraannette instantly regretted her comment. Things had been rough for Toagie and Bill the past few years.

"I don't know what I'm going to do, Toag. You know what I keep thinking, though? I keep thinking about Bobby."

"You think about Bobby way too much."

"I wonder what he'll think if he hears I got rich."

"He'll wish he'd never left you, that's for sure."

"I don't know." Barbaraannette called up an image of Bobby Quinn's face and felt the empty space he'd left inside her. "Six years, who knows what he's been doing. If he's even alive. I think about him sitting in some cabin in Alaska. He used to talk about Alaska a lot. He thought you could go there and find gold."

"He thought a lot of things. That man made my Bill look like the Rock of Gribalcher."

"Gibraltar."

"Whatever. If you can't get your mind off him maybe you oughta take some of that money and get yourself a shrink."

Barbaraannette looked out at the passing landscape, fields of black dirt, here and there a pile of snow. Not as much snow as they had up in Cold Rock, though. Spring came a week or two earlier to the Twin Cities.

She'd been thinking about Bobby a lot, lately. Maybe she should use some of the money to hire another private detective, try to find him, see if he wanted to come home. She'd tried it once before, but the guy had got nowhere, just wasted her money. The thought of Bobby returning set off a whirlwind of confused thoughts, memories of her wedding, Bobby's grin, his thick hair, making love, watching him sleep—Toagie was talking again, something about boats.

"What's that?" said Barbaraannette.

"I said, you could buy a boat."

"What would I want a boat for?" They had turned off the freeway—when had that happened?

"You could go sailing."

Barbaraannette shook her head. If Toagie had won the lottery the money would be gone by the end of the week. "It's supposed to be right up here," she said. "The woman said you could almost see it from the highway."

"There it is." Toagie pointed toward a glass-fronted two-story building. A sign affixed to the wide, white fascia read MINNESOTA STATE LOTTERY. She turned into the parking lot. A white van topped by a thirty-foot-high telescoping pole was parked near the entrance. The top of the pole carried a complicated-looking array of disks and antennae. The lettering on the side of the van read: EYE-WITNESS NEWS.

Toagie pulled into a parking slot. "Looks like you get to be on TV," she said.

Barbaraannette licked her lips. Her mouth was dry and her insides were buzzing.

Brittany, still wearing her paper tiara from the party, woke up and inserted herself between the two front seats. "Where *are* we?"

"We're at the lottery headquarters, honey," said Toagie.

"What *for?*"

"We're here so your aunt can pick up a check, honey."

Brittany said, looking at her aunt, "How come she's breathing so funny?" Barbaraannette was staring at the TV truck, one hand at her throat, breathing rapidly.

"You okay?" Toagie asked.

Barbaraannette nodded, forced a deep breath into her lungs, held it for a moment, blew it out. "I'm fine."

"How come you look so funny?" Britty asked. "Are you gonna cry?"

Barbaraannette shook her head, still staring at the TV truck.

4

*P*hlox was saying how if a person took every nickel they ever earned and put it all into lottery tickets they would have a better shot at getting rich than if they just went along living from paycheck to paycheck clipping coupons and buying generic at the Safeway and hoping a rich uncle they didn't know they had was about to die, because with the lottery a person would get all the money at once. That was the idea. You put money in and in and in, and then one day it all comes out in a rush, the way a piggy bank explodes when it gets too full.

Bobby Steele said from his La-Z-Boy, "When was the last time you saw a piggy bank blow up?" He'd just got home from Wild Wally Wenger's Westernwear Warehouse, Tucson's biggest Western wear outlet, where he worked in the boot department selling pointy toes to the snowbirds. It was better than some other jobs he'd had.

"You buy enough tickets, it's almost got to happen," Phlox said. She stood behind him, messing with his collar. "They don't make this stuff up, you know." Phlox was a devoted lottery junkie. She purchased a couple lottery tickets every day on her way to work at the Desert Diamond Casino where she worked as a dealer. Phlox didn't play cards herself, or put money into the slots. She watched the suckers throwing their money away every day, making the To-hono O'odham elders wealthy. But the lottery, that was another story. That was run by the government, not the Indians, and you could win enough to set you up for life. So far she'd only hit once, last November, a thousand bucks on an instant win ticket.

Bobby stared past the Mexican silver-capped toes of his Tony Lamas at the television. "You want to know what I think?"

"I always want to know what you think, Punkin." Phlox dragged her lavender nails through Bobby's wavy blond hair. From a distance it still looked good but up close, looking down at the top of his head, she could see a lot of scalp. She'd been cleaning a lot of hair out of the bathtub drain lately, but that was okay. He looked good in a hat.

"I think I'd like for you to grab me a beer."

"No problem, Pookie." Phlox sashayed into the kitchen, where she found a cold Miller tucked back behind a sack of yellowed celery. When she returned, Bobby was surfing the channels. She watched the flickering images for a few seconds, then handed her man his beer. "What you looking for?"

"Diamondbacks are suppose to be playing."

Phlox grabbed his shoulders and squeezed. "Wait, go back!" She waited for him to click to the previous channel, a news program. Over the shoulder of the news anchor she could see the Powerball graphic.

"This is about the lady just won it," Phlox said. "You hear about this?"

The news anchor said, "Ever think about what *you'd* do if *you* won the lottery? Well, one Minnesota woman knows *exactly* what she's going to do with her 8.9 million dollars. Val Frankel has a report from our affiliate in St. Paul, Minnesota."

The Powerball graphic spun away to reveal a woman gripping the edge of a microphone-studded podium, coils of reddish brown hair bouncing as she jerked her head back and forth, changing position as her attention was demanded by one or another reporter. A large banner displaying the Minnesota State Lottery logo—a red-eyed, pointy-billed loon—hung behind her. The camera angle made it appear as if the loon was pecking the side of her head. The woman's cheeks were flushed, and when the light hit her just right, her bright blue eyes could be seen darting excitedly.

"She's kind of pretty," said Phlox. "Only she could use a perm."

Several questions were being shouted at her simultaneously. In response to a shouted request, she displayed her winning lottery ticket in one hand and a photograph in the other. The babble of voices faded into a voice-over.

"Earlier this afternoon, shortly after presenting her winning ticket to lottery officials, Mrs. Barbaraannette Quinn announced that she is offering a one-million-dollar cash reward for the safe return of her missing husband."

Closeup of fuzzy photograph: a smiling man, perhaps thirty years old, standing in a boat holding up a stringer of bass.

"Robert Quinn was last seen six years ago when he left the couple's Cold Rock home to go fishing on the nearby St. Croix River. He never returned. His boat was found the next day, his fishing gear and his life jacket still on board, washed up on the bank of the river. The following week, his Jeep Cherokee was discovered, broken-down and abandoned, in Mitchell, South Dakota."

Cut to a photo of a muddy red Jeep Cherokee parked in front of the Corn Palace.

"Since that day, there has been no further trace of Robert Quinn."

Closeup on Val Frankel, the reporter. "Kidnapping? Murder? Abandonment? The fate of Robert Quinn remains a mystery. His wife, Barbaraannette, has held firm to the belief that Robert will one day return. And she's offering a million dollars to the person or persons who can bring her husband home."

Another graphic: a wedding photo. Zoom in on Robert Quinn, a strikingly handsome man with narrow features, sparkling blue eyes, thick, wavy blond hair, and a rakish grin.

Phlox's long nails sank into Bobby Steele's shoulders. She giggled.

"He looks a lot like you, Puddin," she said.

Jayjay Morrow was hanging out at Rudolph's Red Nose, elbows on the bar, watching the news and working on a bottle of Schell's when he felt a hand touch his shoulder.

"Jonathan?" The voice was light, crisp, and familiar. Jayjay looked at the hand—small, delicate fingers, precisely clipped nails—and at the bearded man who was attached to it. The guy from last week, the professor. Jayjay smiled and nodded, then returned his attention to the news story. A million dollars! And it sounded like she'd have plenty left over. Maybe he should write her a letter, see if she'd send him something.

The news program switched to a story about the floods in Missouri.

The bearded man, his hand still on Jayjay's shoulder, sat down on the next stool and said, "Did you know that one has a greater chance of being struck by lightning than of winning the lottery?"

Jayjay said, "I got hit by lightning once." He turned to dislodge the hand. He couldn't remember the guy's name, but he remembered him from last weekend. They'd had a few drinks at the Nose, then dinner at the Olive Tree, and then they'd gone over to the guy's house and he'd stayed all night and the next morning the guy had laid a hundred bucks on him. "I was thirteen I got hit," Jayjay said.

"Indeed!" The bearded man leaned in closer. His breath smelled of wintergreen. "What did that feel like?" A faint whistle from his small nostrils.

Jayjay sipped his bloody Mary. What would it feel like to be hit by lightning?

"Like a bar of hot steel rammed through my body."

"Remarkable!" The man clapped his tiny hands together.

"Yeah." Jayjay grinned. People told him he had a beautiful smile. His teeth were perfect, his cheeks dimpled. "It was just like that. Hot steel."

The bearded man said, "Do you have dinner plans this evening?"

5

Toagie said, "*You know a course you are out of your mind and then some Barbaraannette O'Gara.*"

"My name," said Barbaraannette, "is Barbaraannette *Quinn*." She cut into the slice of cake with the edge of her fork, stabbed it, and placed the small wedge of devil's food into her mouth. Toagie had saved her a piece. For day-old Cowboy Cake it was not half bad. She took a sip of coffee. Cake and coffee—an odd breakfast, but it tasted good.

"Your name, big sister, is I-got-my-head-up-my-rear-end, far as I'm concerned." Toagie lit a cigarette. "I always heard that money makes you stupid, now I know it."

Barbaraannette swallowed. "What's done is done, Toag." After Toagie had dropped her off last night Barbaraannette had locked her doors—something she seldom did—climbed into bed and ignored the phone, which commenced ringing every five or ten minutes until almost midnight. She'd spent the night in fits of sleep punctuated by waves of remorse, embarrassment, and anger. Seven o'clock in the morning the phone had started ringing again. She'd answered it a couple times, thinking it might be Toagie or Hilde or somebody else she wanted to talk to, but both times it was a man, a different man each time, with the investment opportunity of a lifetime. Why did they think she was so hot to make money when she had so much of it?

"You should go back on TV and say you've changed your mind."

Barbaraannette shook her head. "I made my bed, now I've got to sleep in it."

Toagie made an erasing motion with her cigarette. "That's crazy. If I'd known you were going to go on the TV and throw away a million bucks I'd never have driven you down there." Toagie took a ferocious drag on her Salem, thin cheeks sucking in so hard you could see her molars. "Fact is—" She blew smoke. "—and you know it, that man was never worth two cents let alone a million dollars cash money, which, I might add, it turns out you don't even got."

Barbaraannette said, "Have you been throwing up your dinners again, Antonia?"

"That's right, change the fleeping subject why doncha. They give you, what did you say? Two hundred thousand a year?"

"Two hundred eighty-four after taxes."

"Right, so then you got to pay off your Sears card and your car and your mortgage and your groceries and what have you got left?"

"Two hundred eighty-four thousand dollars."

Toagie blinked. "You don't owe nobody? Jeez Louise, what's *that* like? Well, anyway, you won't have nothing like a million bucks."

"I can borrow it."

"Lord God, Barbaraannette, don't even say that. All the things you can do now and you want to go in debt a million bucks for a jerkball like Bobby Quinn? I don't mind being the first one to tell you you're out of your fleeping mind."

"Did you know your hair is a little green?" said Barbaraannette.

"It's not a *little* green; it's a *lot* green—and I've got a few things to say to Rhoda about that not the least a which is she charged me twelve dollars this time." She burned through another half inch of Salem. "Hey, for a million bucks I bet you could buy yourself a good man. One cleans up after his self and doesn't drink much. How would that be? I bet you could buy that Jon Glaus, works at Fetler Ford?" Her hand shot out in the direction of the Ford dealership east of town. The ash detached itself from her cigarette and landed on Barbaraannette's kitchen floor. "He's cute," Toagie added. She bit the knuckle of her right thumb, held it between her teeth. The telephone began to ring.

Barbaraannette removed the whisk broom from its hook in the closet and swept the errant ash into the dustpan. "I'm a married woman, Toag." Barbaraannette dumped the cigarette ash into the sink and washed it down with a two-second blast of tap water. "I've got unfinished business with Bobby. Anyway, I don't think I'd be happy with a man sells Fords."

Toagie let go of her thumb, looked at the tooth marks she'd left behind. "Well if Jon Glaus doesn't do it for you, I could name a half dozen others would be more'n happy to come sniffing after you, big sister, lottery or no." The ringing continued. "Aren't you gonna answer that?"

Barbaraannette shook her head and put away the whisk broom and dust pan.

"What if it's Hilde?" Toagie asked.

"It's more likely some fool with another investment opportunity. Or Mary Beth calling to tell me I'm an idiot."

"You don't need to hear that from Mary Beth. You got me." The ringing continued. "I was you," Toagie said, "I'd get a machine."

Barbaraannette permitted herself a shallow smile. "Instead of Jon Glaus?"

"An *answering* machine."

"I just ignore it."

The two women listened until the phone stopped ringing.

"Why don't you unplug it?"

"Because." Barbaraannette sipped her coffee and eyed the last bite of cake. "One of these times I might just pick it up."

6

"I *can't believe you never even told me your real name.*"

"I told you. It's Bobby. Robert."

"Yeah, but you told me Bobby Steele."

"I *am* Bobby Steele. Bobby Steele Quinn."

Phlox said, "What are you bringing *that* for?" She'd been snipping at him all morning, and she wasn't sure why. Maybe it was because he was all of a sudden worth a million dollars and she wasn't.

"This?" Bobby was folding his lambskin duster into his suitcase. "It's colder'n a welldigger's ass up there. I bet they still got snow."

"You got a jacket already packed. We'll only be on the road two days. How many do you need?"

"One for driving, and one for dress." He grinned. "You want me to look good, don't you?"

Phlox made a sour face, but the fact was, she *did* want him to look good. Looking good was a big part of who he was. Bobby Steele—Bobby Steele *Quinn* was not the richest or the smartest or the nicest guy in Tucson, but he was hands down the best-looking and the best-dressed man Phlox had ever got her hooks into. And he was pretty damn good when he was undressed, too.

She busied herself with her own bag, checking through her makeup kit, tossing in a few extra condoms. Bobby was fitting a pair of cowhide heel protectors onto his boots. He always wore them while driving. He didn't want the backs of his heels to get scuffed on the floor of the pickup truck. Bobby was very particular about his boots.

Sometimes Bobby's fastidiousness got under her skin, and she wished her man was a bit more . . . manly. A little more grizzled, a little dirt under the nails, a shirttail hanging out. But then she would remember her last boyfriend, Bart, whose custom had been to pare his toenails in bed with a pocketknife, and Bobby would start looking good again.

Phlox finished her packing, sat down on the bed and watched Bobby. She'd always liked the way he moved, the way he touched things. He had great hands.

Bobby closed the suitcase, then fitted his straw Resistol onto his head. Phlox felt her nails digging into her thighs. She said, "Aren't you bringing your good hat?"

Bobby pointed to the leatherette hatbox waiting near the bedroom door. "It's packed and ready." The El Presidente, a genuine 100 percent beaver belly fur felt Stetson, had been Phlox's Christmas present to him, nine hundred ninety-nine dollars. That was where her lottery money had gone. It looked great on him. Like a million bucks.

"Put it on," she said.

"Now?"

Phlox nodded. Bobby shrugged, opened the box, and replaced his straw hat with the El Presidente.

"C'mere, you."

Bobby looked at her, frowned. "I thought you wanted to get going."

"C'mere, Bobby Steele." She grabbed him by his silver-and-turquoise belt buckle and pulled him close. "Or whatever your name is."

"Jesus, Phlox, I just got dressed."

Phlox yanked open the front of his shirt, mother-of-pearl snaps popping. "Then you can get all undressed, Pook." She ran her nails slowly down his chest, then went to work unfastening his belt buckle. "Show me again me what that wife of yours is paying the big bucks for." She tugged down his zipper. Bobby's breathing had become audible. He reached up to remove the hat, but Phlox stopped him. "No time for that, honey. You just leave that hat on your head." She worked her thumbs into the waistband of his jeans. "Pretend I'm your wife."

"Jesus, Phlox," he said, shaking his head. But she could tell he was into it. His pupils were huge and his hands were shaking and she had the damnedest time getting his jeans down.

Art Dobbleman parked his Plymouth across the street from Barbaraannette's bungalow. He set the hand brake and put the car in neutral, but left the engine running. He still wasn't sure he should do this. Barbaraannette might think he was being pushy. She might not even open the door to him, what with all the calls and visitors she'd probably been getting.

Not that he had any choice. His boss, Nathan Nagler, had made it quite clear to him that he was to procure the "Quinn account" for Cold Rock Savings & Loan. "I want this institution to be the repository for Mrs. Quinn's money," Nagler had told him, blinking rapidly. Nagler was in his early fifties but had retained his soft, boyish features. His face was the color of cheese curd, his eyes and hair startlingly black. "Unless of course the damn fool woman decides she's going to pay out that reward, in which case I want this institution's money to go to work for her." Nagler had plucked his prized hole-in-one golf ball from its display, bounced it off his leather desk blotter, caught it. "The woman needs us, Art. You make sure she knows it."

The thing of it is, Art thought, it really would be in Barbaraannette's best interest to talk to him. There were things he could help her with, things she would need to know about now that she had her hands on some serious money. He was a professional. Money was his business.

Art sat in his car watching her front door, thinking about how he should make his approach. Should he act professional and impersonal? Try to impress her with facts and figures? Or take the opposite tack, go in all friendly then ease the conversation around to business matters? Neither approach seemed right. Should he leave his rubbers on, or take them off before walking up to her front door? It was pretty sloppy out there, snow rapidly melting in the April sun. His shoes were practically brand new. They had cost him nearly one hundred dollars.

Art rolled his neck, heard it crack. He wished he could wait a few days. It seemed somehow indecent to go charging in looking for business only one day after she'd cashed in her ticket. He felt as if he was approaching a bereaved heiress.

He decided to wear the rubbers, then take them off when she invited him in—*if* she invited him in—so as not to track on her floors.

Art had been sitting in his car for a good ten minutes when the front door opened and Toagie Carlson, Barbaraannette's younger sister, emerged wearing a puffy black parka, purple sweatpants, and knee-high lace-up boots. Art felt a wave of relief—Thank God he hadn't gone in while Toagie was there! Lately, the relationship between the Carlsons and Cold Rock S&L had not been cordial. The foreclosure process on the Carlsons' under-maintained, oversized foursquare was nearing its inevitable conclusion. Toagie had been quite vocal over the past few weeks, telling her side of the story all over town. Naturally, her story made the bank out to be evil incarnate. Art smiled humorlessly. It wasn't as if the bank would lose any business. Anybody who knew Toagie and Bill Carlson knew there had to be another side to the story. Anyway, it was a moot point now that Barbaraannette had won the lottery. Toagie would now have no problem making good on her loan. Still, he was glad he hadn't knocked on Barbaraannette's door with Toagie on the premises.

He watched the younger sister walk quickly up the wet sidewalk, puffing on a cigarette, slightly unsteady in her high-heeled boots. What he should do, he should knock on Barbaraannette's front door right now while she was still in visitor mode, before she had a chance to start making a pie crust or running a bath or doing anything else that might make her resent the intrusion. He was about to go into action when a silver-gray Lincoln glided to a halt in front of Barbaraannette's bungalow.

Art slunk down in his seat. A stolid, steel-haired woman stepped out of the Lincoln, scanned her surroundings, then lifted her over-size purse from the car, closed the door firmly, and marched up the walk toward Barbaraannette's front door preceded by her formidable bosom.

Mary Beth Hultman, the eldest of the three Grabo sisters.

Art felt like a prison escapee who had just been missed by a roving searchlight. He decided to wait a little longer before knocking on Barbaraannette's door.

7

Barbaraannette *was always glad to see Mary Beth, but she often wished it* were some other time. Yesterday, for instance. Or tomorrow. It didn't matter. Though she loved her sister dearly, the time was never quite right for Mary Beth and Barbaraannette. They both knew it and avoided one another when possible, but being sisters in a small community meant they saw each other often.

Barbaraannette said, in a vain effort to get things off right, "Mary Beth, you are looking sensational!"

Mary Beth arched one charcoal eyebrow and unleashed her metallic voice. "Same as I looked last Thursday, dear. What's this I hear about you giving away a million U.S. dollars to that no-good women-chasing wife-abandoning nightcrawler Bobby Quinn?"

Same old Mary Beth, going straight for the giblets.

"How about a cup of coffee," suggested Barbaraannette. "A little caffeine to calm you down."

"Thank you, dear." Mary Beth said, heading for the kitchen. "A million dollars. Better you should pay someone to beat you senseless with a two-by-four than give that man a copper penny." Mary Beth worked at the Grant Anderson Medical Center, Cold Rock's largest hospital, where she ran the Family Planning Clinic with legendary exactitude.

Barbaraannette followed her sister into the kitchen. "I'm not giving anything *to* him, Mary Beth. The reward is for whoever *finds* him."

"Same difference." Mary Beth poured herself a cup of coffee from the Chemex.

"No it isn't."

"Either way, you're a million dollars poorer, dear, and for what? A man hardly worth thinking twice about. You were married to him three years. Were you happy?"

"Part of me was."

"What about the part above your waist, dear?"

Barbaraannette blushed. "I didn't mean anything like that."

Mary Beth said, "Don't think you're the only girl in this town who was part happy with Bobby."

"I'm the only one he married," said Barbaraannette. But she knew that what her sister said was true. Since high school Bobby Quinn had applied great energy toward sowing his oats. Marriage had only slowed him down a little. "I know Bobby was a little wild."

"He was a lot wild, dear." Mary Beth's eyes remained granite, but a faint hint of color came and went on her throat. "That man knew how to charm a woman every which way, and make her thank God she'd had the bad judgment to let him." She sipped her coffee. "By the way, did you know that Art Dobbleman is sitting outside in his car trying to get up the nerve to come knock on your door?"

"Art?" Barbaraannette went to the window and looked past the curtain. "Where? In that gray car? I wonder what he wants."

"He probably wants you to put your money in his bank instead of spending every last dime of it chasing that no-good Bobby."

"I always liked Art. We went out once. He was a perfect gentleman."

Mary Beth nodded. "That was always his problem."

Barbaraannette laughed.

Mary Beth drained her coffee cup. "Are you ready?"

"Ready? For what?"

"It's Saturday, dear. Did you think I dropped by simply to chat?"

"Oh!" Barbaraannette had completely lost track of time. Saturday was the day she and Mary Beth visited their mother, Hilde Grabo. "Did you call her?"

"An hour ago. She should be expecting us."

Barbaraannette nodded. The phone call made it more likely that Hilde would recognize them this time, but it was no guarantee.

8

Hilde Grabo lived in a small apartment in the Bluebird wing of the Crestview Retirement Community. She had her own small kitchenette, sitting room, bedroom, and bath. Every morning at 8:15 a young woman knocked on her door to make sure she had not died in her sleep, and every evening another young woman dropped by to make sure she had successfully fed herself. And if she failed to emerge from her apartment during the day, a young man who called himself the "activity director" would call to ask her why she hadn't shown up to work on the Crestview Peace Quilt, or missed the croquet tournament, or the Thursday Bird Walk, or whatever horrifically boring "activity" it was that she had managed to avoid.

Hilde found it all quite amusing, even on those days when she could not seem to remember why or when she had checked into this peculiar hotel.

On her clear days, Hilde enjoyed writing limericks and reading her favorite publications—*Cosmopolitan* and *Vogue*. It was important to stay abreast of modern fashion trends. She wished she could get out shopping more often, but it seemed as if every time she tried to go, one of the hotel staff interrupted her, insisting that she work on that silly quilt or something. When she called a cab, the cab never came.

She had slipped past them once and borrowed a car, but when

she got to Harold's Fashions, the manager—a rodent-mouthed little twit less than half her age—had refused to let her in, bringing up those ridiculous accusations of shoplifting. It was embarrassing. True, Hilde had on occasion forgotten to pay for a few items, but she was no shoplifter. That chinchilla coat they'd caught her with, well, she'd tried it on and simply forgot to remove it. And the tubes of lipstick in the pockets, what was that? Four or five tubes. That was all. When one bought as many outfits as she had over the years it was natural that one might neglect to pay for a few items. She'd given Harold's plenty of business. It was the height of insolence for them to squawk over a few lousy lipsticks and a coat.

Hilde Grabo had tried her best to instill her sense of style in her three daughters. For the most part she had failed. Her oldest, Mary Beth, appreciated quality tailoring but chose to dress with the humorless severity of a modern-day Carry Nation. And poor Antonia, though she tried so hard, always looked as though she had one idea when she began applying her makeup, but a completely different notion by the time she stepped into her shoes, like a cross between the young mother she was today and the punk rocker she'd been a decade back. Hilde worried about Antonia. Twenty-eight years old and the girl still chewed on her thumb and never left the house without at least one button missing. If she ever became famous—although why that might ever happen Hilde could not imagine—Toagie would rocket right to the top of Mr. Blackwell's worst-dressed list.

But it was Barbaraannette who had provided Hilde with her greatest fashion triumphs and disappointments.

Hilde was paging through the February *Vogue* when she came across a photo spread of Khristianya, a statuesque ice queen recently imported from Latvia. Khristianya wearing fur and lace. Khristianya wearing a ruby-sequined cocktail dress. Khristianya wearing a linen, silk, and alpaca suit. Khristianya, looking very much like Barbaraannette had once looked, except for having green eyes instead of blue, and being narrow-faced and thinner and taller.

Hilde looked up from her magazine.

"Speak of the devil," she said. "Barbaraannette, I was just thinking about you!"

Barbaraannette smiled. She had such a beautiful smile, but she was not wearing a spot of makeup, not even lipstick. Her outfit, some sort of sweatshirt with a big loon printed on the front and a pair of khaki slacks, concealed her figure as effectively as a gunnysack. And those shoes! Like something a foot doctor might prescribe. A far cry from the old Barbaraannette.

Hilde heard a flinty voice: "Mother, we've been sitting here talking to you for the past ten minutes."

"Mary Beth!" said Hilde. "I was thinking about you, too!" She put her hands on the arms of her chair and straightened up, gaining a few inches in altitude.

"I am sure you were, Mother."

"Well then!" Hilde crossed her arms and composed her face. "And have you girls been behaving yourselves?"

"Mother, we are grown women," said Mary Beth.

Hilde frowned. "Of course you are."

Barbaraannette said, "Hilde, did you know I won the lottery?"

Hilde felt her mind spin free for a moment, then experienced an almost audible clunk as concepts meshed and formed complete memories. Of course she knew! Barbaraannette had won millions of dollars! She'd seen it on TV. It was all the other hotel residents had been talking about. Hilde's daughter had won the lottery!

"That's nice, dear," she said.

"And she's offered a one-million-dollar reward to get her worthless runaway husband back," interjected Mary Beth. "I was hoping you could talk some sense into her, but maybe this isn't a good day."

Yes, Hilde recalled as more veils lifted, she had heard about the reward. She had actually seen Barbaraannette, her own flesh and blood, smiling on the TV screen, wearing lipstick for once. A million dollars to get that man back, that Bobby Quinn. That certainly had set the old biddies buzzing around their silly Peace Quilt!

"It's a *fine* day," Hilde said. She shook her finger at Barbaraannette. "Shame on you, Barbaraannette! Making a public spectacle that way. Why, with a million dollars, you could wear anything you want. You could have that mole removed."

Barbaraannette hunched down in her chair, assuming the same stubborn defensive posture she had invented at the age of three. Mary Beth put on a grim smile and sat back.

Hilde said, "Mary Beth, dear, would you excuse us for a few moments? I need to have a talk with your sister."

The moment Mary Beth left the room, Hilde's demeanor changed. Her shoulders relaxed and her mouth widened and opened to show a set of bright white dentures. She winked at Barbaraannette.

"That girl is a trial, I swear. Has she been giving you a hard time, Babba?"

"She's just worried about me," said Barbaraannette.

"She worries about me, too, dear. Frankly, it's a pain in the bejeezuz."

"She thinks I'm making a big mistake, trying to get Bobby back."

"Is that what you think?" Hilde's eyes crackled with alert intelligence.

Barbaraannette had seen these changes in her mother before. The sudden transitions from apathetic vacuity to steely alertness was not typical in Alzheimer's patients, but neither was it unheard of. Her doctor said Hilde might swing in and out of the world for months or years, with each visit becoming more brief. It was sad and disconcerting, but Barbaraannette had resigned herself to her mother's fate.

The other change—from finger-shaking authority figure while in Mary Beth's presence to relaxed co-conspirator the moment Mary Beth left the scene—had been going on ever since Barbaraannette could remember. Hilde Grabo became a different mother for each of her daughters.

"I don't know what I think, Mama. I just did it. Didn't plan it. You know how it was when Bobby left me. I hired that private detective to find him, but that just cost me money I didn't have. I mean, I know there was no way we could have spent the rest of our lives together, but I thought, you know, another year or two. I just wasn't ready. He left without a word and I felt like I'd failed. Like it wasn't finished."

"You always did like to finish things. From when you were three. I never had to tell you to clean your plate."

Barbaraannette nodded. "As soon as I realized they were going to put me on the news . . . I just thought that would be the way to get him back. I didn't think about what I'd do after. I mean, if somebody finds him."

"You didn't?" Hilde was smiling.

Barbaraannette blushed. "Well, I thought about a few things. You want to know something, Hilde? I've been faithful to that man, not that he deserved it."

Hilde's smile broadened. She sat back in her chair. "You, Barbaraannette, you are a case. Twenty years now I've been laying awake nights worrying about your sister Antonia and all the time it was you should have been keeping me up nights."

"You think I'm an idiot."

Hilde said, "Idiot? Sweetheart, I understand completely. You don't have to be an idiot to be stupid over a man. You know, your father was a lot like Bobby."

"Like how, Mama?"

"You don't remember him, do you, honey? See, Sammy, he came between poor Edward, God rest his soul, and Anthony Alan, Antonia's father. You understand, there were nine long years there with only Mary Beth for company. I know you understand, dear."

Barbaraannette nodded. This was no surprise. Her mother made no secret of Barbaraannette's origins. Her father, according to Hilde's most oft-repeated version, had been a disreputable sort, a gambler she had met in St. Paul and lived with, on and off, for three years. She had heard the story several times, but she had never before heard the legendary Sam O'Gara compared with Bobby Quinn.

"What do you mean, he was like Bobby?"

"Well, sweetheart, Sammy wasn't as tall as Bobby, nor as good-looking. He was a small man, truth be told, but he was a man with big ideas. You know what I mean, dear. He had big ideas in the right places. He knew how to treat a girl. I was just crazy for that man."

"Why did you leave him?"

"Oh, sweetheart, I don't know. I was busy with you and your sister, too busy to take care of a man as well. I bought you that little red dress on your third birthday. You looked so cute in that dress. And then I met Anthony Alan. It wasn't so long ago, was it? You were a beautiful child, Barbaraannette."

Hilde smiled, remembering Barbaraannette in her red birthday dress. She thought she had a snapshot somewhere, but where? She had a lot of snapshots someplace. In a closet, if only she could remember which one. Which house. She turned her head to ask Barbaraannette where all her snapshots had gone, but instead of Barbaraannette she found a smiling young man sitting at her bedside holding a clipboard.

"Where did you come from?" she asked. The man was wearing a teal-blue golf shirt that did not go well with his complexion. The name "Reed" was embroidered in white on the left chest of the shirt.

The man's smile wavered. "Do you mean, where did I grow up?"

"You just walk into a woman's room? What kind of manners did your mother teach you, young man?"

"I, um . . . Mrs. Grabo, we were just discussing this evening's croquet tournament."

Hilde frowned. "Where's Barbaraannette?" she demanded.

"Your daughter?"

"Of course she is."

"I'm sorry," said the young man, and he really did look sorry. "Both your daughters left about twenty minutes ago."

"Oh!" said Hilde. She thought for a moment, then smiled slyly. "Would you like to hear a limerick?"

The young man said, standing up, "Maybe I should come back later—"

Hilde recited, before he could reach the door,

> *"There was a young lad in a pickle*
> *Cuz he sat on his favorite testicle*
> *He said, while it smarts*
> *In my tenderest parts*
> *It's better than breaking my dickle."*

"Uh, I'll stop back later, Mrs. Grabo," said Reed as he closed her door.

Hilde giggled. Now, what had she been thinking about?

9

I'm thirty-four and one third years old, Art Dobbleman thought. Six feet four inches tall, one hundred seventy-six pounds. My car has eighty-six thousand, two hundred eleven miles on it. Last month I wrote four hundred sixty thousand dollars in retail loans. I've been working at Cold Rock S&L for nine years and four months. I wear size thirty-six trousers, a forty-four jacket, and I have twenty-eight teeth. My golf handicap is an embarrassing thirty-three. I made forty-one thousand dollars last year. I have been married once, divorced three months, and I am sitting in my car waiting for the woman I have loved for twenty years to come home so that I can lend her one million dollars to help her find her husband.

With his right hand, Art took the web of skin between his left thumb and forefinger and pinched, grimacing. He squeezed until his thoughts shattered and tears spurted from his eyes, held it for an agonized count of ten, released his grip with a blinking gasp. Galvanized, he yanked open the car door and got out and climbed over the snowbank, rubbered shoes sinking into the crumbly gray ice, overcoat flapping in the brisk wind, briefcase held high for balance. Art made his way up the walk to Barbaraannette's front door, his vision spotted with floaters in the bright sun. He lifted the back of his coat and sat on the landing. The concrete felt warm with stored sunlight, and the house blocked the chilly wind. He set his briefcase down, rested an arm on it, stretched his long legs, and began, again, to wait.

Was this better than sitting in his car? Yes, he decided, because now he had, at least, acted. When Barbaraannette returned he would have no choice but to talk to her, even if she was accompanied by the formidable Mary Beth. Art shuddered. Hilde Grabo's three daughters—known locally as the Grabo girls, despite the fact that all three girls had been christened with different last names and then renamed themselves again with marriage—each excited in him a powerful emotion. Mary Beth, whose steely, square-jawed appearance somehow managed to understate her strength of will, excited in Art a primal, hindbrain terror—the sort of raw, unintellectualized fear one might experience when confronted by, say, an approaching tornado. Certain Cold Rock residents referred to her as the Iron Matron, but not Art. Where Mary Beth was concerned, he preferred not to take chances.

The youngest Grabo girl, Toagie, inspired a different sort of fear. Toagie had been a coltish beauty in high school, but the past decade had not been kind to her. A few years riding the punk rock street scene in Minneapolis had given her a sort of tattered, exotic maturity, but one day she had abruptly returned to Cold Rock, dead broke and on probation for a minor drug offense. Before the year was out she'd married local boy Bill Carlson, produced one child, and replaced the gutter-punk language she had adopted with a lexicon of idiosyncratic euphemisms.

When Toagie and her surly husband had walked into the S&L two years ago to refinance their oversize foursquare, Art had known in his heart that such a transaction could only end in sorrow. Bill and Toagie Carlson had long since resigned themselves to a life of bouncing from calamity to disaster with small chunks of weird joy sprinkled throughout the mix. Still, most everyone agreed that Toagie was a lot of fun—even those who had been injured, embarrassed, or arrested while in her company. Despite his misgivings, Art had approved the loan. After all, Toagie was Barbaraannette's sister.

It was Barbaraannette, the middle sister, who stirred within Art the richest emotional soup. He'd fallen hard in the tenth grade and had been in love with her ever since. With age and passing years, his adoration for Barbaraannette had matured and hardened and found its own place inside of him, but it had not abated. He had loved her at close range during her awkward teens, loved her from afar during her college years, loved her still more when she returned to Cold Rock, and loved her with bitter sorrow after she married Bobby Quinn. He had loaned the newlywed couple the money for their house, this very house, despite the fact that Bobby Quinn was a clear and present credit risk. He had done it out of love for Barbaraannette.

Most of Art's friends were married. Most of them had children. At times, Art envied them their coupled, fecund existence. More often, he fantasized about Barbaraannette.

They had gone out on a date once, the memory of which made Art squirm. It had happened shortly before her engagement and subsequent marriage to Bobby Quinn, and before his own ill-fated marriage to Marla Vedeen. Barbaraannette had returned to Cold Rock, moved back in with her mother, and was working part time as a substitute schoolteacher. Art, after several shots of vodka and a great deal of prodding from his friend Steve Lawson, had called her on the phone and invited her to dinner.

He'd had to remind her who he was. "I sat behind you in Mrs. Borson's class. Twelfth-grade English," he'd said, his voice slurred with alcohol.

"Oh!" she'd said. "Of course! How have you been, Art?" Her tone seemed to imply that she did not remember him at all. Ten years he'd been carrying her torch and she didn't know him.

The next night, still slightly hung over, he had appeared at her front door feeling overdressed and underprepared, his armpits caked with antiperspirant, clutching a half-dozen yellow roses.

That date had not gone well. Everything that came out of his mouth sounded stupid and inappropriate. Barbaraannette laughed politely at his jokes, and at several things that were not jokes. The service in the restaurant was insulting, the food abysmal, the lighting bright and harsh. Art heard himself babbling on and on about the Twin Cities Marathon, like she would give a damn. He had finished with a very respectable time of 2:42:27, a fact he had somehow managed to blurt three times. He'd been so nervous, so worried about how he looked to her that he hadn't done a single thing right. He had spilled water in his lap, stepped on her foot while attempting to hold the car door open for her, and, when he got home, discovered that he had a massive chunk of black pepper stuck between his front teeth. No wonder she hadn't wanted to kiss him good night. Not that he'd asked. The last part of the date was a blur in his memory. All he remembered was the awful feeling that he'd blown his big chance with the love of his life and that he wanted to kill himself. But he hadn't killed himself, nor had he asked her out again. A few weeks later Barbaraannette announced her engagement to the irresponsible, handsome, and dexterous Bobby Quinn. Shortly after their wedding, Art himself became engaged to Marla Vedeen and married her, but in the end it had not worked out and, even worse, his marriage had done nothing to temper his obsession with Barbaraannette.

A cloud passed in front of the sun. Art pulled up the collar of his overcoat, drew up his knees and rested his chin on his crossed wrists, trying to understand the forces that had brought him to this place. He drifted through a random string of memories until he arrived, as he often did, at his mental catalogue of long runs. Two months to Grandma's Marathon in Duluth. He began to lope through the remembered course, stride by stride, at a leisurely 7:30 pace.

He had arrived at the twenty-mile mark when he noticed that someone was standing in front of him. He looked up, felt his heart deliver a huge thump.

Barbaraannette said, "Good lord, Art, do you have any idea how pitiful you look?"

Barbaraannette immediately regretted her words. She'd meant it as a bit of playful banter—but had forgotten that Art did not know how to play those games and, in fact, she was pretty lousy at it herself.

"You want a cup of coffee?" she offered, softening her voice.

He nodded gratefully. He followed her into her kitchen and watched, saying little, as she made coffee.

Art took his coffee black. That surprised Barbaraannette. She had always thought of him as a cream and sugar guy. But why would she think that? Maybe it was his strong white teeth. Who knew where these ideas came from?

Art had asked her out only once, the year she'd returned to Cold Rock, shortly before she'd become engaged to Bobby. Dinner at the Four Coachmen—a clumsy and uncomfortable evening, especially for her since she had already decided to marry Bobby Quinn. She'd gone out with Art that night because nothing was official with Bobby yet, and she liked Art, and it was the polite thing to do. She could not remember whether they'd had coffee after dinner. She did remember that Art had dumped a glass of water on his lap, and that he'd been so nervous she could smell the sweat coming off him from across the table, but it hadn't smelled bad. He'd seemed most comfortable when he talked about running. Art ran marathons, twenty-six miles. Twenty-six point two, he'd told her. Barbaraannette had been truly impressed, both by the feat and by his passion for running. How long had he told her it took? She thought for a moment. The number 2:42 came into her mind.

She said, pouring her own coffee, "How long did you say a marathon takes you?"

A visible tremor ran up Art's body. "Me?"

Barbaraannette laughed. "Yes, you."

"Um, my PR is two hours and thirty-six minutes." He cleared his throat. "And twelve seconds. That was three years ago, at the Twin Cities."

"You've gotten faster," Barbaraannette said.

Art stared back at her.

"I mean," Barbaraannette added, "since we talked about it at the Four Coachmen."

"Oh." Art looked at his lap, his cheeks coloring slightly.

"I've seen you running. You run over all six bridges, right?"

Art nodded. "I usually run the bridges, then head up Easton Creek."

"I used to go for walks along there."

"It's a nice spot. I like to run it at night."

"You don't worry about running into wild beasts in the dark?"

Art blinked, unable to follow her through the turn. What did she mean? He fell back to the solid ground of the banking business. "Yes, well, the reason I'm here is that I really need to talk to you, Barbaraannette. I mean, what I mean is, you really need to talk to me."

Barbaraannette laughed, then attempted to imitate Mary Beth's arched eyebrow. "*I* need to talk to *you?*"

Art cleared his throat. "Uh, as a matter of fact, yes. I think you do." He took a deep breath. "What I mean to say is, I've three things to say to you. The first one is, this reward you're offering? It's not too late to call it off, and I think you should. I really think you should."

Barbaraannette narrowed her gaze and pressed her lips together. "And?"

"I really think you should withdraw your offer. Buy yourself a nice car and put the rest of your money into some solid funds."

"I heard you the first time. You said you had three things to say."

"Yes. Are you aware of your sister's situation with respect to her mortgage?"

Barbaraannette crossed her arms. "I know she owes you a pile of money. Why, is she behind in her payments?"

"Yes she is. It's gotten rather serious." He sat low in the chair, knees jutting, back bent forward, head tilted to one side. "Actually, we had planned to foreclose tomorrow."

"And you're wondering if I'm going to bail her out, is that it?"

Art squirmed. "All I'm saying is, if you're thinking about it, I could hold off on the paperwork for a few days."

Barbaraannette nodded. "I'll think about it. What's the third thing?"

Art took a breath and sat up straight. He lifted his briefcase onto the table and unsnapped the latches. "The third thing is, if you go ahead with the reward offer, and if someone claims it, you'll need to borrow the money." He extracted a loan application and placed it beside her coffee cup. "Cold Rock S&L would very much like to be your lender."

Barbaraannette sighed. What ever had made her think he was a cream and sugar guy?

10

Dear Ms. Foster,

I recently saw your excellent movie NELL and it changed my life.

Previous to seeing NELL I was deep in a Clinical Depression. My doctor prescribed Prozac but it made me sick. Also it was expensive. But the fact that I still have the use of my arms after the motorcycle accident where I ran off the road to avoid hitting a bus filled with innocent schoolchildren is a good thing. Life was very hard for me after they amputated my legs, but all the innocent children survived!!!

After my accident I struggled hard to find a purpose in life to go on living. The Clinical Depression made me extremely suicidal so I decided to take an overdose of drugs. But then I read your excellent and profound movie, NELL. Once I read NELL I knew that life was worth living if only to read your other books. You are not merely Talented, you are a Great Actress!!! Maybe you know that already. I am inspired to read all of your books. Unfortunatly, I am on an extremely limited budget. No one will hire me as I am a cripple now and the amount of money I get from also getting wounded fighting Saddam in the Gulf War is very poor. I hardly have enough for food and rent and to support my mother who has Alshiemers.

Do you have any extra copies of any of your inspiring movies?

Preferably with your signature? I would be extremely grateful if
you could spare some. Or if not, if you would send a donation in
any amount, I could afford to buy them myself.

                    Admiringly,
                    Your biggest fan!!!
                    Jonathan James Morrow

"This is quite good, Jayjay. Quite vivid. You write better than
many of my students." André Gideon smiled and set the letter on
the table beside his coffee cup. Sadly, what he had said was true.
He'd read papers from English majors that were less accomplished.
"I am quite certain Ms. Foster will enjoy hearing from you."

"You never know for sure," said Jayjay Morrow.

"Did you actually see *Nell?*"

"Nope. But she was in it. I send out a lot of letters. Mostly I
never hear back, but last week I got a signed book and a picture
from the guy that wrote that book about bridges."

André said, "Bridges?"

"Yeah, *The Bridges of . . .* some country, I think."

"My word! He sent you a book?"

"And a picture of him playing guitar. Only they weren't worth
much, but at least I got, like, five bucks down at the Book Exchange. And a couple months ago this lady sent me a check for a
hundred dollars. But she was an actress. I send them a picture with
the letter." Jayjay reached into the tattered cardboard file folder on
his lap and extracted a color snapshot of a crumpled, bespectacled,
legless man in a wheelchair.

André Gideon looked from the photo to his young house guest.
"My goodness," he said. "You certainly have come around."

Jayjay grinned. His even, white teeth were dazzling, as was the
rest of his twenty-one-year-old body. Once again, André felt the
breath leave his body. It had been two days since young Jonathan
James had moved into his guest room, one week since their first
fateful encounter at Rudolph's Red Nose Bar and Grill, and the
boy's erotic impact remained undiminished. The child was drop-

dead beautiful. Even the pimple erupting from the side of his nose only made the rest of him seem that much more perfect, as did the tiny blue tear tattooed near the corner of his right eye.

He wished he could tell Mother about Jayjay, but she wouldn't understand. She was still waiting for grandchildren. André reached across the table and slipped his fingers into Jayjay's blond curls, feeling the heat of his scalp. The boy tolerated it for a few seconds, then pulled his head back.

"It's not me in the picture, a course. I took it of this guy I saw looked real pitiful."

"He does look that," said André.

"Anyways, this one actress sent me the hundred, so I thought I'd try sending to more actresses."

"I think that is very intelligent, Jayjay," said André. "I like the way you think."

Jayjay beamed. "I sent out a bunch to writers, too. So you think this is okay? Everything is spelled right and stuff? The part about my mom is new."

André looked again at the letter. "There are one or two minor errors here. Nothing terribly difficult to change. The spellings of "unfortunately" and "Alzheimer's," for instance, are incorrect. Also, you refer to Ms. Foster's 'books' when I think you mean to say 'movies.' "

"Oh." Jayjay's face fell.

"An easy mistake to make," André said quickly.

"Uh-huh. So, you're an author—if I sent you a letter would you give me anything?"

"Well, I'm not really an author—"

"You got a book out."

André's face warmed with pleasure. It was so seldom that anyone acknowledged him as a published author—any mention whatsoever gave him a sweet little buzz. It had been seven years since the now-defunct River Time Press had printed five hundred copies of *F. Scott and Papa: Homoeroticism in the Roaring Twenties—A Structuralist Perspective*. Aside from a handful of kindly mentions in a few obscure academic journals, André Gideon's seven-hundred-and-forty-three-page masterwork had made about as much impact on the literary community as Harlequin romance No. 134, and had sold far fewer copies. These days, his book served only to impress his students and the occasional house guest, and to fill two bookcases in his study. He had a second work in progress, a study of the gay roots of late-period French existential literature, but he had made little progress of late. The first two hundred pages of the manuscript had been resting undisturbed in his study for several months now.

"Yes, well, I'm quite certain I would send you something. The part about the bus filled with children—very powerful imagery. One would be hard-pressed to resist so eloquent an appeal."

"Like, how much?"

"Oh, I would think fifty or a hundred dollars."

"How about you give it to me now?" Jayjay smiled. His perfect amber eyes stroked André's graying beard. "Save on postage."

André blinked, not sure whether his young guest was joking or negotiating. Just to be on the safe side he laughed and said, "Of course, dear boy. Fifty dollars? My wallet is on my dressing table. You may help yourself."

Jayjay said, "Thanks, Andy." He grinned. "I already did." He laughed.

André laughed, too. He wondered whether the boy had taken fifty or a hundred dollars. He tried to remember how much he'd had in his wallet. Not much more than a hundred. In any case, it was well worth it to have such a creature gracing his breakfast table. It was only money.

Thank God for tenure.

11

Barbaraannette thought, *My whole adult life I've done exactly two com-*pletely foolish things. The first one was I married Bobby Quinn, and the second was I put myself in front of the whole wide wonderful world and offered one million dollars to get him back again.

Toagie was right. She was out of her fleeping mind. Art Dobbleman was right, too. She should withdraw the reward offer. And maybe she should go to church every Sunday and eat more fresh vegetables and join a health club. Maybe she should donate her lottery winnings to the federal government to help shrink the deficit. There were a lot of things she should do.

The phone began to ring again. Barbaraannette pretended it was coming from next door. She emptied the ashtray Toagie had used that morning, rinsed it and placed it atop the refrigerator. She might be out of her fleeping mind, but at least she didn't smoke cigarettes anymore and it wasn't as if she'd run somebody over with her car or showed up in front of her second-grade class buck naked—which reminded her, she had to teach tomorrow. That would be an ordeal, all the other faculty wanting to know every last blessed detail of her future life now that she was rich. Rich, but stupid. Only not so stupid as that Fred Nyes the music teacher who got caught bare-assed with fourth-grade teacher Wanda Johnson in the janitor's room.

Thinking about Wanda Johnson and her large-breasted, wasp-waisted figure made Barbaraannette suddenly conscious of her own body. She had a momentary fantasy—no more than one second—of Art Dobbleman's enormous hands circling her waist, lifting her as if she were weightless.

The telephone fell silent after a dozen rings.

Barbaraannette locked the front and back doors. She went to her bedroom and stripped off her jeans and the Minnesota State Lottery sweatshirt and unhooked her bra and let it fall to the floor. She examined herself in the dressing mirror. A little soft, perhaps, but not bad for thirty-four. She frowned at the elastic waistband of her panties, which cut a tad deeper into her flesh than she would have liked. Her waist was only two inches larger than it had been in high school, but they were two very soft inches. She should not have eaten that slice of Cowboy Cake.

Her breasts, however, had remained nearly perfect. Perhaps even better than before. Regrettably, it had been six years since she'd permitted anyone to admire them. What a waste! She was reminded of a drawing class she had taken in college. The instructor had taught them to see the human form as a collection of geometric shapes. Barbaraannette saw herself as a collection of circles and ovals. She was all curves. Toagie, on the other hand, would be a clattery collection of triangles, whereas Mary Beth's body could best be depicted by an orderly stack of solid rectangles.

The phone began to ring again. Barbaraannette flopped onto her bed and pulled a pillow around the back of her head, pressing the pillow hard against her ears, crossing her forearms over her eyes to block the light.

The truth was, she'd been letting herself go. Ever since Bobby left she'd done everything she could to make herself dull and uninviting. Dressing like a frump, no makeup, and avoiding situations where she might get asked out. Why? Barbaraannette was not entirely sure. Perhaps she was in mourning for her failed marriage, or punishing herself for being unable to hang on to her man. Or maybe she was simply uninterested in other men, and this was her way of keeping them at bay. The strategy, if that was what it was, was not entirely effective. Toagie was right—despite her efforts to put them off, there were still plenty of men interested in her. Every few weeks another brave soul would make his move, and Barbaraannette would shoot him down. None of them were Bobby Quinn. Barbaraannette closed her eyes and remembered his face.

For six years she had been thinking about what she would do if she ever saw him again. There were times when she saw herself making love to him, then breaking a lamp over his head. Sometimes the small bedside lamp in the bedroom, sometimes the brass floor lamp in the living room. Sometimes she hit him with another type of furnishing altogether. The sofa, for instance. Sometimes she hit him with something and then they made love. She even had fantasies in which he returned to her with some perfectly logical explanation of why he had disappeared and made love to her, repeatedly. Maybe the only reason he had left her was because his little dude ranch scheme had gone awry. He had fled Cold Rock to save himself from his investors. It had been a bad plan to begin with. Hugh Hulke and Rodney Gent, Bobby's old high school buddies, should have known better than to give Bobby their money. It could be—it was *possible*—that Hugh and Rodney had scared Bobby off, and that he had planned to send for her but something had happened to distract him. Maybe he'd been hit on the head and got amnesia. Maybe he was dead. Or maybe he wasn't and if he came back, if she had the chance to remind him of how good they were together, he would not be able to leave her again. He would have to be with her always.

Of course, she knew that was a load of crap. But she thought about it. She'd had six years to develop a wide variety of theories, some of them actually believable. Most of the time she thought he'd taken up with some other woman. Or women.

Barbaraannette had formulated hundreds of plans based on dozens of reunion scenarios, but winning the lottery and offering a one-million-dollar reward had never been one of them. As she had confessed to Hilde, that had been an unplanned, impulsive act. Staring into the television cameras, she had been as surprised as anyone to hear the words coming out of her mouth.

Art Dobbleman was probably right. They were all right. She

should withdraw the reward offer. If Bobby wanted to come back to her—assuming he was even alive enough to do so—he would come back on his own.

But that was not the way Barbaraannette Quinn did things. She had made the offer, and she would stand by it. She would see it through. Her marriage was unfinished business. If the reward offer resulted in Bobby's return, she would decide then and there what to do next. She would take him back, or she would divorce him. Either way, she could finally get on with her life. And if he did not come back? Well, she'd be that much richer.

The muffled ringing of the telephone cut through the pillow. It had been ringing for a long time. What if it was Bobby?

She was not ready for him. Squeezing the pillow hard against her ears, she lay there until the ringing ceased.

This time, Phlox let the phone ring twenty times, hot Oklahoma wind whistling through the phone booth, before slamming the handset back on its cradle. She stomped back to where Bobby was pumping gas into the pickup.

"No answer," she said.

Bobby looked up; a gust of wind snatched his Resistol. His arm shot out and caught the hat by its brim. He screwed it back onto his head and said, "Maybe she's not home."

"Thanks, Kojak. Maybe you gave me the wrong number."

Bobby shrugged. "Or she changed it." The pump clicked off; he removed the nozzle and screwed the cap back on the tank. "Doesn't really matter. We'll get there eventually. Nobody else is gonna be turning me in, right?"

"I just think we should tell her we're coming."

"You can call again later, next time we fill up. Hey, you hungry?" Bobby pointed at a small cafe across the street. Phlox followed his gesture. A yellowed sign in the window read, *Same Cook Since 1946.*

"I don't think so," she said.

"Well I am."

"I don't know how you stay so skinny, all you want to do is eat. You must have a tapeworm the size of a rattlesnake."

"Got to keep my strength up."

Phlox sighed.

The anticipation was almost sexual. Art's hands shook as he tightened the laces of his trainers. He planned to do the creek run this afternoon, a fifteen-miler. He stood up, shook out his long arms, pulled the brim of his baseball cap low over his eyes, loped down his driveway toward the street. The early evening air cut through the fabric of his singlet and raised goosebumps on his shoulders and legs. It wouldn't last. He picked up his pace once he reached the river, and was warm by the time he crossed the third bridge.

It took Art twenty minutes to run the six bridges, crossing and recrossing the small but swift North Rock River that ran through the center of Cold Rock. At the last bridge, a half mile north of town, he turned into the overgrown trail that led to Easton Creek. The thin branches of saplings slapped his bare arms, flensing the tensions of the day. He reached the creek and turned at the dirt path, heading upstream. His soles hitting earth sounded like an extra heartbeat; his breathing became steady and deep. He gave himself to the sensations of silky cool air passing over his flesh, blood racing through dilated arteries. He settled into a steady eight-minute-per-mile pace and fixed his eyes on a point thirty feet in his future. Like a seal underwater or an albatross in flight, Art Dobbleman's everyday awkwardness gave way to grace and efficiency. His anxieties crumbled as he became one with his motion; new thoughts formed and came into sharp focus. He considered buying a pair of the new running shoes from Saucony, and promised himself to call his sister in St. Paul. He remembered that his friend Steve's birthday was coming up, and he made a mental note to send a thank-you to his aunt for the book of Christian meditations she had sent him last month. He decided to change long distance providers, and to cancel his subscription to the Minneapolis paper. Slowly, as the miles fell away, the tiles of his life sorted themselves and fell into place. At mile twelve, heading downstream on the other side of Easton Creek, his mind soft and clear as aspic, he allowed himself to consider Barbaraannette.

12

Nobody said boo to her in the faculty lounge. *They ignored her.* Barbaraannette had braced herself for a storm of Monday morning congratulations and questions, but they were acting as if she were invisible. Sally and Pat sat in their usual chairs drinking coffee and eating cookies and talking and never looked up when Barbaraannette entered the lounge. Henry Stewart hid behind his Cold Rock Gazette, and when Mr. Grunseth, the principal, made his morning pass through the lounge to fill his giant ceramic mug with coffee, his eyes slid off Barbaraannette like a boot off a slick rock. She made her escape to the refuge of her classroom.

All twenty-six of her kids ogled her as though she'd walked in sporting a set of antlers. Even Johnny Kemmel, who was always the last to take his seat and the first to misbehave, sat quietly at his desk and stared at her.

Barbaraannette began class, as was her custom, with a short reading from Winnie the Pooh. She opened *The House at Pooh Corner* to the chapter in which Tigger is Un-bounced, then changed her mind and closed the book and said, "One day while walking through the forest on an ever so slightly cloudy morning, Pooh had a feeling that he was about to trip over something and fall and bonk his nose, so he looked down to see what it was that was about to trip him. There, all white and square on the ground, lay an envelope.

"Now, Pooh had never before seen an envelope in such a location before, and he had particularly not seen such an envelope such as this, with his name, Pooh, printed across it in large clear letters—" Barbaraannette saw a small hand reach into the air.

"Yes, Janey?"

"My mom says you aren't going to be our teacher anymore because you're rich."

Barbaraannette was not sure how to respond to that, so she said, "We can talk about that later, Janey. Would you like to hear the rest of the story?"

"Yes, Mrs. Quinn," said Janey.

Barbaraannette continued. "Naturally, Pooh decided that since it was he that had found the envelope, and because the name Pooh was printed upon it, it would be all right for him to open it. And so he did.

"Inside the envelope was a note, which Pooh attempted to read. He could make out the words 'Pooh' and 'Lucky,' and some Very Large Numbers, and a Very Official-Looking Signature, but the rest of the message was gibberish."

Janey's hand shot up.

"Yes, Janey?"

"What's gibberish?"

"I don't know, Janey. And neither did Pooh. He stood stroking his chin and saying, 'Hmmmmmm. Ahem. Tut tut!' After several *Hmmms and Ahems* and *Tuts* he decided to take the note to Christopher Robin . . . Yes, Adam?"

"Are you going to buy a limousine?"

"No, Adam. I already have a car. Pooh, however, does not drive, so he had to walk all the way across the forest to Christopher Robin's house, where he presented his Mysterious Note. Christopher Robin examined the note carefully.

" 'Why Pooh,' he said after reading it, 'I do believe you have won the lottery!'

" 'A lot of what?' asked Pooh, scratching his head.

" 'Lottery,' said Christopher Robin. 'You have won a Lifetime Supply of honey! You're rich!' "

"Mrs. Quinn?" It was Adam Berg again.

"Yes, Adam?"

"How many is a Lifetime Supply?"

"Oh, let's say a million spoonfuls."

"My dad says you're crazy."

Barbaraannette formed a strained smile. "Your father has a right to his opinion, Adam. Would you like to hear the rest of the story? Good. Pooh was very pleased to learn that he had won a Lifetime Supply of honey, but he soon found out that being rich was not all it was cracked up to be. The first thing he noticed was that he had a lot of Uninvited Guests showing up at all hours of the day and night.

"Now, Pooh dearly loved to be dropped in on, and he believed that the only thing more welcome than an Uninvited Guest was an Invited Guest. Of course, he allowed all of them to sample his Lifetime Supply of honey.

"It wasn't long before things got out of hand . . . Yes, Adam?"

"You should buy all the yellow paint in the world."

Although she was curious, Barbaraannette refrained from asking why. "I'll think about that, Adam. So, one morning Pooh looked out his front door to find a long line of his friends and acquaintances and their friends and relatives, and so forth, and each of them was carrying an empty jar, and Pooh realized that his Lifetime Supply of honey would not last a week if he gave everyone what they wanted."

Barbaraannette stood up and wrote the numeral one followed by six zeros on the green chalkboard.

"Who can tell me how big this number is?" she said.

13

"I think you got mail from every Cadillac dealer in Minnesota," Toagie said, tossing another envelope into the wastebasket.

"A couple dealers from Wisconsin, too," said Barbaraannette, lifting another letter from the pile on her kitchen table. She had arrived home from school to find a corrugated cardboard bin marked U.S.P.S. on her front steps. It was filled to the top with letters. She and Toagie had been working their way through the mountain of mail for more than an hour. "Everybody's so happy for me I just can't hardly stand it. I even got a note from the governor."

"Asking for money?"

"Not yet, but you can bet he'll be begging come election time."

"Well you can't hardly blame 'em, Barbaraannette."

"It was all my students wanted to talk about. Adam Berg asked if I was going to buy a limousine."

"Are you?"

"No. But I might need one of those electric letter openers." She reached into the box and exracted another letter. "I feel like I've got to read every last one. I like the ones that just flat out ask for money. At least I know where they stand." She slit the envelope with a paring knife and unfolded the letter inside. A photograph fell into her lap.

Toagie polished off her third Pepsi, dropped it into the waste-basket.

"That goes in recycling," Barbaraannette said.

Toagie emitted a short belch, picked the can from the waste-basket, and tossed it in the direction of the recycling bin. It fell short, bounced, and rolled under the sink. Barbaraannette frowned at the errant can, then returned her attention to the letter and photograph.

"So, you're not buying a limo. You gonna buy a Cadillac?" Toagie asked, tearing open another envelope.

"Not on your life." Barbaraannette handed her sister the letter. "Take a look at this one, Toag."

Dear Mrs. Quinn,

I recently saw you on t.v. and it changed my life.

Previous to seeing you I was deep in a Clinical Depression. My doctor prescribed Prozac but it made me sick. Also it was expensive. But the fact that I still have the use of my arms after the motorcycle accident where I ran off the road to avoid hitting a bus filled with innocent schoolchildren is a good thing. Life was very hard for me after they amputated my legs, but all the innocent children survived!!!

After my accident I struggled hard to find a purpose in life to go on living. The Clinical Depression made me extremely suicidal so I decided to take an overdose of drugs. But then I saw you win the Powerball. Once I saw that I knew that life was worth living. You are so lucky!!! Maybe you know that already. I am inspired to enter the lottery myself. Unfortunately, I am on an extremely limited budget. No one will hire me as I am a cripple now and the amount of money I get from also getting wounded fighting Saddam in the Gulf War is very poor. I hardly have enough for food and rent and to support my mother who has Alzheimer's.

Do you have any extra Powerball tickets? I would be extremely grateful if you could spare some to give me the same chance as you had. Or if not, if you would send a donation in any amount, I could afford to buy them myself.

Admiringly,
Your biggest fan!!!
Jonathan James Morrow

14

What fascinated André about Jayjay Morrow, aside from his obvious physical charms, was his purity. Jayjay had somehow escaped the taint of original sin. He never looked back, never criticized himself, never examined his own actions. He lived entirely in the present. He did whatever he wanted to do without a second thought. He had no self-consciousness, no conscience, no guilt. He was pure and simple—an animal in human form.

Jayjay had been completely forthright with André regarding his recent address at the Minnesota Correctional Facility at St. Cloud where he had served one year for assault and battery. He had severely beaten a man who, he claimed, had molested him. Jayjay had mentioned this to André at a most awkward moment, then laughed. André did not ask for details. The thrill of the unknown, in this case, appealed to him. Like owning a large and dangerous pet, this walk on the wild side added a bit of spice to his otherwise uneventful academic life.

André watched Jayjay shovel the last of his smoked salmon omelet into his wide mouth, drop his fork on his plate, grin, and leave the table. No "thank you," no offer to help with the dishes, no recognition that André had prepared yet another free meal for him. Just that smile, huge and guileless. A few seconds later André heard the sound of the television coming from the guest bedroom—the theme from *Jeopardy*. In anyone else such behavior would have been inexcusably rude, but coming from Jayjay it was simply part of the package. The boy wasn't rude. He was simply oblivious.

André set about clearing the breakfast table, humming along with the *Jeopardy* theme. *Dee-doo-dee-doo, dee-dooo-dee.* He was finishing the breakfast dishes when Jayjay reappeared wearing the leather jacket André had purchased for him the day before.

"That jacket looks very nice on you," André said.

Jayjay grinned, grabbed an apple from the fruit basket and the keys to André's car from the counter, and headed for the door.

"Are you going out?" André asked.

Jayjay said, "Post Office," as he opened the back door.

"I have a class at eleven o'clock. Will you be returning by then?"

If Jayjay replied, his words were cut off by the slamming door. André blinked, then smiled ruefully. The *Jeopardy* theme was still coming from the guest bedroom, and he was sure that the bed remained undressed. A bit like having a teenage son, he supposed.

He thought of his mother, sitting in her little house in Diamond Bluff, Wisconsin. He had not called her in two days. If Mother could see him now, what would she think of Jayjay? He could almost hear her dry voice: "Someone ought to take a switch to that child." Shortly thereafter, she would find occasion to remark upon André's unmarried status. He had tried to tell her that marriage was not likely with him. He had even, once, come right out and told her he was gay. If the words had entered her ears, they had died before entering her conscious mind. She could not or would not hear him.

But if she *could* hear, if she understood who and what he was, then how would she feel? Would she be happy for him? Watching him serving breakfast to a young man—a child, really, who could not spell the word "unfortunately," who had once by his own admission nearly beaten a man to death, who treated him like a servant? How would she feel to see him teaching Sophocles to farm kids at the barely accredited Cold Rock College for sixteen thousand four hundred dollars a semester? If she understood who he really was, would she accept him? Would she be proud?

André felt his eyes filling with warm tears. Of course she would. She would be as proud as any mother. He had achieved a great deal.

He had a well-stocked wine cellar, a comfortable home, a tenured teaching position, and an exciting new house guest. He was a good person and a respected member of the academic community. He had money in the bank, a roof over his head, his health, and Jayjay Morrow. What else could a woman want for her only son?

All things considered, in the first year of his second half-century, André Gideon was a happy man.

"What's the matter, honey bun?" Phlox asked. "You keep slowing down. Something the matter with the truck?"

Bobby shook his head and brought the speedometer back up to sixty. "I guess I'm just not looking forward to Cold Rock."

Phlox gazed out at the passing snowbanks, gray with road grime. A lone billboard, brown with yellow lettering, stood in a sodden field a few hundred yards from the highway:

Taxidermy & Cheese Shoppe
8 miles

Suppressing a shudder, she said, "Just keep thinking about the money."

"That's what I'm doing. But I'm thinking about Barbaraannette, too. The woman scares me, and that's no lie."

Phlox rested a hand on his thigh. "Pookie, I just can't imagine a big strong man like you being scared by a little girl like that."

"She's not so little."

"I saw her on TV, sweetie. What's so scary?"

Bobby pushed out his lips, saying nothing.

Phlox said, "She funny in the head?"

"It depends what you call funny. I ever tell you what she did to me that New Year's?"

"You never even told me you were married, Pook." Phlox dug her nails hard into his thigh.

"Ow!" Bobby swerved and slapped at her hand. "Jesus! You want me to have an accident?"

"What did she do?" Phlox asked.

Bobby rubbed his leg. "The New Year's before I left, we go to this party? You know, having a few drinks, a good time. Anyways, we get separated, right? I go off with some other people and lose track of Barbaraannette. I finally get home about three or four and Barbaraannette's already in bed, and I get in there next to her, pretty loaded, and she doesn't say a word, so I go to sleep. Next thing I know, I feel something hot on my face and I open my eyes and she's holding a lighter over my mouth close enough to burn nose hair. She says, 'I just wanted to see if you were flammable drunk, or just regular drunk.'

"I sit up and go, like, 'What the hell you doing?' And she starts going on about me and Tanya McElliot and all this other stuff, and finally she lets me get to sleep again, and then something hits me in the face and I wake up and she's sitting there in bed with a knife slicing up a zucchini squash. Staring at me and cutting slices off the zucchini and throwing them at me. I had to go sleep in my Jeep."

Phlox said, "Who's Tanya McElliot?"

"Just this girl."

"You don't plan on seeing her, right?"

Bobby frowned. "Anyways, it was more than just that. One time she got the idea I'd had this other woman in our bed and she hauled our mattress down to the river and threw it off the bridge."

Phlox said, "Was she right?"

"She ruined the damn mattress! What's right about that?"

"I mean, was she right about you messing around with somebody on her bed?"

"Her bed? It was *our* bed, and what difference does that make?"

"It made a difference to her."

"No shit. But forget about Barbaraannette, I got other things to worry about, too. I had a business go sour on me, too. Some folks might not have forgot about that."

"What sort of business?" This was the first Phlox had heard of it.

"We were gonna start up a dude ranch, me and these other guys. I had my eye on this property out in Wyoming, and I got these guys to go in on it with me. Actually, they were the ones putting up the money."

"What happened?"

"Nothing."

"So what's the problem?"

"*That's* the problem. See, I kinda-sorta didn't get around to buying the land."

"Oh. But you kept some of the money?"

"I didn't keep it, I spent it."

"Oh." Phlox stared out at the landscape of dirty snow and frozen mud. Somehow none of these things about Bobby's past surprised her. "So you owe a few people some money. What are we talking?"

"Just a few thousand." Bobby's cheek twitched. "About twenty, actually."

"Pookie! How many guys do you owe it to?"

"Two. Three, counting some I got from Barbaraannette, only she doesn't need it now."

Phlox laughed. "Punkin, you are a case."

Bobby pointed. "There, you see that little blue thing sticking up there? That's the water tower." The pale blue globe with white lettering peeked above the horizon for a few seconds, then sank below the horizon as they entered a dip.

"What'd it say on it?" Phlox asked.

"You'll see." The highway followed the base of a low hill, then began to climb. The engine pinged as the truck strained for elevation. Bobby down-shifted and muttered, "Goddamn gasohol." They crested the hill; the town of Cold Rock lay below them spread across a broad valley. A glittering gray river sliced through the town, which was stitched together by a series of six low bridges. "That's the North Rock River, where Barbaraannette threw our mattress in. Use to have a couple mills on it, I guess, but now it just looks good and every few years it floods all of downtown and everybody threatens to move their businesses away. But they never do."

The water tower, Phlox could now see, read, *Home of the Crockettes.*

"Crockettes?"

"Women's softball. They won the state championship back in eighty-something."

"It's bigger than I thought." Phlox could pick out at least three church spires, a small downtown area straddling the river, and a complex of grain elevators a mile or two upstream.

"Twelve thousand people. Maybe fifteen by now. They even got a college here." Bobby pushed in the clutch and let the truck coast down the long hill into town. They passed a McDonald's, a Pump-n-Munch, and a Taco Bell. "The Taco Bell is new. You hungry?" Bobby asked.

"No," Phlox said, still recovering from the Taxidermy & Cheese Shoppe concept. "How about we just get this over with? We go to your wife's and I collect the reward and we get the hell out of town. You can eat all the way back to Tucson."

Bobby looked longingly at the Taco Bell as they drove past. "She might not let me go so quick. Don't forget, she's shelling out a million bucks."

"What's she going to do? Tie you up?"

Bobby's face contracted into a pained expression. "Hell, I never understood the woman when I was living with her. I got no idea what's on her mind."

Nothing. Not even a letter. Jayjay peered through the open back of his Post Office box. He could see right through to the mailroom. Nobody looking. He peered through the tiny window in the brass box next to his. The guy had a couple of letters and a magazine. Jayjay pushed his arm through his open box, turned his wrist back to reach into his neighbor's box from the rear, grabbed the magazine, and drew it back out through his own box. *People* magazine, one of his favorites. He left the Post Office feeling as though he had not wasted his time and walked back to the car wondering what he should do with the rest of his morning. It was a nice sunny day. Probably get up into the sixties. He could stop in at the Nose, have a bloody Mary, hang out for a while. Or go for a long drive in the country, watch the snow melt. He didn't feel like going back to the professor's house. Eating the guy's food and drinking his wine was okay, and he didn't mind the sex, but he didn't want to spend a whole morning with André, have the guy fawning over him and telling long stories about people Jayjay didn't know and worst of all wanting to go for walks. Nothing Jayjay hated worse than walking down the street with a queer. A little town like this you didn't want people thinking you were light in the loafers. Jayjay was not inclined that way himself. He'd been with a few other older guys, and of course there was his time in jail, but he was no freehole punk and he damn sure wasn't gay. He'd been with plenty of women, too. Whatever. No more walks with the old fag, he decided. Especially not here in Cold Rock.

That was the problem with small towns. You never knew who you were gonna run into. He might see his aunt Nadine, who would want to know where he'd disappeared to and why he hadn't showed up for work at Souvenir Specialty Supply. Why? He could tell her why. Because gluing little cloisonné plaques with the names of the states onto the handles of miniature teaspoons, forks, and butter knives was not work, it was slow torture. He had taken the job because it was a condition of his parole that he be employed, and because his aunt Nadine had agreed to hire him, but after three weeks of gluing plaques onto flatware Jayjay had had enough. Now that he had someplace to crash other than Nadine's back bedroom, he could see no reason to continue his employment.

Jayjay decided on the long drive, maybe head up to Grand Casino, throw a few bucks at the Indians, maybe hit a jackpot on the slots. He started the car, then noticed the gas gauge was near empty. His smile collapsed, his face contorted and reddened. He drew back a fist and punched the steering wheel hard, ten times in rapid succession, screaming, "Fuck, fuck, fuck, fuck!" He locked both hands on the wheel and became motionless for several seconds, breathing shallowly, slowly bringing his features back to neutral. When he had composed himself sufficiently, he reached out and snapped off one of the knobs from the climate control panel and threw it out the window. That made him feel a little better.

Putting the car in gear, Jayjay headed up the street to the Mobil station. He pumped ten bucks into the tank, paid the guy inside, and was about to pull out when he noticed the cowboy pumping gas into an old white pickup. He was sure he'd seen the man's face somewhere before—in the paper, or in a movie or something. Jayjay sat perfectly still, hands on the steering wheel, his eyes locked on the man in the cowboy hat, waiting for his brain to sort things out.

A few minutes before the lunch bell, Principal Grunseth tapped on the glass door of Barbaraannette's classroom, interrupting her explanation of why the United States doesn't have a king. He pointed at her, then at himself, then up toward the second floor, then raised his eyebrows. Barbaraannette nodded. He wanted her to come up to his office after the kids were released for lunch. He disappeared from the glass, and she returned to her explanation.

"So you see, instead of having a king, every four years all the people vote on who they want to run the country."

Adam Berg raised his hand. "My dad says that the country is run by Jews."

"Our country is run by many different kinds of people, Adam."

"He says that school is turning me into a little robot. Robots are cool. My dad smokes cigarettes."

"I'm sure he does."

"He said that you're as rich as a Jew now."

Thankfully, the lunch bell rang. Barbaraannette herded her kids out into the hall and in the direction of the cafeteria, then climbed the stairs, rapped on Principal Grunseth's door, and let herself into his office.

Lewis Grunseth held his forty extra pounds high in his abdomen, giving him the look of a man perpetually holding his breath. He had small, round eyes, an upcurved smile, and he kept his thinning hair cropped close to his skull. Grunseth was only six years older than Barbaraannette, but he had embraced middle age early on. He demanded that the students call him "sir" and that the faculty address him as "Mr. Grunseth," even in private conversation.

Barbaraannette, who remembered him mowing their lawn when he was a teenager, had trouble with that, so she usually called him nothing at all.

"Well, well, if it isn't the lottery winner!" said Grunseth, standing and gesturing for Barbaraannette to take a seat. "That's quite a thing! Quite a thing."

Barbaraannette sat down. "I'm still trying to get used to the idea," she said.

"Quite a thing! Yes sir!" Grunseth said. "Yes sir!"

Barbaraannette realized with a start that he was nervous, like a man with bad news to relate. Her first thought was that Hilde had had a stroke, or gone for an unsupervised walk and been hit by a car.

"Is something wrong?" she asked, gripping the plastic arms of the chair. "Is it my mother?"

"Your mother? No! I just wanted to talk to you, Barbaraannette. Talk about what you're going to do now. All that money?"

Was he going to ask her for money? Barbaraannette waited, more curious than anything.

Grunseth cleared his throat. "Ah, I assume that you, ah, won't want to go on teaching?"

"Why would you assume that?" She hadn't actually thought about it. Even with her lottery money she would still need something to do during the day.

"Well, ah, I mean, since you obviously don't need the money . . ."

Barbaraannette waited.

Grunseth cleared his throat again and continued. "I mean . . . I mean, since, you know. You don't have to work . . . and then of course there is the Pooh problem. I really don't know what you were thinking about, Barbaraannette. We've had complaints!"

Pooh problem? Barbaraannette said, "What are you talking about?"

"Several complaints. I understand that yesterday you told your students that Pooh had won some sort of lottery?" Grunseth paused.

"Something like that," Barbaraannette admitted.

Grunseth slapped his palm down on his desk blotter. "You can't go around making up stories that aren't in the texts!"

"Winnie the Pooh? That's not a textbook."

"For God's sake, Barbaraannette, it's Winnie the Pooh!"

"Tell me you're joking, Lew," said Barbaraannette.

Grunseth was too agitated to take offense at the familiar use of his first name. "You told them that Pooh won the lottery, for God's sake!"

"And what's wrong with that?" Barbaraannette asked, genuinely puzzled. "It was simply a way of introducing them to their arithmetic lesson."

"Barbaraannette, people don't want to think about you having all that money. It makes them feel like they don't have enough."

"People felt that way before I won it, Lew."

"And now you're using up a job that maybe somebody else needs to make ends meet. There are a lot of young teachers out there looking for work, you know."

"Are you asking me to quit?" Barbaraannette asked.

Grunseth pursed his lips and looked down at his desk blotter. "I just think you should consider the effect you are having on other people's lives," he said, adjusting the position of his desk calendar.

"This isn't about Winnie the Pooh, is it?"

"We had complaints."

"How many, Lew?"

He shrugged. "Oh, you know." He dragged his forefinger across his desk blotter, following impressions invisible to Barbaraannette. "The usual. George Berg, Adam's father."

Barbaraannette felt her face heating up. "Have you seen what that man has on his truck?"

"I . . . what?"

"Adam's father. He has a bumper sicker that says 'My Kid Beat Up Your Honor Roll Student.' I really don't think we should be designing our curriculum around his opinions."

"Yes, well, you're right of course." He drew a figure eight on his blotter, lifted his finger. "Look, the Pooh thing is no big deal, Barbaraannette. I don't know why I brought it up. I just thought that if you were thinking of leaving us . . ." He stared down at his invisible drawing with the intensity of a seer reading tea leaves. "I wanted to let you know that I've got someone willing to step in and take over your class."

Barbaraannette remembered something then, a rumor she'd heard about the college. They were cutting way back on their Liberal Arts program to make room for the new veterinary school. She heard they were eliminating a dozen tenured positions. "Is your wife one of the professors getting laid off at the college, Lew?"

Lewis Grunseth's face bloomed bright red. He slapped his palm down on his desk. "You leave Angie out of this! And don't call me 'Lew'!"

Barbaraannette sat back, startled by the outburst, but continued her thought. "Let me guess. Angela is your candidate for taking over my class, and you want me out of here as soon as possible. Right?"

Grunseth's eyes bulged; he squeezed his fist so hard Barbaraannette could read the bones through his skin.

She said, "That's going to be quite an adjustment, going from teaching Kant and Hegel to reading *The House at Pooh Corner* out loud. From the text."

Grunseth took a deep breath. He touched his fingertips to his temples, shaking his head slowly. "There aren't a lot of teaching positions in Cold Rock."

"I know that."

"Damn it, Barbaraannette, you've won nine million dollars! You can do anything you want! Why do you want to spend your days with a bunch of seven-year-olds?"

Barbaraannette licked her lips. She could taste blood now, and maybe that was enough. She said, "The fact is, Lew, I'm not sure that I do."

Grunseth's shoulders dropped. He stared at her, lips parted, eyes naked with hope.

15

B*obby Quinn stood with one hand resting on the handle of the gas pump,* his mind drifting through a maze of memories. Six years ago he had filled up at this very same Mobil station on his way out of town. He wondered what had happened to that old Jeep of his. He'd left it broke-down in Mitchell. Planned to sell it, but then he'd met a gal named Dora on her way to Denver and the easy thing to do had been to hop in her little Mazda and ride her west. Denver Dora. She'd been a stand-up comedian working the comedy club circuit. He'd about bust a gut every time she started talking. Funniest woman Bobby ever met. He'd stayed with her a month until it got cold out and he headed down toward Tucson.

The gas pump clicked off, interrupting his reverie. Bobby gave the handle another squeeze, brought the total up to twenty dollars even. Now he was back in the land of the Crockettes and about to face Barbaraannette, a former Crockette herself. A cold, loose feeling slithered over his bowels. She was going to be kinda upset with him. Bobby thought about the million bucks, and that helped a little, but he was still plenty nervous. He looked toward the office where Phlox was trying once more to call Barbaraannette. A million bucks. Who knew what Phlox would do once she got her mitts on that kind of money? Half of him was thinking she might just take off and leave him, and the other half was thinking that he might just decide to stay with Barbaraannette, see what it felt like to be a rich woman's husband.

He climbed into the back of the pickup, unzipped his travel case, lifted out the hat box containing his El Presidente. Nothing like a fresh hat, especially an El Presidente, to make a man feel better. He removed his everyday straw hat, lifted the El Presidente from its nest and fitted it onto his head. There. He felt better already, knowing that he wore the finest chapeau in Cold Rock and maybe even in the whole state of Minnesota. He stood up in the back of the pickup, feeling tall.

"Well I'll be goddamned to hell and back, look what we got here!"

Bobby twitched at the familiar voice. Hugh? He looked down at the heavyset man staring intently at him from the other side of the pumps. For a moment, Bobby felt himself relax. It wasn't Hugh Hulke, just an older, balding guy who sounded like Hugh. Then his mind stripped away forty pounds, put some hair back on the guy's head. The man's lips curled back, revealing a gold-capped incisor. It was Hugh, all right.

Bobby wondered if he could jump down, get behind the wheel, get the truck started, and make it out the driveway without Hugh getting his hands around his neck. Hit the door lock with one hand while turning the key with the other. Unless Hugh had something he could bust the window with, Bobby figured he had a chance. He was about to go for it when a second voice came from behind him.

"That who I think it is?"

Rodney Gent, looking even bigger than he had six years ago, draped his oversize hands over the tailgate. That pretty much destroyed any chance Bobby had of getting into the pickup unscathed. Rodney would put his fist through the windshield as easy as punching through drywall. Bobby cast an anxious glance toward the store, hoping Phlox would read his mind and come running out, start yelling or something, give him a chance to get away.

Hugh said, "It sure does look like him, Rod Man. Only maybe even slimier. That's you, ain't it, Bobby? Where you been? Hiding out on your pretend dude ranch?"

Bobby took a half step back, looked over his shoulder. Both

Hugh and Rodney lowered their heads and shifted positions. Back in high school the two men had played defense for the Cold Rock Chiefs. Bobby hadn't played any football himself, but in that moment he knew how it felt to be a quarterback with no open receivers.

Hugh said, keeping his eyes hard on Bobby, "You know what he looks like to me, Rod Man?"

"What's that?"

"Looks like cash on the hoof, that's what."

Bobby made his move, scrambling over the truck cab and off the hood, hitting the ground running, one hand holding his hat to his head. He pounded down the sidewalk, no idea where he was going, heard the roar of an engine, tires squealing. How had they gotten into their car so fast? Bobby ducked between Smitty's Auto Body and the bowling alley, jumped a chain link fence, and cut through somebody's backyard to Fifth Street. He stopped, gasping for air. Had he lost them? He heard a roar, looked back to see an eggplant-colored van coming around the corner. He saw Hugh's face through the windshield. Bobby took off, jumped another fence, ran down an alley. He was crossing Elm Street when a green Ford Taurus screeched to a stop in front of him. The driver, a smiling blond-headed kid, reached over and opened the passenger door.

"You need a lift?"

Bobby looked both ways, then saw the van again, coming fast down Elm. He got into the Ford and shouted, "Go! Go! They're after me!" The kid stomped on the gas, made the turn onto Main Street, tires skittering, turned again at Fifth, doubled back on Maple.

Bobby looked back.

The kid said, "Don't worry, there's no way they're gonna catch us in that old thing."

"Good." Bobby slumped in the seat, some of the tension draining out of him.

"How come they're after you?"

"I don't know. They think I owe them some money."

"You need a place to stay?"

"I've got to get back to my truck. My girl's gonna be wondering about me."

"Sure, that's no problem. Only I've got to stop off at home, first. You don't mind, do you?"

Bobby looked back, again. No sign of the van. Maybe it would be best to wait a while—Hugh and Rodney might be waiting for him back at the station. He could hook up with Phlox later, somehow. He took a closer look at his savior. A college kid, blond-haired and smiley. Nothing to worry about there.

"That's fine by me," he said.

The kid, grinning like a fool, bobbed his head happily. "I got to stop at the hardware store, too. Pick up some of that duct tape." His grin widened. "And maybe a pipewrench."

"Doing some plumbing?"

"Yeah."

Bobby knew almost nothing about plumbing, but he said, "Maybe I could give you a hand." It would kill some time while he figured out what he should do next.

"I appreciate that." Nodding and grinning.

Bobby figured the guy had a few loose connections, but that was cool. Nobody was perfect.

16

Phlox hung up the phone. Still no answer. She heard a man shouting and looked out the service station window. She saw two men jumping into a maroon van, the driver taking off before the other guy even got his door closed. At the same time, a green car fishtailed out of the lot, leaving a cloud of dust and smoke. Within two seconds they were both out of sight.

Phlox said to the kid behind the counter, "What was that about?"

The clerk shrugged. "I dunno. The guy in the hat took off running, then all hell broke loose."

"Hat?"

"Like a cowboy hat."

Phlox pushed through the door and ran out to the truck. No sign of Bobby, just the pickup truck. She went back inside.

"You say you saw him run off?"

"Like he was being chased."

Phlox nodded, putting the pieces together. She should have realized. Letting Bobby show his face in public in this town was akin to wearing the Koh-i-noor diamond to a convention of thieves. She paid the clerk for the gas, then went out to the truck and sat in the driver's seat staring out the windshield trying to think it out. He got away, or he didn't, or he got caught and he'll get away, or he won't. He's hiding or he isn't. He'll come back to the gas station soon, or never. After a time, the clerk came out and asked her to move away from the pumps. Phlox drove the pickup to the corner of the lot and sat there for another twenty minutes. Finally, the image of Bobby being dragged back to his wife by faceless men prompted her to act.

She went back inside and said to the clerk, "If my friend with the hat comes looking for me, tell him I went to talk to his wife."

Of the three, it was Barbaraannette who'd got the looks and the fashion sense, though she hadn't really blossomed until the year after she graduated from Henry High—the year after her first romance with Bobby Quinn.

Hilde remembered the day Barbaraannette had come home late from the Henry High graduation party, swollen-lipped and bright-eyed with nothing to say. Hilde had been concerned like any good mother, but she'd known the day had long been coming and there wasn't a damn thing she could do to stop it. She took Barbaraannette to Dr. Fox, got her a prescription for birth control pills, and then bought her a root beer float at Lang's Pharmacy.

That boy Bobby had given Barbaraannette a few heady weeks of young love, then cast his eye in other directions, the way boys will. The breakup had been hard on Barbaraannette. That fall, wounded and bitter, she had left Cold Rock to attend college in Florida.

The next time Hilde saw her daughter, it was as if God herself had reached down from heaven and transformed her. She'd dropped twenty pounds of baby fat, her skin and auburn hair had gone coppery with Florida sunshine, and her eyes carried in them the color of the sea. Even more striking, her personality had taken on a vivacious, self-confident sheen. For four years Hilde watched Barbaraannette become increasingly beautiful with each return visit to Cold Rock.

Then Barbaraannette had stopped visiting. Hilde had heard almost nothing from her middle daughter for three long years—a brief letter, now and then, with a new address in San Francisco, then Chicago, then New Orleans, then New York, each note citing another man's name, a new job. She'd signed her letters Barb, a name Hilde hated because it sounded so hard and sharp. She had not come home, not even for Mary Beth's wedding, for three long years.

"Mama?"

Hilde looked up from her plate of macaroni and cheese at the young woman sitting across from her. She said, "Most of the people here are old."

"Mama, it's me, Barbaraannette."

What a coincidence! She'd just been thinking about Barbaraannette. "Of course you are," she said, scooping up another forkful of the orange matter on her plate. It was salty. Hilde liked salt. "Five years you don't come home, now look at you. Barely twenty-six, you could be thirty."

"I'm thirty-four, Mama."

"Thirty-four what?" Hilde hated these games. She wished the hotel management would put a stop to them.

"Years, Mama. I have to tell you something."

"I can't stop you."

"I just quit my job at the school."

"Now why did you go and do that?" School? What school?

"They asked me to leave. They don't want me there anymore."

"Why, that's ridiculous! What's wrong with those people?"

"I think they're jealous of me."

"Well they should be! You're a beautiful girl. Will you be coming back to Cold Rock now?"

"I've been back nine years, Mama."

Hilde blinked and looked away. She heard the voice go on speaking to her, but other voices drew her into another less confusing time. She remembered now that Barbaraannette had finally returned to Cold Rock, her eyes narrower, her lipsticked mouth hard and red over the pale curve of her chin, her voice husky from cigarettes and alcohol. She had become more beautiful than ever, though it had become a sadder, more mature beauty. What Hilde remembered most vividly was the way the men of Cold Rock, even the married ones, had swarmed the new Barbaraannette.

The girl really knew how to fix herself up.

These days—Hilde abruptly found herself back in the present—

Barbaraannette did not seem to care what she wore. Her wardrobe was plain, plain, plain—all earth tones and practicality. Such a shame. Such a beautiful girl.

Hilde herself had never held back when it came to making herself look good. She'd had her breasts worked on back in the 1970s, had her face lifted twice, and had undergone a number of tucks, peels, and excisions. She'd put in four decades with Jack LaLane, spent hundreds of thousands of dollars on her wardrobe, never appeared in public without her makeup, and always kept her hair big, bold, and bright. This year she was a redhead. It was a wig, but one had to make allowances for age. After all, she was sixty-six years old.

Or was it seventy-something? She'd been sixty-six when Barbaraannette had returned to Cold Rock and renewed her romance with Frances Quinn's boy, Bobby. Sixty-six when they'd married.

Hilde said to her daughter, "You could've done better."

But when she lifted her eyes, she was alone.

17

S*he could take a trip around the world, buy herself a Rolls-Royce, feed ten* thousand hungry children, or try to get Bobby back. Or she could buy that cherrywood Hoosier she'd seen down at Eggers' Antiquarium—six foot tall and a hundred years old if it was a day. Barbaraannette wondered which course of action Hilde would recommend if she still had her wits about her—if Hilde had *ever* had her wits about her. She might have told Barbaraannette to blow the first quarter-million on clothes and hairstyling and then go find a man who had at least as much money as she did. That was how Hilde thought. On the other hand, Hilde had always understood about Bobby. That was one thing about Hilde. She always understood, even when she had no idea what was going on.

Barbaraannette made a right turn onto Foster Avenue and heard the familiar *thunk* come from the front of the car. Nang, the mechanic down at the Shell station, told her she was going to need major front-end work soon, something called CV joints. She didn't need a Rolls-Royce, or a limousine, but a new car would be nice. According to Art Dobbleman, even if she had to borrow the million bucks, she'd still have some money to play with. Maybe not enough to travel around the world and feed the starving children, but she could certainly afford a new car. Maybe a minivan, in case she bought that Hoosier and had to haul the thing home.

Barbaraannette pulled onto her street and into her driveway—

thunk–pleased to see her front steps free of reporters, family members, and bankers. She noticed a white pickup truck parked across the street, a woman with fluffy blond hair behind the wheel. Another reporter? Barbaraannette walked quickly from her car to the front door, but not quickly enough.

"Excuse me!" The woman was out of her truck, trotting across the street. She wore tight, faded blue jeans, a white snap-button Western shirt with cacti embroidered above the pockets, and dangerously pointed cowboy boots. No jacket. Everything looked as if it had been intentionally purchased one size too small except for the Mexican tooled-leather bag big enough to hold a TV set bouncing off her left hip. "Are you Mrs. Quinn?" Pale eyebrows arced over frosty blue eyes.

Barbaraannette said, "That's right."

The woman smiled and thrust out a hand. Her nails were sky blue, the same color as her eyes, and jutted half an inch beyond the tips of her fingers. "Fiona Anderson. People call me Phlox."

Barbaraannette nodded, but did not shake the dangerous-looking hand. "Are you a reporter?" she asked.

Phlox shook her head. "Not me, honey." She smiled, and hundreds of fine crinkles appeared on her face. Her hair was bleached nearly white on top, with the more protected locks retaining an ash-yellow hue. Barbaraannette guessed her to be about thirty, with a good chunk of those years spent in the sun.

"Are you going to ask me to buy something, or to donate money to a worthy cause? Because if you are, you might just as well go talk to that tree." She pointed at the maple beside her driveway.

Phlox laughed, a big, chesty laugh that made Barbaraannette want to smile. She liked women who weren't afraid to laugh loud.

"I suppose a lot of folks have been bothering you," Phlox said.

"A few," Barbaraannette admitted.

"Well I'm here about your husband."

Barbaraannette felt her heart miss a beat, then deliver an artery-swelling thump. "Bobby?"

"That's right, honey. I brought him all the way from Arizona, fresh off the desert."

"Where is he?" Barbaraannette looked past Phlox toward the pickup. The air seemed suddenly too rich; her head swam. Barbaraannette reached out and put a hand on her front door, drawing strength from its solidity.

Phlox laughed again, a little less chest in it this time. "I said I brought him, honey. I didn't say I *had* him."

Barbaraannette swallowed and heard herself say, "Would you like to come inside and sit down?" She needed to rest her rear end on something. Not waiting for Phlox to answer, she opened the door. All those years of wanting Bobby back, and now that it was happening she suddenly could not remember his face. She headed for the kitchen, needing its bright familiarity. Phlox followed.

Barbaraannette said, "Would you care for a cup of coffee?" Coffee would make sense of things, calm her down.

"Honey, coffee's the last thing I need." Phlox reached into her enormous purse—for one weird moment Barbaraannette thought she was going to pull Bobby's head out of her bag—and came out with a twelve-pack of Budweiser. She planted the twelve-pack on the counter, tore into it expertly, her long blue nails somehow surviving the process, and came out with two cold cans. "Have you a beer, sweetie pie."

Walking the two miles from campus to his home, briefcase bouncing off his thigh, André Gideon imagined himself giving young Jayjay a piece of his mind. "You had better learn to be more responsible, young man, or you will find yourself out on the street," he would say. "I will only be pushed so far!"

He imagined Jayjay laughing at him, which caused his cheeks to redden further. André moved his briefcase to his left hand. He'd been late for his class and to make matters worse, Malcolm Whitly, dean of the Liberal Arts College, had chosen today to audit Humanities 1022, giving him that wall-eyed, high-browed William Buckley gaze for the entire hour. Forty-nine minutes, actually. And then, piling inconvenience upon irritation, Whitly had asked André, with his usual absurd precision, to meet in his office in Brewer Hall at 2:40 that same afternoon.

"Might I ask what this is in regards to?" André had inquired.

"I'm meeting with several of the department heads today," Whitly had replied, offering no further information.

André was more peeved than curious. Two-forty was an odd, inconvenient time. What could it be about? At least now, having been granted tenure last fall, he didn't have to worry about getting fired.

Looking at his watch—it was after 1:00 already—André ignored the complaints coming from his legs and picked up his pace. He planned to make lamb curry for supper, and given the quality of lamb available in Cold Rock, it would have to simmer for a good three hours. He wanted to get the meat in the Dutch oven, then drive—assuming that Jayjay had returned with his car—back to campus for his meeting with Whitly.

His calves were starting to burn; André slowed down. It wasn't good for him to get angry like this. What was there to be upset about? The meeting with Whitly might be nothing, and Jayjay might have a perfectly good explanation for not returning the car in time. Maybe he had not understood that André needed it to go to work. Or perhaps something had happened, something out of his control.

André forced himself to breathe deeply, to settle down. He didn't want to scare the boy off. They were so good together, like prosciuttto and melon. He knew that Jayjay was not exactly Mr. Responsible. He was more like Mr. Feckless, not a care in the world. If one wishes to ride the wild ride, André mused, thinking in terms of carnivals, one must be willing to pay the price.

He pushed Jayjay aside and thought about the curry. Did he have any coriander seed? If not, and if Jayjay was home, he could send the boy to the store. And if Jayjay wasn't home . . . André chose not to brood upon it. Negative thinking led to negative realities. He visualized his green Ford parked safely in his driveway. Could his thoughts influence the physical world? He believed that they could. A few blocks later he came within sight of his neat little bungalow and his faith in positive thinking was borne out. His car was parked in the driveway much as he had seen it in his mind's eye. André felt his shoulders drop; the tension draining from his body. He realized how afraid he had been that Jayjay had left him.

Of all the challenges posed by advancing age, applying lipstick had to be among the most vexing. Hilde pushed her face closer to the mirror and made another swipe at her upper lip. There were so many crevasses to fill. Tubes of lipstick just didn't last like they used to. Fortunately, she rarely left the hotel these days. It was just too much trouble.

Hilde capped the lipstick and drew back from the glass, regarding her reflection. Not bad for seventy-one—or however the hell old she was. The auburn wig helped. She tucked in a stray wisp of white hair. The wig was more than auburn—it had some real color to it, a lot of style. Hilde smiled and winked at herself, opened the window of her room and climbed out, being careful not to snag her Liz Claiborne slacks on the rose bushes.

Phlox said, "Aw, that's really tough, honey. She don't recognize you ever?"

"Usually she does. Some days she's really good." Barbaraannette took another sip of her third beer. She and Phlox had been talking for nearly an hour and somehow they hadn't quite got to the Bobby issue head-on. They'd kind of brushed around the edges of it—Barbaraannette knew that Phlox and Bobby had been living together in Tucson, and that they'd arrived in Cold Rock that morning, but she still didn't know where Bobby was. Somehow, Barbaraannette had found herself telling Phlox about her family. The woman knew how to listen. Barbaraannette liked her brash confidence and her big laugh. Phlox reminded her of the woman her sister Toagie might have become—bigger, bolder, and with a reservoir of joy.

"My mama died young, but she died in gear. I guess maybe it was a blessing. Never had any sisters, just a couple of snaky-mean big brothers use to do awful things to my dolls. So all three of you girls had different daddies?"

"That's the way Hilde always told us. We're so different I have to believe it's true. Toagie's kind of like you."

Phlox laughed. "Well I'm different from *you*, that's for damn sure."

"Then how come we both ended up with the same man?"

Phlox finished her beer, cracked the tab on another. "You got to be pullin' my reins, sweetie. Bobby Quinn? Who wouldn't want Bobby? The man's gorgeous. Not to mention he's hung like a race-horse, and don't you tell me you never noticed."

Barbaraannette felt her face heat up, then something gave way and she started to laugh, and Phlox was laughing, too, and deep behind her laughter Barbaraannette thought, Is that really why I want Bobby back? Her laughter subsided into hiccups; she wiped her eyes with a napkin and watched Phlox do the same.

She said, "If you like him so much, how come you're willing to give him up?"

Phlox looked surprised by the question. "Honey, you've got to be kidding. For a million dollars I'd give up oxygen."

Phlox thought, Does she like me? I hope to Christ she likes me. Everything might depend on it. She didn't know what else she could have done. Bobby running free, hiding out someplace, or caught by those men. Any minute now somebody else might be knocking on the door demanding the million dollars. *Her* million dollars for *her* man.

Was it true that she would give up Bobby for the money? Phlox pushed the thought aside. All she knew to do was to get in tight with the wife, convince her that whatever happened—whether Bobby showed up on his own, or was hogtied and dragged up the walk by the men who'd chased him—it was Phlox Anderson who had brought Bobby back to Cold Rock. *She* was the one who deserved the reward. And she was damn well going to sit here in Barbaraannette's kitchen until she was sure they had some kind of understanding. Or until hell froze over.

"Jayjay? I'm home!" André closed the front door and listened for a response. He heard water running in the bathroom. Jayjay taking a shower. André smiled. It felt so right, so *domestic*. He set his brief-case down and took off his coat, then cocked his head, listening to another less familiar sound. A thumping noise. It sounded as though it was coming up through the heating vent. Coming from the cellar. The furnace acting up again? André opened the stairwell door.

The thumping became louder. A thrill of fear scampered up his body, and he stood for several seconds, his hand squeezing the doorknob, listening. An animal trapped in the ductwork? If it was an animal, it was a big one.

He shouted, "Hello?"

The thumping became more urgent. Could it be Jayjay? André couldn't imagine what might have happened to him down there. And if it *was* Jayjay, then who was in the shower? He had a sudden vision of Jayjay trapped in the furnace room, caught beneath a col-lapsed wall. The image overcame his fear and propelled him down the steps.

The thumping was definitely coming from the furnace room, a room André had entered only two or three times since he had bought the house four years ago. He pushed the door open and felt for the light switch. A single hanging bulb flickered, then glowed.

What he saw did not make sense at first. A man dressed up as a spaceman? For Halloween. Except it wasn't Halloween and, André quickly realized, the man was not so much dressed up as he was *taped* up with yard after yard of silver duct tape. A few dozen loops of tape wrapped his torso and the back of a chair. His hands were duct-taped together, as were his cowboy-booted feet. There had to be several rolls of tape involved. The man's mouth and chin were thoroughly duct-taped and, most peculiar of all, his big felt hat was taped to his head. Only the man's eyes, cheeks, and nose were visi-ble. Nevertheless, he managed to look thoroughly frightened. With his eyes fixed upon André, the man rocked the chair, banging the back of his duct-taped, cowboy-hatted head against a furnace vent. André suddenly recognized the chair as the eighteenth-century Windsor he had been restoring.

"Good lord!" he exclaimed. He had purchased the rather delicate antique last fall for thirteen hundred dollars. André shouted, for lack of any clear or intelligent thought, "What on earth are you doing in my chair?"

From the stairwell behind him he heard Jayjay's voice answer, "I told him he could stay with us a couple days, Perfesser. That's okay with you, isn't it?"

18

The last time Barbaraannette had drunk this much had been in New Orleans more than ten years ago. That, too, had been a very bad time to overindulge. She'd been in a restaurant, she recalled, a seafood place on Lake Pontchartrain. Bunyons? Bronson's? She couldn't remember the name, but she did remember that she'd had four or five gin martinis, which was four or five more than she should've had, waiting for her soon-to-be-ex-boyfriend, Dave whatsisfaace—her memory was fuzzy with the drink, both then and now—to show up. She'd come to the restaurant to tell him to kiss off and go paddle his pirogue up some other woman's bayou—something like that, she had her speech ready—mad as hell at him for several reasons including one named Catfish and another named Joleen, and she'd been a little bit scared of him, too, him being big and also a cop, which was why she'd scheduled the kiss-off for a busy night in a popular restaurant with good lighting in the parking lot.

This was how she'd felt then—giddy, bulletproof, and invisible. Like watching it happen on TV, putting off the future one martini at a time, having a good time despite what was to come. And what *was* to come? In Louisiana, when she'd finally gotten around to telling the guy it was over, there had been a scene in the restaurant which had become a scene in the well-lit parking lot, and then Dave punching her windshield so hard he broke it. Drunk as she'd been, she'd almost driven straight into the lake on the way back to her apartment.

Maybe the martinis had made it easier to deal with Dave, like the beers were making it easier now for her to sit chatting with this Phlox woman, touching on Bobby now and then but mostly just gabbing like old friends. But now, as then, the time came to talk turkey, drunk or not, and Barbaraannette said, her voice unnaturally loud after four beers, interrupting a story Phlox was telling about how hot the summers got in Tucson, "Let's cut the cake here. Where's Bobby?"

Phlox met her eyes, tapping a blue nail on the top of her beer can. She said, "Honey, I drove that man two thousand miles to bring him here to you. In good faith I brought him, and I want you to remember that."

"I understand," said Barbaraannette. She was getting an inkling.

"See, I think maybe what might happen is you might get some other party knocking on your door, and I want you to understand the situation. What happened was Bobby and me we were down the road gassing up the truck and I was inside trying to get hold of you on the phone—"

"I've been letting it ring," said Barbaraannette.

"No shit, honey. So anyways, I look out the window and—" Phlox was interrupted by ringing. Both women looked at the phone. "You gonna get that?" Phlox asked.

Barbaraannette shook her head.

"Could be Bobby," said Phlox. Before Barbaraannette could reply, she crossed the kitchen and picked up. "Bobby?" Her brow crinkled, lips pouted. She extended the phone to Barbaraannette. "It's for you."

Barbaraannette stood up, slightly miffed, said, "Well, I *live* here, don't I?" She put the phone to her ear. "Hello?"

"Barbaraannette?" It was Mary Beth. "Who was that?"

"A friend of mine." Barbaraannette spoke carefully, not wanting her sister to detect the alcohol in her voice.

"Who?"

"Her name is Phlox."

"*Fox?* What kind of name is that?"

"Phlox."

"*Flocks?* Well, never mind. Mother has disappeared again."

Barbaraannette felt her innards begin to roll. She grabbed the edge of the table and sat down.

Mary Beth said, "They think she's stolen another car."

"Oh." This had happened before. "What's she driving this time?"

"She's got Dr. Cohen's sports car. He's the one who called me. He was quite perturbed. We've got to get out and look for her."

"Oh." Barbaraannette was not prepared for this. She'd had too many beers to be driving all over the county searching out Hilde's old haunts. There were a hundred places she could be, and that was just counting the places she might go to intentionally. Barbaraannette said, again, "Oh."

"Are you all right?"

"I'm fine. Did you call Toagie?"

"I'm calling her right now. You get out and start on the old neighborhood and the park. I'll send Toagie out to Klaussen Lake, see if she's gone to the farm." The farm, two hundred acres of rock-ridden land capped by a dilapidated stone farmhouse, had been purchased by Hilde's second husband. Barbaraannette had not been there for several years, but it was quite possible that Hilde had made it her destination. Revisiting her past had become a theme with Hilde.

"Good. Where will you be?" Barbaraannette asked.

"I'll cover downtown. The car she took is black. It's a—just a moment—it's a Porsche Carrera, whatever that is."

"It looks like a squashed-down Volkswagen."

"Oh. Well, Dr. Cohen thought it quite important. He kept repeating the kind of car it was. Porsche Carrera. But I don't think there are too many black sports cars in Cold Rock. If you find her, call me on Jim's cell phone. You have the number?"

"BUY PORK."

"Good. Call me every half hour to check in. Let's find her before she drives it up a tree."

Barbaraannette hung up the phone. She wished she could throw up, undrink all those beers.

Phlox said, "Buy pork?"

"That's Jim Hultman's number. Mary Beth's husband. He owns a feedlot."

"Who's . . . oh, never mind. I can see you got troubles, honey."

Barbaraannette said, "My mother's a car thief, and I'm a drunk."

Phlox shrugged. "You could do worse, honey."

"And I've got to go driving around now so my mother doesn't climb a tree."

"Now you're not making sense, girl. You don't want to be out driving drunk, and that's for damn sure."

"I've got to."

"You got to be someplace you just sit back and let me do the driving."

"You're drunk, too."

"Me?" Phlox laughed. "Honey, I'm just getting warmed up." She stood and hoisted her bag onto her shoulder. "You coming? You better be, 'cause I haven't got a clue where we're headed."

Barbaraannette opened her mouth to object, then gave in to Phlox's self-confident momentum.

Phlox said, on the way out the door, "So where is this tree, sweetie pie, and why the hell does your mother want to climb it?"

Hilde headed into the loop at sixty miles per hour. She could feel the tires, hear them squealing, the sound changing pitch as the rear tires broke loose. Her hands gripped the wheel; she eased back on the accelerator, keeping the slide under control, then punching it hard as she came up over the bridge, bringing the speed back up to sixty as she entered the next leaf of the clover, heading down now.

The cloverleaf south of town was the only such interchange within fifty miles. It had been built in the 1960s during a period of high accident rates and low employment, despite the fact that the traffic volume in no way justified the multimillion-dollar project. Hilde remembered when it had been built, but she could not remember where it went.

On the other hand, what did it matter? She was having fun. She hadn't had a lot of fun lately. This cloverleaf was better than the craziest carnival ride, and free! How many times had she gone around? Twenty ramps, or leaves, or whatever they were, at least.

Under the bridge, then up and around the next leaf. What's this? A white car with red lights on the roof, chugging along, getting in her way. She leaned on her horn, swerved around it, inches to spare, catching a glimpse of a young man's startled white face. She smiled at him and kept going.

Any moment now her destination would come to mind.

Mary Beth answered on the first ring.

"Any luck?" Barbaraannette asked, pressing the pay phone receiver against one ear, holding a hand over the other to block the sound of a pneumatic wrench hammering from the service station bay.

"No. I swear, Barbaraannette, teaching Hilde to drive was the dumbest thing you ever did."

"I thought you said offering the reward for Bobby was the dumbest thing I did."

"I was wrong."

A few years back, before it became apparent that Hilde's grip on time and space had begun to soften, Barbaraannette had dropped by Hilde's house one afternoon to find a sporty-looking new car in the driveway. She'd wondered who was visiting her mother, but Hilde had been sitting alone on the front porch, absorbed in a thick booklet. This had surprised Barbaraannette, as her mother rarely read anything other than *Vogue*.

"What are you reading?" she'd asked.

In answer, Hilde had held up the booklet: *Toyota Celica User's Guide*.

"Why are you reading that?"

"Well, I bought one is why."

"You bought a car? That's *your* car?"

"That's right."

"But you don't drive!"

Hilde jabbed a forefinger at the booklet. "I'm learning, aren't I? And it's about time!"

After some discussion and a couple of family meetings Barbaraannette had volunteered, over Mary Beth's objections, to act as Hilde's instructor. There had been a few unsettling moments, but Hilde had learned quickly, and for the next four years she and her red Toyota had terrorized Cold Rock and amassed a notable collection of traffic citations. Barbaraannette had loved to see her mother running wild, though she'd had to conceal her pleasure from Mary Beth.

Barbaraannette said, "It wasn't dumb, but I know what you mean."

"We'll probably find her in Rochester again. Or Fargo." Those were two of the places Hilde had gotten to in her Toyota, both times lost and unable to remember her own address. The second time, after Barbaraannette had flown up to Fargo to drive her mother home, Hilde had been diagnosed with a chronic brain disorder that might or might not be Alzheimer's disease. That had been Hilde's last legal road trip. A few years later, after a series of nearly disastrous kitchen fires, the girls had been forced to sell the homestead and move Hilde to Crestview where the kitchens had smooth-top electric ranges, smoke detectors, and someone to check on her.

"As long as we find her," Barbaraannette said. She hung up the phone. She walked back across the service station island to Phlox's pickup and climbed inside.

A few seconds later, Phlox emerged from the office. "This is the place Bobby took off running," she said as she slid in behind the wheel. "He hasn't been back." She started the truck. "The guy says that the guys Bobby was talking to were Rodney Gent and Hugh Hulke. You know them?"

"They were friends of Bobby's. They were having some problems."

"Those the dude ranch guys?"

"Bobby told you about that?" Barbaraannette pressed a hand to her forehead.

Phlox asked, "You feeling okay?"

Barbaraannette shook her head. Whatever small pleasures the alcohol had brought had now devolved into disorientation and fatigue. Blades of reflected sunlight cut at her; dust motes flashed like microscopic novae. A knot had begun to form behind her right eye. "I could use a bite to eat. And some aspirin."

"You want to stop back at your house?"

"No." Barbaraannette swallowed. Nausea, too. "Let's keep on looking. Let's try the Bingo Hall. She used to go there a lot . . . wait . . ." Barbaraannette cocked her head and leaned out the window. "Hear that?"

"What? The siren?"

"I think it's coming from the highway." She pointed south.

"Say no more." Phlox spun out of the service station.

19

"The thing is, *Perfesser, you have to do it right or they don't pay the re-*ward. You have to call and talk to the right cop so when you bring him in you get credit. A thousand dollars."

"I don't understand. If the man is wanted, why can you not simply call the police and have them come pick him up?"

"Yeah, I know, it's weird. But you're supposed to call first." Jayjay leaned against the door jamb, one bare foot atop the other. Black jeans, no belt, no shirt.

André shook his head. "It seems a rather unsavory way to make a living, Jonathan. You never told me you were a bounty hunter."

"It's sort of a sideline. Don't worry, though. I'll have him out of here real soon now."

André frowned and removed the leg of lamb from its butcher paper wrapping. "I certainly hope so."

"I'll call again." Jayjay turned to the kitchen phone and dialed. His jeans rode low on his hips, almost ready to fall to the floor. André began to hone his cleaver on a sharpening steel. Frowning, Jayjay worked a finger into his navel as he listened to the phone, then hung up. "No answer," he said.

"How strange."

Jayjay shrugged. "It's a special number. They don't always answer. I'm gonna go watch some TV."

André watched the boy leave, considered following him, then

decided that his advances would not be welcome at this time. Jayjay was more acquiescent in the evening hours. He returned his attention to the lamb.

The lamb that had once owned this leg, André thought, must have stood waist high at the shoulder. Mutton for sure. He hacked through the tendons with the cleaver, his nostrils flexing at the rich, tallowy smell. Ah well, a few extra cloves of garlic, two tablespoons of his homemade masala, a handful of dried curry leaves, and three hours on the range would overcome the pissy smell and restore the lamb to the tenderness of its youth. He set aside the cleaver and went at the leg with a boning knife, removing strips of bright red meat and trimming them of all visible fat. Every minute or so he stopped cutting, jogged from his rhythm by a thunk or a rattle or some other peculiar sound drifting up from the cellar. The duct-taped man slowly destroying his chair.

The cold lamb felt both sticky and slippery. André felt a stirring low in his gut, and he shuddered. Fear, hunger, nausea, or lust? Rather than analyze it further, André snatched up the cleaver and hacked energetically at the defatted meat, chopping it into bite-size pieces. He heard the sound of canned laughter from Jayjay's room.

The thumping sound ceased. The man in the cellar had tired, or given up. André could hear only the gentle murmur of the stock simmering in the Dutch oven, filling the air with a rich, chickeny fog. He forced himself to evaluate his situation. Stripped to its most basic components, it was simply this: Jayjay had captured a man and duct-taped him to André's antique Windsor chair. He claimed that the man had a price on his head, and that he was going to turn him in for a reward. Those were the facts, as supported by the presence of the duct-taped man in the cellar on the one hand, and by Jayjay's testimony on the other.

Nevertheless, several vexing questions remained: What crime had the man committed? Jayjay had been vague on every particular. André understood that the law was flexible where bounty hunters were concerned, but he knew nothing of the specifics. Did one have to be licensed with some government agency to bounty-hunt? If so, he was fairly certain that Jayjay, having spent time in prison, was not properly certified. And at what point was the bounty hunter required to present the criminal to the proper authorities? Clearly, one could not hold a man captive for weeks or months, but what about holding him for a few hours, or days? And if the man was being illegally detained, how did this impact André's own legal status? If he stood by and did nothing, would he become an aider and abettor? Was it already too late?

It occurred to André that he might talk to the man and get his side of the story. He looked at the glistening pile of lamb chunks, and at the remains of the leg on the cutting board. Perhaps another quarter-pound of lean meat remained to be coaxed from the bones, but the thought of slicing through more sinew and membrane had lost its appeal. He scooped the meat into the Dutch oven, stirred in the chopped garlic and spices, applied the iron lid, adjusted the flame, then took the boning knife and walked purposefully down the cellar stairs.

The man was sitting quietly when André entered the furnace room, but became agitated at the sight of the knife.

André said, "Please do not be alarmed, I am simply going to remove the tape from your mouth so we can talk." The man stopped straining against his bonds, but his eyes remained wide. André examined the layered duct tape, trying to decide where to cut—or should he simply find the end and begin unraveling the man? How many layers were there? What had Jayjay been thinking of? Why tape the poor man's hat to his head? Maybe that was the place to start. André wriggled the thin blade between a strip of tape and the hat, cut through the tape. He grasped the cut end and slowly pulled. It came away from the felt easily, but adhered with greater force to the man's cheek. André pursed his lips, gave it a yank. Tears erupted from the man's eyes. Once again, André felt the stirring low in his abdomen, and this time there was no doubt it was of erotic origin. He ignored the sensation as best he could and set about cutting and peeling away enough of the tape to free the man's lips.

"Are you able to speak now?" he asked, setting the knife atop the furnace.

The man licked his lips and worked his jaw up and down, then said in a hoarse voice, "Something to drink?"

André nodded. The man had been bound and gagged for hours, of course he was thirsty. "I will get you something shortly, but you must promise me something, ah, what did you say your name was?"

The man stared back at him. "You don't know?"

"I do not."

"It's Bobby."

"Excellent. Bobby. Now, Bobby, I do not wish to hear any shouting, carrying-on, or other noise-making. And please do not rock to and fro, or bang the back of the chair against the wall, or otherwise strain against your bonds. That is a very valuable chair, Bobby. It is more than two hundred years old."

"I didn't ask to sit here."

"Be that as it may, there you are, though I hope for not terribly much longer."

"I gotta take a leak."

André frowned. This had not occurred to him. "You may have to hold it a while longer."

"I may have to piss all over your chair."

André pursed his lips. He did not like this Bobby. He said, "Do you want me to put this tape back on your face?"

"No."

"Then tell me, Bobby, why are you wanted?"

"Wanted?"

"What crimes did you commit?"

"Crimes?" He appeared to be genuinely surprised. "I didn't do anything."

Perplexed, André crossed his arms and regarded Bobby. "You must have done something or you would not be a wanted man."

"I'm not wanted. All I know is, your friend psycho boy hit me over the head with a pipe wrench and taped me to this goddamn chair. Are you gonna get me a glass of water?"

André flexed his jaw. He did not care to be ordered about by this Bobby. "Not until you answer my questions," he said.

"Well, hell, I'm trying!"

"What do you mean, you're not wanted?"

Bobby hesitated, then flexed his torso in a way that in an un-
bound man might have become a shrug. "I mean, you make it
sound like the cops are after me. Well, they're not. It's just Barbaraannette."

"Who?" The name had a familiar sound.

"My wife," he said. "That's why your buddy cold-cocked me, ain't
it? For the million bucks?"

"Million dollars?" André experienced a moment of disorientation, then it hit him. The lottery winner, that ridiculous woman
who wanted her husband back. He'd seen her on the television.
This was her husband? André stood in stunned silence as his mind
absorbed and collated this new information. Jayjay was planning to
collect the million-dollar reward. Collect the money, then move
on. André felt his face glowing with shame and anger.

Bobby said, "Hey, you didn't know about this?" Pressing his advantage, he continued. "Well you won't be able to spend it even if
she gives it to you, which she probably won't if you're in jail for kidnapping. You better cut me loose right now or you're gonna be in
big trouble."

André took a step back, seeking a clear channel of thought. He
feared that the man was correct. If he was not wanted by the law,
not a fugitive from justice, there could be no excuse for duct-taping
him to a two-hundred-year-old Windsor.

"Let me go. I'll just walk out of here and you'll be done with me.
You hear what I'm saying?"

He needed time to think. André's eyes darted wildly, landed on
the roll of duct tape on the floor beside the furnace. He picked it up
and unrolled a long strip.

Bobby said, "You better not—" André slapped the length of tape
across the man's mouth, wrapped it twice around his head. The rich
smell of concentrated urine rose up around him. André fled up the
steps.

Jayjay stood in the kitchen holding the phone to his ear. As André emerged from the stairwell, he hung up the phone and asked,
"What's going on?"

"I was checking on your guest," said André. "How long do you plan to keep him here?"

Jayjay sat down. "I just tried to call again. They're still not answering."

"Oh? Tell me again. Who are you trying to call?" André felt his heart speed up, felt his fingernails digging into his palms.

"I got it written down." Jayjay leaned forward and fingered a scuff mark on the toe of his right Doc Marten.

"I have spoken with him, Jonathan." André's voice rose in pitch.

The boy looked up, startled.

André reined himself in, took a calming breath. "I know who he is. Listen to me, Jonathan. Even if you should collect the reward money, you will be charged with kidnapping. You cannot just grab a man off the street that way."

"How else was I gonna get him?"

André clenched his teeth. "In my house! You kidnapped a man and brought him to my house!"

"Where else was I gonna bring him?"

André restrained the urge to seize the boy and shake him. "You will simply land yourself in jail, Jayjay—and me with you! I insist that you let him go. He told me that if we let him go he will not press charges."

"Uh-uh. No way, Perfesser. I caught him fair and square. I want my money."

"Money?" André banged his fists on his hips. "You little ingrate! Money? A thousand dollars? You told me a thousand dollars! You lied to me you, you ingrate." He moved closer to Jayjay and shook a finger in the boy's smirking face. "I want that man out of my house now. Do you understand me?"

Jayjay leaned back away from the finger. "Hey, take it easy."

André's hand curled into a fist. "If you do not do as I ask, you will live to regret it!"

Jayjay raised his hands in front of his bare chest, palms forward, laughing nervously. "Hey! No prob. Whatever you say, man."

"Arre you laughing at me?"

"No!" Jayjay forced his features into an approximation of sobriety. "I hear you, man!"

Every muscle in André's body was contracted. His mouth was a white pucker; short breaths whistled through his nostrils. He took a step back. Would the boy do as he asked? A small part of him was disappointed. He had been about to do something. Something physical. Throw the boy out on the street where he belonged! André lowered his fist, let his hand open. For a moment there he had almost forgotten he was standing in his own kitchen. He caught sight of the wall clock. Two-thirty! Anger suddenly became alarm. He was late for his meeting with Whitly. He stripped off his apron.

"I must leave immediately. Where are my car keys?"

Jayjay pointed at the key hook by the back door.

"Thank you." André grabbed the keys, then went to the hall closet and put on his brown tweed sport coat. He checked his reflection in the hall mirror, ran his fingertips through his beard. "Mark my words, Jonathan. Unless you wish to end up in jail, you must set that poor man free. I will be home by four o'clock, and when I return I expect to hear no thumping coming from my cellar. I expect that man and all of that awful silver tape to be removed from my Windsor chair." He draped his Stewart plaid scarf around his neck. "I will not tolerate your disobedience, Jonathan. The man must go, and that is my final word."

André closed the door firmly behind him, thinking, There, *that* should put the boy in his place.

Driving somewhat more rapidly than was his usual practice, André maintained his tight-lipped indignation all the way to campus. The situation was really quite stimulating. He had actually threatened the boy with physical harm, and it seemed to have worked! The appearance of the duct-taped man in his cellar was both frightening and inconvenient, and unfortunate as far as his Windsor chair was concerned, but it did get a man's juices flowing.

Jayjay did not move from the kitchen chair for several minutes after André left. The guy was a know-it-all faggot professor, but a few of the things he'd said made sense. Cashing in the cowboy might not be as easy as he'd hoped. He might collect the reward and land his ass back in prison with nothing to spend it on but cigarettes and jailhouse hooch. Getting his hands on this Robert Quinn might be the worst thing ever happened to him.

On the other hand, he'd never had anything worth a million bucks before. There was no way he was going to let the guy walk. There had to be a way to get the money. He stared at the burbling iron pot on the stove, awaiting inspiration. After a few seconds he felt a squirming in his belly, so he grabbed a fork and took the top off the pot and speared himself a chunk of meat. He waved it in the air until it had cooled, then put the whole thing in his mouth and chewed. The meat was tough and not very flavorful. Jayjay remained unimpressed by the professor's weird gourmet cooking. Why couldn't the guy just fry up some burgers? He noticed a jar of dried red peppers above the stove and added a generous handful to the stew. They might not make it taste any better, but it would damn sure make dinner more entertaining. He built himself a peanut butter sandwich and retired to his room to watch TV.

Some time later a shuffling sound followed by a muffled crash roused him. Jayjay ran down to the basement. The guy had tipped over the chair somehow. He had one hand loose and was clawing frantically at the tape around his chest.

"Fuck!" Jayjay rushed forward, kicked him in the face, jumped back. The man screeched—Jayjay could hear it right through the duct tape.

"Shut up or I do it again," Jayjay shouted.

The squeal subsided.

"You try that again and I'm gonna kill you. She didn't say nothin' about you got to be alive." Jayjay edged closer. "Man, you pissed yourself, didn't you?"

The man lay on his side, staring at him, breathing loudly through flared nostrils.

"You lookin' at me?" Jayjay stepped in and kicked him again, this time in the face. "That'll teach you." He picked up the roll of duct tape. "I'm gonna wrap you up a little more now, hear? Don't you fucking move. Okay? I want to see you nod."

The man's head bobbed. His nose was bleeding.

"You just do like I say and nobody's gonna get hurt, understand? Everybody's gonna get what they want."

With the light out and the basement door closed, the darkness was complete. Bobby Quinn focused on his breathing. Air in; air out. His left cheek pressed cold concrete. Cold Rock, sucking the heat right out of him. He knew he shouldn't have come back, no matter how many millions Barbaraannette waved under his nose. One of his nostrils was swollen shut. Breathe in, listen to the air whistle through his nose, let it out. This was all Barbaraannette's fault. He tried to visualize what he'd seen of the basement. The guy with the beard had left a knife on top of the furnace. It might as well be on top of the house. Was there anything sharp and pointed he could wriggle to, dragging the heavy chair—a nail or a sharp stick or something that would pierce the duct tape covering his mouth? Air in—it took him nearly ten seconds to get a lungful—air out. It occurred to him for the first time that he might not survive this.

Air in; air out. He wondered what had happened to Phlox.

20

When Barbaraannette and Phlox arrived at the cloverleaf the eastbound ramp was blocked by a Cold Rock PD squad car, lights flashing, and by Police Chief Dale Gordon's unmarked Crown LTD. Two Cold Rock cops crouched behind the protection of their squad car, guns drawn. Chief Gordon, hatless and dressed for golf in yellow trousers and a green knit shirt, stood behind his car holding a bull-horn. Their attention was focused on a small black Porsche stopped halfway up the ramp, its engine revving.

"Get out of the vehicle and put your hands on the roof," Gordon's amplified voice crackled.

Barbaraannette, headache forgotten, jumped out of the pickup and ran past the policemen toward the sports car.

"Halt!" Gordon shouted.

Barbaraannette ignored the amplified warning, focusing on the blur of orange wig visible through the Porsche's windshield. She opened the door, reached in, and pulled the keys from the ignition. Hilde, fingers white on the wheel, stared through the windshield and continued to pump the accelerator for a moment, but when the engine refused to respond her fingers relaxed and her face melted into apathy.

"You okay, Hilde?" Barbaraannette asked.

Hilde did not reply, but she apeared to be uninjured. Barbaraan-nette felt the fear drain away, making room for anger. She looked down the ramp at the Cold Rock cops holding their guns, and at Chief Dale Gordon in his yellow pants holding the bullhorn, all of them looking at her as though she had crashed their party.

Gordon raised the bullhorn to his mouth. "Step away from the vehicle, Barbaraannette."

Barbaraannette's eyes narrowed. She walked directly up to Gordon and grabbed the bullhorn. Surprised, he let her take it.

Dale Gordon was only a few years older than Barbaraannette, but he looked ten years older. The flesh beneath his chin jiggled when he spoke; wind cutting across the highway fluttered his thin hair. Tiny red veins brought a blotch of color to his tuberous nose.

Barbaraannette said, "Dale, what on earth do you think you're doing?"

Gordon, licking his lips, took a step back. "Just following standard procedure."

"That is my seventy-three-year-old mother in that car!"

"Well, now, I *know* that's your mama, Barbaraannette."

Barbaraannette raised the bullhorn and pointed it directly into his face. "THEN WHAT ARE YOUR MEN DOING WITH THOSE GUNS?"

Gordon staggered back, clapping his hands to his ears.

Barbaraannette directed the bullhorn at the two officers hiding behind their squad car. "PUT THOSE GUNS BACK WHERE THEY BELONG!"

The cops lowered their guns, looking to their chief for confirmation. Gordon made an incomprehensible waving motion with his hands. The cops looked at each other in confusion.

Barbaraannette dropped the bullhorn on the road and strode back to the Porsche. She helped her mother out of the car and was walking her back to the pickup when she was intercepted by Gordon and his men.

Phlox said, "I thought he was going to put you in handcuffs for sure, honey."

Barbaraannette helped Hilde into the truck. "So did I," she said. "Let's get out of here before he changes his mind."

"You got it." She backed down the ramp and pulled out onto the highway. "I about bust a gut when you put that horn in his face."

"I get carried away sometimes."

Hilde suddenly became restless. Barbaraannette leaned forward and looked into her mother's face. "Hilde?"

Hilde perked up and took an interest in her surroundings. "Barbaraannette? Are we there yet?"

"Are we where?"

"Foreman's! I hear they're having a going-out-of-business sale!"

Barbaraannette sighed. "That was a long time ago, Hilde." Foreman's had closed its doors two years ago, and even if they hadn't Hilde would not have been welcome. For every dollar she had spent there she'd stolen two. Hilde's kleptomania had spun out of control around the time her mental faculties began to deteriorate. Barbaraannette sometimes wondered whether she had actually begun to steal more, or had simply gotten caught more often.

"Well then, let's go to Harold's."

Barbaraannette was experiencing a core meltdown behind her right eye. Her headache had returned in a more intense, localized form. She touched her temples lightly with her fingertips. "Not today, Hilde. They're still upset about that chinchilla coat you walked out with."

Hilde grinned, remembering. "That was an accident." She shot her left elbow into Phlox's ribs. "You want to go shopping, don't you? Let's you and me get serious, fill up the back of this pickup truck."

Phlox brought her arm down to protect her side. "Nothing I'd like better, doll, but I think we'd best get you home."

"You're not taking me back to that hotel, are you?"

"You're staying with me tonight, Hilde," Barbaraannette said. "And I don't want to argue about it. It's either that or you spend the night in jail."

Hilde frowned and turned to Phlox. "You know, she acts just like my daughter."

Barbaraannette closed her eyes. If her head didn't hurt so bad she would either be laughing or crying.

The scene at the cloverleaf would make a good story to tell Toagie at some later date, but right now, Barbaraannette felt fortunate to have recovered her mother and to have avoided arrest herself. There had been a few tense moments, but Dale Gordon had not been unreasonable once the ringing in his ears had stopped. He was a patronizing, chauvinistic, self-important bureaucrat, but he had a thing for Barbaraannette and after several minutes of portentous scolding, he had agreed to release Hilde into her custody.

"On one condition," he said. "I want you to promise me you'll keep her off my streets," he warned.

"I'll do my best," said Barbaraannette. She did feel bad about blasting the poor man's eardrums. "I hope she didn't make you miss your tee time."

"I was on my way home. Your mama really had us going. You know how many times my boys chased her around this interchange?"

"She would've run out of gas eventually," said Barbaraannette.

"If the owner decides he wants to press charges, it could go hard for your mama."

"Dr. Cohen won't press charges. He doesn't want to lose a resident. In any case, he shouldn't leave his keys in his car."

"I'll mention that to him." Chief Gordon permitted himself a smile. "Fact is, your mama drives that little thing better than he does."

"I'm sorry she caused so much trouble."

"And I'm sorry for your troubles, too, Barbaraannette. But I guess all that lottery money will help."

"So far it's just made things more complicated."

"Uh-huh. I hear you're trying to get Bobby back."

"That's right."

"Having any luck?"

Barbaraannette looked over toward the pickup truck where Phlox and Hilde sat waiting. "Not exactly."

"If I see him, I'll bring him on by your house before I throw him in jail."

"Why would you do that?" Barbaraannette was surprised.

"I still got that warrant. Hugh Hulke and Rodney Gent got a civil judgment against him. He owes them money. But I wouldn't worry your little head about it. You can afford to settle up for him now, can't you?"

"Hmmm."

"Or if Bobby doesn't show up, maybe I could just stop on by anyways."

Barbaraannette didn't get it. "Why?" she asked.

Dale Gordon shrugged and crinkled his eyes. "Just to see how you're doing. Maybe we could have dinner sometime?"

"How is Sheila doing?" Barbaraannette asked.

"Oh, she's fine. We're separated, you know."

"I didn't know that. Well then. I guess I'd better get going."

As they rode home in Phlox's pickup truck, Barbaraannette told herself that Dale Gordon was not a problem she needed to think about. She was frying other fish, and she had a volcano rumbling in her head. The brightness of Hilde's wig actually caused her physical pain. Barbaraannette regarded her mother's profile, inches away. Hilde had stepped out again—her mouth slack, her eyelids drooping, her fingers moving purposefully in her lap. Was she scratching herself? Barbaraannette stared at Hilde's hands, perplexed, then realized that her mother was typing, transported forty years into the past, to a time when she had worked as a secretary. Barbaraannette reached over and covered Hilde's hands with her own. Hilde slowly turned her head, bewildered, and stared at Barbaraannette as if at a phantasm. She asked, "So, where do you work?"

Barbaraannette held Hilde's hands, kneading them. "We'll be home in a minute, mom."

Hilde was nearly asleep by the time they got home. Barbaraannette led her mother to the spare bedroom where she got her undressed and into bed. Hilde was gone within seconds, snoring vigorously. Barbaraannette rejoined Phlox in the kitchen.

"You doing okay?" Phlox asked.

"I've got a little headache." She sat down at the table.

"You want me to work on it?"

"I took some aspirin."

Phlox got behind her chair. "Lean forward a little. There you go." Barbaraannette felt Phlox's nails on the back of her neck, felt her fingers moving. "Just let your head hang loose."

"I don't know if a massage will help. It feels like I've got a knife in my brain. I think I've got a migraine."

"You don't have a migraine, honey. You got a mother who swipes cars and a few stale beers in your gut." Her fingertips explored the back of Barbaraannette's head, probing. "You got a nasty knot here."

Barbaraannette felt pressure, then a bright, sharp pain as Phlox dug in with a knuckle. The new pain disappeared as quickly as it had arrived, leaving behind a node of warmth. Barbaraannette felt the dagger in her skull soften. Phlox's fingers continued their explorations, pausing now and then to work on a troublesome area.

"You sure are popular with the boys," Phlox said.

"What do you mean?"

"I was watching that policeman talking to you. He was all monkey business."

"Dale is having trouble with his marriage. He just wants to think he's still got it."

"Does he?"

"I doubt it." Barbaraannette laughed. The throbbing had subsided.

"Fact is," Phlox said, "I'm surprised you haven't taken up with another fellow by now. I mean, I like Bobby, too, but six years is a long time, honey."

"I guess I just got in the habit of being by myself."

The telephone rang. Phlox's fingers stopped moving.

Barbaraannette said, "I guess I better answer that." She stood, took a breath, and picked up the phone. "Hello?"

"Did you find her?"

Barbaraannette relaxed. "She's here, Toag. She's fine. Where are you?"

"Where am I? I'm at Klaussen Lake is where I am. It took me a fleeping hour to get out here, and then I got stuck in the mud trying to drive in to the house. I had to walk a mile to the neighbor's, and he hauled me out with his tractor, and I've been dialing EAT PORK for half an hour now and not getting through–"

"It's BUY PORK, Toagie."

"That's not what she told me."

"Are you unstuck now?"

"Yeah, I am, and Hilde's not at the farm which of course you know on account of she's with you. Where'd you find her?"

"She was driving around the cloverleaf. Dale Gordon found her."

"I'm surprised he didn't throw her in jail."

"He would have if we hadn't got there. How's the house look?"

"Like a pile of rocks with a leaky roof. I think there's a skunk living in the cellar. I didn't even go inside. We should get Hilde to sell the place. Is she staying with you?"

"For tonight." Barbaraannette hadn't allowed herself to think it out any further. "It might take some talking to get Crestview to take her back."

"Yeah, well, we'll sic Mary Beth on 'em. I'll see you."

"Bye." Barbaraannette hung up. "That was my sister," she said to Phlox. Three seconds later, the phone rang again. "Ten to one that's her again." She picked up the phone. "Hey, Toag."

"I've got your hubby," said a male voice.

Phlox saw Barbaraannette's neck muscles go rigid, saw her fingers go white on the phone.

"Yes," she said. Her voice sounded hollow. "That's right. Well then, bring him on over." She listened some more, nodding. "I don't have it in my purse, you know. I'll have to borrow it." Barbaraannette frowned and cleared her throat. Her cheeks blotched pink and her mouth, which had been hanging open, became a hard, straight line. "Listen to me—what did you say your name was?" Her voice turned brittle. "I see. Well, Mr. Smith, they don't pay all the money at once, you know. It's an annuity spread out over twenty years. That's right. Now, are you going to let me talk to him?" She tipped her head toward the phone, listening intently. "Is that a fact? If that's the way you're going to be, I guess you better just keep him." She returned the handset to its cradle. Her pupils had constricted to pinpoints and she was breathing rapidly. Barbaraannette hugged herself.

Phlox said, "You okay? You're shakin' like a leaf, honey." She put her hands on Barbaraannette's shoulders to stop her own hands from shaking. "You want to tell me what they said?"

"He said he had Bobby."

"Take a deep breath and hold it a second. There you go. Was it that Hugh and Rodney?"

Barbaraannette shook her head and let her breath out slowly. "I don't think so. He sounded young. He said he had Bobby but he wouldn't let me talk to him. I told him—you heard me—I said, 'You can keep him.' Good God, what have I done?"

Phlox's heart was thrumming. She said, "He'll call back. Where else is he gonna get a million bucks for Bobby?"

Barbaraannette nodded. "You're right. Only he wouldn't let me talk to him and maybe that's because he doesn't even have him. Or maybe he does."

"Don't you forget, honey, I'm the one brought him here. Bobby was with me."

Barbaraannette stared off through the walls of her kitchen. Her breathing had returned to normal, and the color in her cheeks had evened.

Phlox said, "You aren't gonna give him the money, are you?"

Barbaraannette said, "I've really started something, haven't I?" A faint smile toyed with her lips.

"Don't you forget who dragged that man all the way across the country."

"I'm not forgetting anything," said Barbaraannette.

The two women locked eyes. Phlox felt a strain on the bond she had forged. She turned away abruptly and started for the door.

"Where are you going?" Barbaraannette asked.

"I'm going to find your husband for you," Phlox said.

21

For *several seconds after the click, Jayjay kept the phone pressed to his ear.*
She'd hung up on him! "You can keep him"? Where did *that* come
from? One day she wants her husband so bad she says she'll pay
a million bucks, the next day she doesn't want him at all. And
what was that about not having the money? Was it true that the
money didn't get paid out all at once? This was getting way more
complicated than it was supposed to. He slammed down the
phone and got a beer from the refrigerator and went into his room.
Now what was he supposed to do? Call her back, of course, but
maybe he should let her hang for a while. Give her time to think,
and himself, too. He thought about writing letters to some more
actors, but the few dollars such a letter might bring seemed paltry
next to the unnegotiated million he had taped up in the basement.
Jayjay sat on the bed and turned on the TV with the sound off. He
watched the cartoonish antics of the Power Rangers, seeking inspiration. Maybe he could sell the cowboy to somebody else, like the
two men who were chasing him at the gas station. Let them figure
out how to get the million. He heard the front door open. Damn,
the professor was home. He hoped the guy wouldn't flip out on
him. At the very least he'd have to listen to the old fairy's complaints all night, or at least until he figured out what to do with the
cowboy. He heard the squeak of a cork, the clink of bottle against
glass. A few moments later André appeared in the bedroom door-

way cupping a nearly full brandy snifter in his tiny hands. He looked pale.

"Jonathan?"

"Hey, Perfesser. What you drinking?"

"Rémy Martin." André sat beside him on the bed and took a large sip of cognac. He shuddered and said, "My life is over, Jonathan." His eyes were puffy, as if he had been crying.

"Oh yeah?"

"The very fabric of my existence has been sundered." Something on the TV caught his eye. He said, "Good Lord, Jayjay, what on earth are you watching?"

"Power Rangers."

"Would you be so kind as to turn it off?" André took another swallow of his cognac.

Jayjay gestured with the remote; the screen went dark. The professor was making him nervous. He'd never seen him this way.

"Thank you," André said. He set the snifter on the bedside table and swung an arm around Jayjay's shoulders. Jayjay stiffened, wondering what was coming.

"Jonathan, do you think that I am a good person?"

"Sure I do."

André shook his head. "Well I am not so sure. I have been thinking, Jonathan, thinking a great deal. Is our guest still in the cellar?"

Jayjay nodded, braced for an onslaught of four- and five-syllable words, but to his surprise the professor simply nodded dreamily. "Do you remember what I told you before? About not being able to spend your money in jail?"

"Yeah, well . . ."

André's delicate fingers squeezed Jayjay's shoulder. "I may have been somewhat hasty in my assessment of the situation. There may very well be a way to capitalize on the present state of events." The cognac was having its effect. André's face had become suffused with red, and his voice had gone hoarse. Jayjay squirmed uncomfortably in the professor's embrace.

"A man is allotted only so many days," André mused, "and to

live out one's life while remaining strictly within the arbitrary bounds set by society would be such a shame, such a pity, such a waste." He put his hands on Jayjay's cheeks and turned his face toward him. "Is it worth the risk, to experience all that life has to offer? Are the laws of men made for such as we? Have I told you what a beautiful child you are?"

Jayjay shook his head free and jumped up. Those little hands creeped him out. "Jesus, Perfesser! Jack down, would ya?"

André laughed and reached for his cognac. "Ah, Jonathan! And to think that I nearly passed up the opportunity—" He inhaled from the snifter. "—to inspire the aroma of *les fleurs du mal*." He drank deeply, draining the glass, and fell back onto the bed shouting, "Thank you very much, Malcolm Whitly, you subhuman excretion. You sniveling sack of bureaucratic slag, you slime-mold, you putrescent pile of rat dung . . ."

Jayjay backed out of the room. The guy had definitely gone off the deep end.

André called after him, "Where are you going, my little chickadee?"

Jayjay did not reply.

André laughed. He had actually managed to frighten the boy! Jayjay the imperturbable had finally recognized that he, André Gideon, was a force with which to be reckoned, a man who could step beyond the pale as easily as most men step out of their underwear. Unlike that worm Whitly, whose only power came via bureaucratic fiat, who got his jollies shattering the lives of hardworking academics such as himself, who would sacrifice the classics simply to address a minor budget crisis.

Whitly had actually enjoyed telling him he was out of a job.

"But," André had sputtered, "I have *tenure!*"

"I'm terribly sorry, André, but it's not just you, you see, it's the entire Humanities Department." His lips trembled, holding back, but André detected the suppressed smile. "We've been forced to streamline the Liberal Arts College. Rather than a separate and distinct Humanities Department, we will be offering a single core curriculum class called Western Classics which will, of course, be taught by Jim McCready."

"McCready? But . . . but he's Poli-Sci!"

"Yes, another department which has been eliminated."

"But . . . why is he teaching the *classics?*"

"He's senior to you, André." Whitly allowed himself the smile now, spreading his hands as if displaying an invisible model of the ineffable, capricious universe. "What can I say?"

"But . . . the *humanities!* My *job!*" André winced as he remembered the whining, pleading tone he had taken in the face of Whitly's smarmy dismissal. He could almost see Whitly's grin in the textured ceiling of Jayjay's room. He closed his eyes, squeezing them tight, losing himself in an ocean of phosphenes. For a few moments he enjoyed the sensation, floating a few inches above the mattress, then the whirlies hit. André's eyes snapped open and he sat up. He could see himself in the mirror over the dresser, a Stickley piece he'd picked up for next to nothing. He saw a sallow, bearded, red-eyed man on the downslope of his prime. For a moment he feared he was about to vomit, and then he was sure of it. Seconds later he was on his knees before the toilet bowl. Three times his abdomen clenched, each time firing out a thick rope of umber slime. Gasping, wiping his mouth with a handful of wadded-up toilet tissue, André slumped against the edge of the bathtub and waited for his viscera to rearrange itself. He closed his eyes. Another swell of nausea came and went, this time without dramatic consequence.

André could not remember the last time he had vomited. He was surprised by the burning sensation, the feeling that his esophagus had been singed. Maybe it only burned when one vomited cognac. Maybe it was middle age. In either case, he did not like it. His throat was raw, his stomach hurt as if pummeled, and his hands—he held them out—were trembling. Cautiously, he lifted himself up onto the edge of the bathtub. He tossed the wad of tissue into the toilet and dropped the lid so that he would not have to look at it.

There is a metaphor here, he thought.

For his entire adult life André Gideon had lived within, even embraced, the strictures of higher education. He had placed himself in thrall to the university system, and had never questioned the limitations imposed upon him. Even as a student he had eagerly given himself to Academia. He had taken on its philosophies and taboos and had made its belief system a part of his core being. In an even larger sense he had lived his life within the arbitrary ethical structure of Western Civilization, a set of approved social behaviors that dated back to the ancient Greeks, and before. He did not steal, kill, or destroy that which belonged to others. He was a good citizen, a good person. He was homosexual, true, but even in this he remained true to the classical Greek ideal, devoting himself as he did to an appreciation of the arts, and to the enlightenment of younger men.

He had followed their rules, and now they had ejected him as surely as he had ejected his bellyful of spirits. There was the metaphor.

André felt something shift in his abdomen. His mind returned to the wild, drunken thoughts he had voiced to young Jayjay a few minutes earlier—it seemed like hours! Could he really collect the one-million-dollar reward? The woman had said nothing about the manner in which her husband was to be returned. Nevertheless, there would be repercussions. One could not kidnap and imprison a man without raising ethical and legal questions, and if he attempted to reap the reward he would be as culpable as Jayjay. But what of it? Was it really such a terrible thing to cause one man a day or two of discomfort in exchange for a fortune? Was not a good person such as himself permitted one questionable act?

The image of the duct-taped man swam into view. Silver tape. His two-century-old Windsor. André frowned, drawing a mental curtain across the disturbing tableau. He depressed the toilet handle. The sound of rushing liquid reactivated his nausea, though only momentarily. Sitting on the edge of the bathtub, tweed elbows on corduroy knees, he listened as the guttural flushing sound gave way to the hiss of the filling toilet tank. By the time the hissing ceased he felt much better. The perspiration had dried on his face and the feeling in his stomach now resembled hunger. He stood, enjoying the solidity of the tiles beneath his feet, and turned on the tap and threw cool water onto his face. He scrubbed his beard dry with a clean bath towel. He ran his fingers through his hair, gray now but still growing thick and low on his forehead. He took a good, hard look at his mirror image, at his rumpled beard, at cheeks ruddy from the towel, at his small, hazel eyes. Everything he saw was in sharp focus. He could see the individual whiskers and pores, and the minute, spidery veins beneath the surface of his skin. He felt alert and sober, as if his mind had been flushed clean, as if reality, for the first time since early childhood, was reaching him unfiltered. He did not now see the slight, precious, mannered, slightly pompous Humanities professor to whom he had become accustomed. He did not see the middle-aged homosexual academic with one foot in the closet and the other in Rudolph's Red Nose seeking youthful companionship. He did not see a fearful man hiding behind a doctorate and a beard.

He saw a man who was going to do something with his life.

22

"Hello, Mother," *André said.*

"Andrew? Why haven't you called?"

"I am sorry, Mother."

"The country is falling to wrack and ruin."

"Yes, Mother."

"Negroes and Chinamen are breeding like mink, while good women go without grandchildren."

"Mother, I have good news. I am about to become a rich man."

"Your father often said that very same thing, yet all he left me was you. I'm destitute."

"You are not destitute, Mother. You have your pension."

"My pension is a pittance."

"You also have your Social Security, Mother."

"Yes, but for how long?"

"That will not matter, mother. I will take care of you. It is true what I said. I am coming into a fortune."

"That's nice, dear. Women are drawn to a man with money. You will become very popular, Andrew."

André sighed. "How is your gout, Mother?"

"I'm walking on it, dear. Pins and needles. You know, the daffodils are showing on the south side of the house."

"Really!"

"If you came to visit your mother more often, you would know these things."

André lifted the lid from the Dutch oven and leaned over it, letting the curry-scented steam fill his sinuses. The odor was sublime. Feeling reckless, he crumbled three Saanam peppers into the curry, then set about measuring basmati rice and chicken stock into the rice steamer.

"Jayjay!" he called. "Where are you, Jayjay?" He locked the top on the rice steamer and turned it on.

Jayjay emerged from the basement stairwell.

"Ah! There you are! Dinner will be ready shortly. How is our guest?"

"He's okay. He's asleep."

"You have removed him from my chair, I trust?"

Jayjay shrugged disinterestedly.

"Jonathan?"

"Don't worry about it. He's not sitting in your chair anymore."

"Excellent." André felt a lessening of the anxiety he had been gathering. The image of the man taped to his Windsor chair had been haunting him all afternoon. He removed several jars of Indian chutneys and pickles from the refrigerator and began spooning them into assorted bowls and plates. He liked a variety of colors and flavors on the table. "I have been thinking, Jonathan. I may have come up with a way we can collect that reward—without serving time in prison."

"We?"

André nodded, spooning the last of the lime pickle into a pink Fiestaware bowl. "That is correct. You and me, Jonathan. Academia no longer commands my attention. Would you like to hear my plan?"

Jayjay sat down and nodded.

"All right. Now, the problem as I see it is that if we turn in the husband the reward will probably be in the form of a check, correct?"

"I s'pose."

"And very shortly thereafter, the husband is likely to accuse us of kidnapping him. We will doubtless be arrested."

"We could just take off."

"Yes we could, and we will, but that is not enough. Once we receive the check, it must be cashed. They are likely to stop payment." He pointed a forefinger toward the ceiling to emphasize his point.

Jayjay looked up. "So we cash it right away and just take off."

André frowned. The boy was as obtuse as he was beautiful. "Jonathan, you cannot simply walk into a bank and cash a one-million-dollar check. In the first place, it is unlikely that any bank in Cold Rock would have that amount of currency on hand. In the second place, the husband will most likely be talking to the police within minutes of our releasing him into his wife's custody. No, what we must do is open a local bank account under a fictitious name. Then we set up an offshore bank account, in the Grand Caymans, perhaps. We deposit the check to the local account, immediately have it wired to the offshore bank, then transfer the money to another account in, ah, Switzerland."

"How do you open a bank account in a place you never been to?"

"I do not know," admitted André. He had once seen something of the sort in a film. "But I am quite sure it can be worked out. We then board an airplane for Europe, spend a few months traveling, then perhaps rent a villa in Italy. I could write my book under a *nom de plume*."

"A what?" Jayjay was scratching his nose. "What about the cops? The way you're saying, they'd be on us in, like, seconds. We wouldn't even get to the airport."

"As I said, Jonathan, I have a plan. The problem as I see it is one of time. If we could cause the husband to delay contacting the police for—let us say eight hours—then we would have time to make our move, correct? How, then, do we accomplish this?"

"We could superglue his mouth shut."

"Yes, well, ah, he would still be able to communicate. He could still write."

"We could break his fingers."

"Good Lord!" André was genuinely shocked. It was one thing to kidnap a man and incarcerate him in one's cellar, but breaking fingers? That was far too crude. Although if the man in the cellar were Malcolm Whitly, he might feel differently. "No, no, no, Jonathan! What I propose is that we give him a dose of sleeping pills, enough to render him unconscious for a few hours."

Jayjay nodded. "I could get some good pills."

"Excellent. You procure the pills, and I shall see to the banking arrangements."

André carried the lime pickle and the mango chutney into the dining room. With uncharacteristic helpfulness, Jayjay began to set the table. "I still don't get it about the bank stuff."

André smiled tolerantly. "It is nothing you need worry about, Jonathan."

" 'Cause I was thinking that it might be easier if we just have her pay us cash."

André began to object, but he could find nothing to object to. Cash. What a thought. He imagined himself on an airplane with an attaché case filled with cash and Jayjay in the window seat.

Jayjay pulled a scrap of paper from his pocket. "I got her phone number right here."

The Mobil station manager who had identified Rodney Gent and Hugh Hulke did not know where either of them lived, but he offered Phlox the use of his Cold Rock telephone directory. Hugh Hulke was not listed, but Phlox found Rodney and Susan Gent with a five-digit address on Highway 23. The manager gave her directions. Phlox thanked him, got in her truck, and headed west.

One of the things Phlox had noticed as a dealer at the Desert Diamond Casino was that the winning poker players always projected an air of confidence. They acted aggressively, without hesitation. She wondered whether they were ever as scared as she felt now, alone in a strange town searching for her man.

She wished she felt just a bit more confident, more certain that if she did find Bobby that everything would be okay. The problem was that this whole plan had never sat quite right with her. She had no objection to the money, of course, nor of having it supplied by Bobby's ex—which was how she thought of Barbaraannette. Her problem was that at bottom the million dollars seemed an abstraction, a dream. She feared that Bobby would stay in Cold Rock and she would wind up with nothing. No money. No Bobby. She loved the man to death but she didn't trust him much.

But now she was in the middle of it and there was nothing for it but to go forward. If things worked out she would be rich and still have her man. Or maybe she would have one, or the other, and she could live with those options, too.

An air of confidence. Phlox took several deep, calming breaths as she pulled up in front of Rodney and Sue Gent's small, moderately dilapidated two-story farmhouse. Without hesitating, she marched up and knocked on the screen door.

Sue Gent was a tall, large-bottomed, long-necked woman with a round head, a red face, and a cap of curly mustard-color hair. Her head bobbed like an angry jack-in-the-box as she told Phlox that as far as *she* was concerned Rodney was not home now or any other time and that she should take her little country ass back to whatever house of sin had spawned her and beg the Good Lord to forgive her for bringing shame and misery upon the households of good people such as herself.

"He's not home then?"

Sue Gent's narrow shoulders rose and her eyes seemed to emerge from their sockets.

"I guess not," Phlox said, taking a step back. "Could you tell me where Hugh Hulke lives, then?"

When Sue Gent slammed the door, a confetti of paint chips flew from its crackled surface. Phlox brushed off the front of her denim jacket and returned to the truck. Now what? Aside from driving around aimlessly, she could not think how to proceed, confidently or otherwise. Maybe she should head back into town and start asking people at random—Cold Rock was small enough that sooner or later she would find someone who knew where to find Hugh and Rodney and, possibly, Bobby Quinn. It wasn't much of a plan, but it was all she had. She started the truck and pulled out onto the flat, empty highway.

She had traveled less than a mile when she passed a mailbox with the name Hulke printed on the side. That was another way to go—she could get lucky.

Phlox made a U-turn and pulled into the dirt driveway. On either side were fields of turned-black earth, still spotted with patches of snow. She followed the drive for a quarter mile before arriving at a pale yellow, vinyl-sided ranch house surrounded by a motley collection of outbuildings: two collapsed silos, a long, dangerously leaning corn crib, and a pair of sheds held together with tarpaper and mismatched sections of roll roofing. The driveway continued another hundred yards to a newer-looking metal pole barn with a triple-wide twelve-foot-high rollup door. Several vehicles, including a rusted Camaro, a derelict snowmobile, and a faded green John Deere tractor, were parked in front. Phlox parked the truck and picked her way across forty feet of half-frozen, rutted mud, wishing she wasn't wearing her good Justins, aiming for the small door at the corner of the building.

As she neared the door she heard voices. She turned the knob and eased the door open a crack. The first thing she saw was the rear end of a maroon van. She opened the door a few more inches until she could see the entire vehicle.

From the other side of the van came a whining protest. "You prick! I swear t' God you are the luckiest summabitch I ever seen!"

A deeper, slower voice replied. "Yeah? I'm so lucky what the hell am I doing hanging out with you?"

"Like I said. You're a lucky prick is what. It's your goddamn deal, Hugh."

Phlox slipped through the doorway, squatted down and looked through the van windows. She could see the bottom half of a wooden cable spool and two sets of winter boots. If Bobby was present, he was out of sight. She moved around the back of the van to get a better look at the two men, presumably Hugh Hulke and Rodney Gent. Several beer bottles studded the top of the spool table. Both men were on the plus side of hefty. The one on the left wore a camouflage down vest over a checked flannel shirt. An undersized

Minnesota Vikings stocking cap perched atop his head as if to cover a bald spot. A small cigar jutted from his yellow grin. He was dealing cards, which made him Hugh Hulke.

The other man, Rodney, was slightly larger in every physical dimension. He too wore a down vest, although with a different camouflage pattern. A blaze orange wool cap sat low on his forehead, the visor nearly touching the tip of his bulbous nose. He looked at his cards, grimaced, discarded. "I s'pose you want a goddamn seven." He picked up a longneck, held it up to the light to make sure it wasn't empty, and drank it down.

"Matter a fact, I believe I do, Rod Man."

"Jesus Christ Almighty!" Rodney slammed a fist down on the spool. The bottles wavered but remained upright. Hugh laughed.

Phlox weighed her options. It did not appear that these men had Bobby in their possession, but it was still possible. But if they did have him, why would they be sitting around playing gin rummy? She decided to stand quietly for a time, see whether the subject came up on its own.

Her question was answered almost immediately when Rodney said, "I still can't believe we let him get away."

"Me neither," said Hugh. "We'd have caught him if you weren't such a damn jelly belly."

"Me? You're the porker here. You look in a mirror lately?"

"I got big bones." Hugh discarded.

Rodney scowled at the discard. "Yeah, and I'm a damn rocket surgeon." He drew a card, fitted it into his hand, discarded.

Hugh said, "I wonder who that was in that car."

"Some asshole prob'ly didn't even know who he picked up."

"Then how come he took off that way?"

"On account of we were chasing him."

Hugh shook his head. "You're not just fat, you're stupid, too."

"Yeah? So?"

"I'm just trying to make a point here."

"And what's that?"

"How the hell should I know?"

Phlox couldn't help herself. She burst out laughing.

23

The wallpaper, the ceiling, and the bed were unfamiliar, but Hilde thought she recognized the maple dresser. Mary Beth had used it in her room until she'd moved out. Hilde couldn't remember where it had gone from there. She sat up and explored her more recent memories. She remembered borrowing the Porsche but she could not remember how her ride had ended, or how she had gotten to this room, or how long—hours? days? weeks?—she had been here. Hilde swung her legs over the edge of the mattress and let her feet drop to the nubbly carpet; her feet were bare. Looking at the rest of her body she discovered that she was wearing an unfamiliar nightgown. She reached back with one hand, pulled the neck around and out so that she could view the label. *Eileen West.* Hilde smiled. She must be at Barbaraannette's house. She leaned forward and transferred her weight to her feet, then straightened up. Her ankles, knees, and hips all registered their usual complaints. Interesting how, at her age, simply standing up became a sequence of conscious, considered acts. It was no wonder that she had become so forgetful with so much of her mental energy now devoted to such mundane matters.

Hilde found Barbaraannette in the other bedroom sprawled on top of the bedspread, fully dressed, one arm thrown over her eyes, her mouth hanging open, snoring quietly. She closed the door and went in search of the kitchen. Yes, this was most definitely

Barbaraannette's house. Was she living here now? Had she been kicked out of the hotel? Or was this just a visit? This forgetfulness was becoming a real problem. She hoped that no one had noticed. A cup of tea might help get the old gray matter pulsing. Hilde filled the teakettle and put it on the stove and sat down to wait for the whistle. While she was waiting, the telephone rang. Hilde picked it up quickly, not wanting the noise to awaken her daughter.

"Hello?"

"Good evening! Am I speaking with Mrs. Quinn?" The man had a very cultured voice.

"Yes?" said Hilde. She was not Mrs. Quinn, of course, but she was Mrs. Quinn's mother, which was more or less the same thing.

"I am calling in regards to your husband."

"Oh?" Hilde waited.

"I would like to deliver him to you, as per your request."

"As per?" Hilde switched the phone to her other ear. "Hello?"

"Yes, hello! Mrs. Quinn?"

"Yes?"

"I would like to discuss, er, the reward with you. The manner of payment?"

"Yes?" Hilde was certain that any second now the gears would mesh and she would understand what this man was talking about.

"We are wondering if it would be possible for you to pay us the amount in cash."

"Is this a collection call?"

"Excuse me?"

"The check is in the mail."

"Is this Mrs. Quinn?"

"Yes?"

"Is this the Mrs. Quinn who is married to Robert Quinn?"

Hilde hesitated. It was one thing to claim to be Mrs. Quinn, but another thing altogether to claim to be married to her own son-in-law. She said, "Hello?"

"Yes. Mrs. Quinn, do you want your husband returned to you?"

Hilde blinked. "Which one are we talking about?" she asked.

A younger, ruder voice interrupted. "Don't fuck with us!"

"Excuse me?" Hilde said.

"Listen, lady, you want your husband you better quit fucking around here or your old man's gonna be in some serious shit."

Hilde said, "There's no need to be rude." Barbaraannette appeared in front of her, gesturing frantically. "Just a moment," Hilde said to the man on the phone. She put a hand over the mouthpiece. "I think I'm having an obscene phone call," she said.

"Get off the phone!" André hissed.

"She's just jacking you around, Perfesser," Jayjay said. He was on the cordless, standing in the kitchen doorway.

"You let me handle this—hello?"

"Hello?"

"With whom am I speaking, please?"

"This is Mrs. Quinn. Who are you?"

"Mrs. Quinn, I have located your husband."

"Oh!" She said nothing for several heartbeats. "You aren't the person who called earlier, are you?"

"No I am not. Mrs. Quinn, I'd like to arrange to deliver your husband to you and collect the reward you have offered."

"I see." Another long pause. "I'd like to talk to him, please."

"Of course, of course." André did not want to go back into that cellar. "It is not convenient at the moment, however."

"Well, when it's convenient you give me a call back. Or just bring him on by and we'll see about the reward. By the way, what is your name?"

"That is of no importance. Perhaps I haven't explained myself sufficiently, Mrs. Quinn. I will be happy to let you speak with your husband at the appropriate time, but I think we need to make some arrangements first. To be precise, I would like to be paid the reward money in cash. Would that be possible?"

"I hadn't really thought about it."

"That is precisely why I am calling you now—" André became aware that his shirt was soaked with sweat, and that his hand hurt from squeezing the phone. "—so that you have time to get the money. The cash."

Mrs. Quinn cleared her throat. "How do I know you have Bobby? Is he okay?"

"He's fine."

"Yes, well, Mr. Voice-on-the-phone, this is all very suspicious. You bring my husband to me and I'll see about your reward. Good-bye, Mr. Voice—"

Jayjay cut in. "You hang up and your old man's dead, lady!"

For a moment no one spoke, then André said, keeping his voice carefully under control, "Mrs. Quinn, there's no reason for this situation to become adversarial."

"Then why are you threatening me?"

"I'm not. I—"

"This is bullshit," Jayjay interrupted.

"Please—" André said, feeling the situation slipping out of his control.

"You get the fucking money or else, lady!"

"I don't think I like your attitude," she said.

"You think I give a shit?" Jayjay shrieked. "I got my ass blown up fighting Saddam! I'm a goddamn war veteran. You think I care what you like?"

André snatched the cordless away from Jayjay. "We will be in touch," he said, then hung up both phones.

Jayjay said, "Hey!"

"I told you I would handle this," André snapped. "Are you trying to ruin everything?"

"No! I—"

"We agreed that I would be the one to talk to the woman. Me. Now she knows there are two of us working together."

"So?"

"It was a stupid thing to do, Jayjay."

Jayjay tucked his chin; his face darkened. "Don't call me stupid."

André threw his hands in the air and turned his back.

Jayjay said. "You think I'm stupid? You're stupid. You're the fucking stupid one."

André, hugging himself, looked down at the stovetop. He needed time to think, to calm down. Being surrounded by his pots and pans and the smell of lamb curry helped.

Jayjay grabbed him by the shoulders and spun André to face him. "*You're* fucking stupid. She's not gonna just pay us the reward, y'know, unless she has to—" He jabbed André in the sternum with two fingers, producing an audible thump. "—*stupid.*"

"What do you mean?" André covered his chest with his hands.

"She's not gonna give us a fucking dime unless we show her we're serious. We gotta send her one of his ears or something, like they do in Italy."

André stared at the red-faced young man standing in his kitchen. This was the beautiful Jonathan James? It hardly seemed possible. Cutting off people's ears? Was he planning to do him harm as well? Inconceivable, after all he had done for the boy. Change the subject, he thought. He turned back to the stove, groping for words. "When were you in Italy?" he said over his shoulder.

"I was never in fucking Italy," Jayjay said. "Jesus Christ, talk about *stupid!*"

André could feel the boy's breath on the back of his neck. Slipping on a pair of oven mitts, he lifted the Dutch oven from the stovetop and turned around.

Jayjay backed away from the hot iron pot. He said, "Look, we gotta call her back, let her talk to the guy or she's not gonna do nothing."

André carried the curry to the dining room and set it on a trivet. "We'll call her back after dinner." It was important that he retain some semblance of control.

"We gotta call her back now or she might call the cops or something."

Unable to stop himself, André said, "Why on earth would she do that? Simply because you threatened to kill her husband? How unreasonable of her!"

Jayjay's normally full lips compressed into a thin white slash. He picked up the cordless and hit the redial button. André felt in himself a powerful urge to strike the boy, to pick up a utensil of some sort and swing it against the side of his head. He even went so far as to consider the specific items at hand—the top to the Dutch oven, the serving spoon, the ceramic candlesticks—but nothing seemed quite right.

Jayjay said into the phone, "You still want to talk to your old man? Hold on." He gave André a triumphant look, mouthed the word "stupid," and descended into the cellar.

André felt an unfamiliar expression come and go on his face. He made a clucking sound with his tongue, stripped off the oven mitts and followed Jayjay into the cellar.

24

The cold concrete floor smelled of piss and dust and his throat was dry as ash. The furnace turned itself on again, producing a faint orange glow near its base. Bobby squirmed closer to the heat, dragging the heavy wooden chair, trying to be quiet about it, trying not to throw his breathing out of sync. With his mouth taped over and one nostril swollen shut the slightest effort left him desperate for oxygen. Air and water. He had never before had to worry about either of those things. All he'd ever worried about was money and sex and looking good but right now he would give up all those things, at least for a while, for a glass of water and a lungful of clean air.

He could hear voices from upstairs, the two crazies. What had he done to deserve this? Leave Barbaraannette? That one little thing he'd done six years ago? No. A lot of guys just like him made their move for one reason or another and none of them got hit over the head and taped to a chair. Then again, none of them had been married to Barbaraannette.

The voices got louder. He heard one of them coming down the steps saying, "I think he's taking a little nap. I got to wake him up." The door opened and the light went on. Bobby could see boots; it was the young one, the one who'd kicked him.

The kid said, "You move? I told you not to fuckin' move."

Bobby tensed, waiting for another kick, but the kid squatted down in front of him, holding a phone in one hand. With the other he began to pick at the duct tape. "Shit, man . . ." He put the phone down and started digging in with his nails, trying to tear the tape away.

Then Bobby heard another voice. "Good Lord, what have you done?"

The man was still taped to the chair. Worse yet, the man and the chair were tipped over, and one of the chair legs had broken off. Two hundred years old and now it lay sundered on the cellar floor. André's hands met and clutched. He heard his voice, complaining in high-pitched and anxious tones. "Do you know what you've done?"

Jayjay had frozen in position, crouched over the chair, his hands on the man's face, looking over his shoulder, his eyes small and glittering. He looked to André like an evil troll, an underground creature come to prey upon his antique furniture.

André shouted, "Get him off it! Get him off!"

Jayjay the troll-boy stood up. "Just calm down, Perfesser."

"You told me he was off it, damn you!" André pushed Jayjay aside, knocked the bare light bulb swinging, fell to his knees and went at the duct tape with bare hands, ripping through it with desperate strength, muttering to himself. He managed to tear through a few loops, then encountered a twisted rope of tape that resisted his efforts. André grasped the tape and pulled with all his strength. The tape held, but one of his fingernails folded back, sending a shock of pain up his arm. André gasped and tears spurted from his eyes. "Damn you!" he wailed and punched the man in the side with his good hand.

"Take it easy, Perfesser. Let me give you a hand, okay?"

André looked up, saw Jayjay the troll-boy smiling, showing his teeth.

"What's so funny?" André demanded.

"Nothing!" The light bulb, still in motion, moved the boy's eyes in and out of shadow. "Here, let me help." The boy moved a hand and André saw the thin blade, still greasy with raw lamb, projecting from his fist.

His boning knife. He'd left it sitting atop the furnace, he remembered, and now the boy had it. Yellow light struck the blade and flashed directly into his eyes. André stepped back, hit the wall. The room became smaller. André could not take his eyes off the knife. Again, it caught light from the bulb and sent it lasering into his brain. André tore his eyes away and looked to the doorway, suddenly realizing that he might never leave this dingy, brutal little room.

"What's the matter?" The boy asked, stepping toward him, cutting off his escape, lowering the blade as if to conceal it, or readying it for an upward thrust. André's eyes darted wildly, delivering a mad slide show of images. The amputated leg of the Windsor lay on the floor between them. André felt himself suspended in time, knowing that he was about to act, feeling a weird, sensual joy as he gave himself to the moment. Was this what a man felt as he stepped off a precipice? He bent forward at the waist, his knees flexed, he saw his hand grasp the chair leg, bring it up above his head—

"Hey!"

—and down, striking the boy on the shoulder.

"Ow, shit, man, fuck, you—"

The boy still held the knife. André swung again, hit fingers, heard a gasp overlaid by a high-pitched scream, swung again and felt the chair leg strike skull. The knife clattered to the floor but the screaming went on. The boy staggered back, tripped over the man in the chair, fell against a pile of old storm windows. André leapt over the chair, raised his club and struck again. The sound of shattering glass sliced through the scream; André struck again, and again until the screaming stopped and he realized that the awful sound had been coming from his own throat. He backed away from the clutter of broken glass, averting his eyes from the boy's bloodied head. He backed up until the far wall, cold gray block, struck his shoulder blades. He sank to the concrete floor, gasping, his throat raw, his body buzzing and twitching, tiny hands still gripping the bloodied chair leg, his torn fingernail throbbing with each enormous, rib-shivering heartbeat. He did not move until his eyes fell upon the cordless telephone on the floor, inches from the duct-taped man's wide, staring eyes.

•   •   •

Barbaraannette said, "Hello?"

No response, only a hollow sound, and something that might be distant breathing. What had she heard? A fight of some sort, but who? The one who called had told her she could talk to Bobby, then she'd heard a lot of cursing and banging, and then that awful screaming, like a pig getting killed.

"Hello?" she repeated.

She heard a scraping sound, then a soft click. Now she could hear nothing, not even the hollow sound. Barbaraannette hung up the phone and looked down at her mother sitting quietly on the sofa, her hands folded in her lap, her face devoid of expression.

Barbaraannette made herself smile and said, "I think you're right, Hilde. It was definitely an obscene phone call."

Hilde showed no sign of having heard her. Barbaraannette sat down beside her mother and looked into her face. "Mom? Anybody home?"

Hilde's pupils were constricted to pinpoints, letting in as little light as possible. Barbaraannette waved a hand in front of her face. Hilde blinked, a tear rolled down her cheek, joined a bead of drool at the corner of her slack mouth, hung there.

Barbaraannette felt suddenly and terrifyingly alone. She needed to talk to somebody, but Hilde was unavailable and she didn't want to tie up the phone. What if those people called back? She would have to wait. A half hour, at least, then she could call someone. But who? Not Toagie. Toagie would freak out. Not Mary Beth. She wasn't ready for Mary Beth, who would doubtless put all her energy into telling her it was all her fault. Maybe she should call the police. She thought about Chief Dale Gordon and grimaced. The last thing she wanted was to owe that man another favor.

She stood up and said, "You're tired, Mom. Let's get some rest." She tried to bring Hilde to her feet, but encountered only deadweight, so she pushed her mother gently onto her side and straightened her legs. She fetched a thick wool blanket from the linen closet, covered her, then sat on the floor in front of the sofa and rested her head on Hilde's blanketed hip. She watched Hilde's face until her eyes closed and a soft sputtering sound came from her lips.

"There you go," Barbaraannette said. "I don't know where you go, but I hope you find a fast car when you get there." Hilde began to snore in earnest, and Barbaraannette shifted her eyes from her mother's gaping mouth to the telephone, waiting.

For several seconds after the bearded man turned off the phone and picked up the knife, Bobby thought he was about to die. He closed his eyes and tensed every muscle in his body, but when the cut came it was duct tape rather than flesh that parted. Was he being set free?

Making little *tut-tut* sounds with his tongue, the man sliced quickly through layers of tape. "You saw it, yes? Saw him with the knife. A witness, I have a witness. You saw it all."

Bobby did not know whether that was a good thing or a bad thing. He was afraid to nod or shake his head.

"I had no choice," the man said as he cut the last few bands of tape and pulled the chair away. "Oh dear. Oh my." He was looking at the broken leg. Bobby tried to move, but his arms and legs were still taped together. He lay on his side watching as the man tried to fit the bloodied chair leg back onto the chair. "Awful, simply awful." The man shook his head sadly, peeling scraps of silver tape from the back of the chair. "What a waste." His eyes rediscovered Bobby. "You poor man," he said.

Bobby felt a surge of gratitude fill his chest, but his hopes had evaporated when the man picked up the roll of duct tape and said, "I suppose you think that I am a bad person." He rolled Bobby onto his stomach and began adding layers of tape around his wrists. "But that is only because you do not know me." The man stood up—Bobby could see a spot of blood on his Hush Puppies—and ascended the basement stairs.

From his new position on the basement floor Bobby found himself staring directly into the dead boy's face, less than six feet away. He thought, it serves you right, you sorry son of a bitch. The thought brought him no satisfaction.

He closed his eyes and breathed. His swollen nostril had opened slightly. He no longer feared suffocation, but he was more certain than ever that he was going to die in that basement. He could hear the bearded man moving around upstairs, talking to himself. He could still hear the weird screaming and the wet thud of the kid's head being caved in.

Bobby wished for a lungful of clean air, for a glass of water to appear. He forced his thoughts out of the basement, imagined himself sipping a cold one, watching Phlox in her denim shorts washing the truck. He saw himself driving, wind blasting his face, sun on his arm. He opened his eyes. The dead boy was still there, wedged into the mass of shattered storm windows, one eye open, the other battered closed and crusted with drying blood. He wished he had never come back to Minnesota. He wished that someone would turn off the light.

25

You mean to tell me all this time he's been hiding out in Tucson?"
"Five years, honey."

"Damn! I been to Tucson five, six times." Hugh Hulke looked at the butt of his cigar, grimaced, threw it to the floor. "I always figured Bobby'd head for Wyoming or Montana, way he talked about it all the time. Tucson. Damn. I coulda run across him anytime."

"You would've if you'd been shopping at Wild Wally's." Phlox sipped her beer. She and Hugh were sitting at the spool table. Rodney, reclined on a ratty sofa against the back wall, balanced a beer bottle on his chest. Hugh shifted his chair and leaned in close to Phlox. "What'd he go to Tucson for? You?"

Phlox shrugged. "I don't know what got him down there. Maybe he wanted to sell cowboy boots." She lifted one of her feet onto the table, the tip of her boot nearly catching Hugh's nostril. "He got me these. Sixty percent off."

"I never did get those pointy toes," Hugh said, sitting back.

"You like 'em or you don't." She brought her other foot up and crossed her ankles, smiling with what she hoped was an air of confidence.

Hugh grinned. "You're a feisty one."

"You think so?" It was working.

"You come here looking for Bobby, what were you gonna do if he was here?"

"Take him off your hands. Collect the reward."

Hugh raised his eyebrows in mock astonishment.

Phlox said, "In fact, that's still my plan. Of course, I understand Bobby owes you boys some money. I'd make sure you're taken care of."

"Aren't you the generous one!"

"I'm the only chance you've got to recoup your investment. All you have to do is help me find him."

Hugh tipped his head and frowned as if waiting for an unfamiliar sound to repeat itself. After a moment he said, "Now don't you take this wrong, sweetheart, but if I knew how to find Bobby, what would I need you for?"

"On account of I'm the only one who can collect the reward. I've already arranged things with Barbaraannette."

Hugh made a sour face.

Phlox continued. "She knows I'm the one that brought him back here. Besides, suppose you hogtied Bobby and dragged him over to Barbaraannette, and suppose she paid you the money. You don't think Bobby would turn around and have you arrested for kidnapping?"

"He wouldn't if he knew what was good for him," Hugh growled.

"But Bobby wouldn't know what was good for him, would he? You'd end up in jail for kidnapping, and you'd probably have to give the money back because the court wouldn't allow you to profit from a criminal enterprise."

Hugh nodded, either in agreement or to show that he was following her logic.

"So what I'm suggesting is, you help me find Bobby and I'll cut you guys in. Ten percent. A hundred thousand dollars. That's five times what you lost on Bobby's land deal."

Hugh worked his lips for a few seconds, then said, "A hundred thousand each?"

Phlox shook her head. "Total. You divvy it up however you think."

"You think he's out there running loose?"

"I think somebody's got him. You saw him jump into a car, right? And whoever it is, they've got the same problem as you would've. They can't turn him in without getting charged with kid-napping. The only person can do that is me."

"I don't suppose you know who's got him?"

"If I did, I wouldn't be here. The only thing I know is, at that gas station where you boys saw Bobby? There was somebody there in a green car that took off the same time Bobby did. Only I didn't get the make or license."

Hugh said, "Hey Rod Man, you catch the license on that car?"

"Nope. But it was a green Ford Taurus, maybe a ninety-four, ninety-five. That's all I seen."

Hugh shrugged and returned his attention to Phlox. "Okay, suppose whoever was in the green car put the snatch on our Bobby. How are we supposed to find him?"

Phlox said, "How did I find you?"

"I got no fucking idea."

"This is Cold Rock, Minnesota, Hugh. It's not that big a place."

"So?"

"So how many green Tauruses do you think a town this size can hold?"

Art Dobbleman was five slices into a fourteen-inch veggie pizza and ten minutes into the six o'clock news when the telephone rang. He was pretty sure it was Marla, his ex-wife. They'd been separated for four months and officially divorced for three months now, but she still made it a practice to interrupt his dinner three or four times a week. Making sure he was being a good divorcé. He took a large bite of pizza, pressed the mute button on the TV remote, picked up the phone and issued a muffled hello.

"Art? It's me. Barbaraannette."

"Bar—oh!" He forced the half-chewed mouthful down his throat. "Hi!" He followed it with several ounces of apple juice.

"Are you busy?"

Art looked down at his long, bare legs. He hadn't changed clothes from his evening run, a little six-miler. "I'm just sitting around."

"Art, I need to talk to you."

"I'm here."

"About borrowing some money."

"Sure! Sure, we could do that." He felt foolish now. He'd thought she might be calling *him,* but it was just business. He asked, "Is this— has someone found Bobby?"

"Maybe. I'm not sure. But I want to be ready. I think I better sign some papers or something, whatever you have to do, because when I need it—if I need it—I'm going to need it fast."

"How fast?"

"Art, I can't tie up the phone right now, I'm waiting for an important call. Could you come over here?"

"Now?" He hoped he'd have time for a shower.

"If you're not busy?"

No shower. "I'm on my way," said Art.

The first bite nearly turned his tongue into a twisted cinder. André guzzled both wine and water, gasping. What had happened to his wonderful curry? Could those three little peppers have produced such a mouth-searing effect? André wiped the tears from his eyes and examined the plateful of curry, poking at it with his fork. He discovered several whole Sanaam peppers hidden amidst the lamb and onions. André's face, already flushed, turned a deeper shade of crimson. Fury rose in him with the image of Jayjay's smirking face. Jayjay's dead face.

The events of the past three hours scrambled for his attention; André squeezed his eyes closed, pushing away the thought of the dead boy in his cellar. The very idea was absurd! So absurd, in fact, that he found it easy to pretend that it was not so. Casting about for a tolerable replacement thought, he found himself once again in Italy, he and Jayjay—no, some other person—enjoying prosciutto and fresh fava beans, looking out over the Mediterranean. André in an off-white linen jacket, cotton trousers, and sleek calfskin loafers, no socks, the sea breeze caressing his ankles. His companion speaks, a rapid sequence of Italian words which André understands to mean that he, André, is a remarkable and mysterious man. He smiles and extracts a sheaf of lira notes—ten thousand? A hundred thousand? What was a lira worth these days? He would have to do some research. He permitted himself to consider, for a moment, the duct-taped cowboy. The man was worth a million dollars. The man could also put him in prison for the rest of his life. No prosciutto, no fava beans, no antique chairs.

There had to be a way. He could stick with the plan, call the woman back, return her husband to her and collect the money. It would take him several hours to get safely out of the country, and even then, how safe would he be? Did the Italians extradite kidnap-pers and murderers? Also, if he became a fugitive, would he have to abandon his antiques?

André impaled a piece of lamb, placed it upon his tongue, chewed thoughtfully. The heat filled his mouth. This time he let it burn. The flavor was fiery and sublime. He swallowed, felt the heat flow down his throat into his stomach. He took another bite, felt his sinuses open.

André considered actions, reactions, scenarios both probable and improbable. He followed each scheme from outset to conclu-sion, saw himself free, imprisoned, wealthy, poor, alive, dead. He worked his way slowly through the plate of curry, letting its heat fire his imagination. By the time he finished the last bite he knew ex-actly what he had to do.

26

Art *would be arriving any minute. Barbaraannette looked down at her-*
self, frowned. She tiptoed past the snoring Hilde to her bedroom,
stripped off her jeans and T-shirt, and flipped through the contents
of her closet until she found a navy blue dropwaist dress—she'd
bought it for the last MEA conference in Minneapolis—that hit a
mark somewhere between frumpy and sexy. She looked in the mirror, ran her fingers through her hair, considered and rejected lipstick. Art was a banker. He probably wouldn't notice, and besides,
this was business. She pulled on a pair of burgundy flats, returned to
the kitchen, put a teakettle on the stove, turned on the flame, fitted
a filter into the Chemex, added a few scoops of coffee, then waited.

The man who said he had Bobby hadn't called back yet.
Something had happened. Had it happened to Bobby? Had Bobby
even been there? Was he even in Cold Rock? Was he even alive?
Barbaraannette's head whirled with doubts. The woman, Phlox,
claimed that she had brought Bobby to Cold Rock. Barbaraannette
had believed her, but what if that had been a lie, an attempt to extract
money? And maybe the man who had phoned was up to the same
thing. Maybe Barbaraannette had foiled their plans by insisting on
talking to Bobby. So far, she had no concrete proof that Bobby still existed upon this earth. Barbaraannette did not know what was going
on, but she did know one thing. Everybody wanted her money.

The teakettle began to whistle, shattering her thoughts. Barbaraannette turned off the burner and slowly poured hot water into the Chemex, letting the coffee-scented steam warm her face. She didn't usually drink coffee this late in the day, as it gave her strange dreams and a fitful sleep, but on this evening she craved the bits of clarity, or at least the illusion of clarity, brought by caffeine. She watched the dark stream trickle into the glass urn, the water magically drawing flavor and power from the grounds. That was exactly what she needed to do with her life. Distill it down to its essence. Figure out what she wanted.

Until now, she thought, she had never had to think too hard about what she really wanted. Bobby had left her, and she wanted him back. She had seen herself as a martyr without a cause. So long as he was gone she had led a peacefully deprived life, waiting for something to happen, as if losing her husband had absolved her from the responsibilities of volition. At some point she had lapsed into a kind of comfortable stupidity. Was it when Bobby left, or before that? When had she stopped being her own person? She let her thoughts drift back to her wedding. No, it went back further than that, perhaps to the moment she had first seen Bobby Quinn pumping gas into his El Camino at the Shell station. She'd been seventeen years old back then, shortstop and number three batter for the Crockettes, and a straight A student at Cold Rock High. Bobby had been nineteen and the best-looking guy she'd ever laid eyes on. She'd gotten stupid all right. She'd stupided herself all over him and the luckiest thing about it was that she hadn't gotten herself pregnant right then and there. If she had—and this new thought made her feel very strange indeed—if she *had,* her child would now be the same age as she had been then, letting Bobby have his way with her in the woods in the back of his El Camino. Of course, she had been having her way with him, too, but no matter whose script they'd been playing there could be no question but that as a result she had been stupid and confused for seventeen years now, more than half her life. And in another thirty years, if her genes held true, she would become even more bewildered. Maybe getting pregnant wouldn't have been such a bad alternative. At least she'd have had someone to take care of her in her dotage.

Something will have to change, thought Barbaraannette. She poured herself a mug of coffee. The doorbell rang.

The single most wonderful moment of Bobby's recent life had to be when the bearded man handed him a tall glass of cool water. Moments before, the man had cut the tape from his mouth and his arms. Bobby's legs were still immobilized but he could sit up. The block wall of the basement felt cool against his back.

Bobby's hands were shaking as he raised the glass to his lips and sipped. The water hurt going down his swollen throat, as delightful a pain as he had ever felt.

The bearded man, still holding the knife, stood back a few feet, staring at him intensely.

"Thank you," Bobby said. His gratitude was real and overwhelming. He drank some more. "Thank you, sir," he said again.

The bearded man said, "My name is André."

"Thank you, André."

"You are welcome, Bobby."

Bobby drank again, a small sip, savoring it.

André asked, "How are you feeling?"

"Better. I'm sorry about your chair."

André nodded. "Yes, well, these things happen. I must tell you that I, too, am sorry—about all of this. It was not my idea, you know."

Bobby's eyes moved to the corpse, then quickly away.

André said, "It was Jonathan who brought you here. I asked him to let you go, but . . ." He shook his head ruefully. "Our lives take strange turns, do they not?"

Bobby waited, then gave a shallow nod when he saw that André required a response.

"Strange turns indeed. You and I, for instance, are very different people. I am an academic. I live in a world of ideas. I make my way through life by exercising the powers of my intellect, whereas you . . . what is it you do?"

Bobby said, "I sell boots."

"Yes, of course. We are each of us concerned with different ends of the human form. And then one day, through pure chance, your wife wins the lottery. Suddenly we are brought together. Do you believe in fate, Robert?"

"I guess."

"That is because you are a boot salesman. But you do not want to be a boot salesman the rest of your life, do you?"

"I reckon not."

"And you won't be. Tell me, Robert, what were your plans here? Were you planning to return to your wife to become a rich woman's husband?"

Bobby thought quickly, trying to figure out which of the many lies available to him would be most likely to get him out of this basement, but because he didn't know what André wanted from him, he fell back on the truth. "My girlfriend was supposed to turn me in."

André said, "Ah! I understand. Were you then planning to stay with your wife, or were you going to split the money with the girlfriend?"

Bobby cleared his throat. "I kinda hadn't decided."

André nodded. "Because your girlfriend and you would have split the money, a million dollars, but your wife has far more money than that."

"Something like that. Only, I think Barbaraannette might make life kinda rough for me. Like I said, I was thinking it out both ways."

"That is very intelligent." André smiled. "Let me ask you this. How would you like to return to your wife and, at the same time, have one-half-million dollars of your own money. Escape money, if you will, just in case things don't work out for you. You could even go back to your girlfriend, if you wished."

Bobby didn't move a muscle.

"You are interested?" André asked, a smile forming in his beard.

Bobby nodded. It sounded like a way out of the basement.

André's smile broadened, showing teeth. "Excellent. Let me explain to you how this is going to work, and why."

•   •   •

"There's really not much to it," Art said, touching the tip of his ballpoint pen to the loan agreement. They were sitting at the kitchen table. "You're already approved. Your lottery payments are all the collateral we need. I'm authorized to make the loan at one-quarter point over prime, adjusted quarterly, plus a small origination fee, with a fifteen-year repayment plan. Your payments would be, initially, eight thousand four hundred and one dollars and twenty cents per month, or slightly more than one hundred thousand dollars per year. All you have to do is stop by the bank tomorrow morning and we'll get everything signed and notarized, and you can write checks on the full amount beginning immediately."

Barbaraannette said, "Suppose I need it in cash?"

Art clicked his pen a few times, searching her face. "The entire amount? In cash?"

Barbaraannette nodded.

"We could get you cash. It might take an extra day. I can't say I recommend it."

"How much space would that take up? Could one person carry it?"

"Sure." He thought for a moment, imagining a hundred packets of hundred-dollar bills, one hundred bills in each small bundle. He indicated his briefcase. "It would fit in there. Can I ask why you'd want it in cash?"

Barbaraannette did not reply immediately. Her eyes slid away, and her hands met around her coffee mug. Art watched thoughts come and go on her face. There was an instant when he believed she might be about to cry, then her mouth tightened and two kidney-shaped blotches of red appeared on her cheeks, as if she was about to explode in anger. He drew back, bracing himself, but her face changed again, her mouth softening. In every manifestation, he found her face to be a thing of beauty. When she had answered the door he almost told her how nice she looked in her dark blue dress but then it was too late. To say something now would be awkward.

Barbaraannette raised her hands and pressed them against her cheeks, massaged her jaw, dropped her hands and shook her head slowly. "Art, if I tell you why I want cash, you'll think I'm the biggest fool in the whole blamed state."

Art took a breath. "Barbaraannette, let me put your mind at rest. There's nothing you could do or say that would strike me as being more idiotic than offering a million bucks to bring Bobby Quinn back to Cold Rock in the first place. Okay?"

Barbaraannette cocked her head. "You mean, since you already think I'm an idiot, what difference can it make?"

Art felt a grin turn up his mouth.

Barbaraannette began to giggle.

Art started laughing, too, then he heard a strange cackle and turned around to see Hilde Grabo, orange wig askew, standing in the archway, a huge grin on her wrinkled features. The moment their eyes met, Hilde's mouth snapped shut.

"What's so funny?" she asked.

Barbaraannette and Art both fell headlong into laughter. Hilde pushed out her lower lip, walked around them and began to look through the cupboards.

Barbaraannette got her laughter under control and watched. After a minute she asked, "What are you looking for, Hilde?"

"Do you have any raisins?"

Barbaraannette got up and located a box of raisins. Hilde took the box from her and poured a generous portion into a cereal bowl. She sat down beside Art at the table and began to eat them with her fingers.

Barbaraannette gave Art a helpless look and shrugged. "Hilde's version of raisin bran. So, you can get it for me in cash?"

"You still haven't told me why you want cash."

"The man who called—there were two men, actually—demanded cash. But I still don't know for sure whether Bobby was with him, or if they were lying to me. They were arguing. I could hear on the phone that they were fighting. Then they hung up, and then one of them called me back and said he was going to put Bobby on the phone, and then there was all this screaming and they hung up again." Barbaraannette winced. "Maybe it was some kind of joke."

Art was not smiling. "Do you think he's being held against his will?"

"Maybe. I don't know."

"What about the woman who was here. Do you think she's part of it?"

Barbaraannette shook her head. "I don't think she knows what's going on. She said she was going to go find Bobby, but I don't know how she thought she was going to do that." She remembered the way Phlox had driven her around, helping her search for Hilde. "She's a pretty resourceful woman. I liked her." She reached across the kitchen table and patted her mother's shoulder. Hilde, intent on her raisins, did not seem to notice.

Art said, "But you do think that Bobby came to town with her?"

"She knows Bobby, that's for sure. I think he was with her. She says he was chased off by Hugh Hulke and Rodney Gent. You remember them?"

Art nodded. "Hugh took out a home equity loan to invest in Bobby's dude ranch. He's still trying to pay it off. Was it Hugh who called?"

"No. This was a very cultured sounding man. He had a way of talking, not quite British, but almost. And the first man was very rude, said he was a Gulf War veteran."

Art lifted his coffee mug and peered into it as if reading tea leaves. "Barbaraannette, I really think that you should call the police about this."

"That's the last thing I need."

Art looked up, surprised. "Why is that?"

"I don't need to be owing any more favors to Dale Gordon."

"What do you mean favors? It's his job."

"Not really. We don't even know for sure if there's been a crime."

"At the very least, you've been threatened over the phone."

"They didn't threaten me. They threatened Bobby."

"Nevertheless—"

The telephone rang. Barbaraannette was on it before the second ring.

"Hello?"

"Mrs. Quinn?" It was the man who had called before, the polite one with the educated voice.

She said, "Who is this?"

"I understand you are trying to locate your husband?"

"You know very well what I'm doing."

"Pardon me?"

"You and your foul-mouthed friend."

"I'm sorry, I don't know what you're talking about. Perhaps you have confused me with another."

"I don't think so."

"Yes, well, in any event, I have your husband here. Would you like to speak with him?"

Barbaraannette nodded, then said, "Yes."

"A moment, please." Muffled conversation came over the wire, then a voice she had not heard in six years.

"Hey there, Barbie doll."

Her body went prickly, as if touched by ten thousand pins.

Hilde flicked a raisin at Art, hitting him on the cheek. She said, "You better get busy, Arthur. It's him."

Art turned his attention from Barbaraannette, whose face had gone pale, to her raisin-flicking mother. A second raisin hit him, this one right on the nose. Hilde's eyes had narrowed. She pointed a finger at her daughter and said, "Look at her!"

Barbaraannette, her eyes focused on a far horizon, said, "Bobby?" She listened and swallowed. "Are you all right?" Some color, a blotchy pink, remained on her throat.

Hilde put a raisin in her mouth, chewed, and said, "She's like a car."

Art said, "What?" He was watching Barbaraannette, and not sure he had correctly heard Hilde's words.

Barbaraannette said, "Uh-huh. But where have you been?" She listened. "You're right, we can talk about it all later. But are you really okay? That man you're with, are you, is he making you say these things?" Her brow wrinkled. "Oh, uh-huh . . . do you know a woman named Phlox?"

Hilde reached over and poked a fingernail into Art's ribs. "Like a *fast* car," she said.

Art shifted his chair away from Hilde, trying to focus on Barbaraannette.

"I see. She just gave you a ride? Bobby? Hello? Oh! Yes." The color was rising; her cheeks now held a trace of pink. "Yes? Tomorrow? That would be fine. I'll have to go to the bank. All right. Okay then. Yes, Cold Rock Savings & Loan, on First Street. All right then. Goodbye." She hung up the phone, blinked and reacquainted herself with her surroundings. "Excuse me," she said, and abruptly left the kitchen.

Art stood up to follow her, but Hilde grabbed his arm.

"Give her a minute, Arthur. Can't you see she's ashamed?"

"I thought you said she was like a car."

"You young people are so literal."

Art shrugged and sat down.

Hilde said, "I like Porsches. What do you drive?"

Art shook his head, bewildered. "A Plymouth?"

Hilde laughed. "You know what you ought to be driving, don't you? You ought to be driving Barbaraannette."

The water was blue. Who had ever thought it might be a good idea to make toilet bowl water blue? Why not green, or lilac? Or yellow, for that matter, which seemed more natural. Or clear. Why not leave it clear? Why did she put those things in the toilet tank, anyway? Because her mother had?

Barbaraannette, kneeling before the porcelain bowl, waited for herself to spew. She knew there was something in there that had to come out, she just hoped it wasn't her liver or a kidney or some other vital organ.

The tile floor was hard on her knees and her head hurt. She closed her eyes and imagined the tangled mass inside her. It would be green and ragged and dry, made of stale beer and coffee and lottery tickets and six years of mourning and confusion. The thought of such a conglomeration erupting from her body was terrifying, but the thought of it remaining within her was worse. She opened her eyes onto the still blue pool.

Tomorrow morning at ten o'clock a man would bring her husband home, and she would give him a check for one million dollars.

And then what?

She could stick a finger down her throat, but that scared her, too. The blue pool had begun to look too much like an eye. Barbaraannette closed the toilet lid and sat down upon it and observed the shape of the floor tiles imprinted on her knees. Maybe it wasn't nausea she was feeling, but disgust. She was paying a million dollars to get Bobby back. At the moment, she would pay twice that for him to never have existed.

Did she even want to see him? They had not been all that happy together, she and Bobby. In fact, except for the sex and the dancing, it had been pretty lousy. On the other hand, there had been the sex and the dancing. On the *other* hand, there had been Bobby's chronic lack of employment, his expensive taste in clothing, and the fact that he had never washed a dish or dropped a toilet lid in his life. On yet another hand, there was the overwhelming fact that when Bobby left her, Barbaraannette had discovered a huge, gaping hole in her heart. It may be that the hole had been there all along, but until Bobby disappeared it hadn't bothered her so much. So what was it she wanted? Did she want Bobby, or just a load of clean fill?

Barbaraannette massaged her knees in an effort to eliminate the marks left by the tiles. This kind of thinking would get her nowhere. She had put her foot in it and what was done was done and that was all there was to it. Besides, she had guests.

"Did you know that raisins are made out of dried grapes?" Hilde asked.

"Really?" said Art.

"There's a song about grapes." She began to hum a tune, and as she hummed her face relaxed, the small muscles that kept her flesh close to the jaw seemed to lose tension, and her cheeks slid down a good half inch to form jowls. Art could not identify the tune at first, but after a few bars he recognized "The Battle Hymn of the Republic." A song about grapes? Art smiled, but he was having some trouble. Hilde was amusing, but much more than that she was sad and frightening. The old Hilde, who had been one of the bank's more flamboyant customers, had by no means disappeared, but there was not as much of her in this body as before. Little flashes, like when she'd flicked the raisins at him, that was pure Hilde, but this humming, jowly woman was somebody else. He lifted his coffee cup, which was empty, and pretended to drink. Another thirty seconds, he decided, and he would go find Barbaraannette, make sure she was okay.

He was up to twenty-five when Barbaraannette breezed back into the kitchen, all smiley and chipper. "So then," she said, "I'll drop by the bank first thing in the morning, and we'll sign all those papers, all righty?" She picked up her mother's raisin bowl, now empty, and put it in the sink. "Would you like more coffee?"

Art said, "No thank you. Uh, Barbaraannette? That was Bobby, wasn't it?"

Barbaraannette nodded, still with the smile, and took his cup and saucer.

"And?" he persisted.

"And I don't need the cash. The man said a certified check would be fine. He's bringing Bobby to your bank at nine-thirty tomorrow morning. Is that okay?"

Art nodded guardedly. "Was this the man who threatened you?"

Barbaraannette's smile lost a few watts. "I don't know." She brightened. "But everything is okay. I talked to Bobby and he sounds fine. He said that this man talked him into coming home, so I guess I have to pay the reward."

"What about the woman?"

"Bobby said she just gave him a ride."

"Where is Bobby now?"

"I don't know."

Art could see that she was struggling to maintain a cheerful demeanor. She was still holding his cup and saucer, her fingers white with pressure. He gathered his papers and fitted them into his briefcase. "I had better get going," he said. "I'll see you tomorrow morning."

"That will be nice," said Barbaraannette.

27

J*on Glavs could drink a bowling alley—ten Budweiser longnecks—every* night of the week without feeling hungover in the morning. It was a matter of pride with him. He would drink his first one immediately upon arriving home from the dealership and would build his triangle of empties on the coffee table in front of the TV one bottle at a time. If he sold a car that day he would top it off with a shot of bourbon, which would give him a mild headache the next morning, but it was worth it. If he sold two cars, which didn't happen that often, he'd continue to drink shots until he fell asleep. Those made for some rough mornings, but fortunately he didn't have that many two-car days.

Once or twice a week he would go out with his buddies or, rarely, on a date, but most nights he simply sat at home and drank beer and that was okay with him. He was only thirty-three years old, renting this little house on Walnut Street, and could still get into a pair of thirty-six-inch-waist Levi's. Gallons of Rogaine and some judicious combing had reversed his hair loss, and of course he always had a sharp car to drive. This week he was driving a red Mustang. A lot of women thought he was good looking. Plenty of time to get serious about marriage and career and health and all that crap.

He cracked his number seven beer and thumbed the remote until he came across a rerun of *The Simpsons*. Jon liked to watch Homer Simpson. What a loser.

The doorbell rang. What the hell? He turned off the TV sound and went to answer it, beer in hand, curious to see who would be calling on him so late. Maybe it was some gorgeous large-breasted long-haired woman asking directions. You never knew. He swung the door open.

"Hey there, Jon boy!" A broad-bellied, long-armed guy in a Vikings stocking cap. The guy needed a shave. Jon smiled uncertainly. He recognized the man, remembered selling him a truck a couple months back. No, not a truck, a van. He looked past the man, saw the very vehicle parked at the curb. A six-year-old Econoline, maroon, high mileage. He'd been glad to get it off the lot.

"You remember me, don't you?"

Jon remembered that he'd got thirty-five hundred for the van, but he couldn't remember the guy's name.

Jon said, "Ah, how's that Econoline running?"

"Fine, fine. You mind if I come in a minute?"

Jon frowned. "What for?"

"I wanted to talk to you about a car," the man said.

"It's not exactly business hours."

"You like easy money, don't you?"

Jon thought for a moment, but only one response suggested itself. "Sure," he said. "Who doesn't?"

The trip odometer read three point one miles. Three point one miles from Barbaraannette's house to his house, almost five kilometers, a distance he could run in under sixteen minutes. Art got out of his car and went inside and called Nathan Nagler at home and told him that he had just written a one-million-dollar loan to Barbaraannette Quinn. Nagler was pleased. He told Art that he had done a fine job, and invited him to dinner next Sunday. Art, who had sampled Mrs. Nagler's cooking on one previous occasion, accepted with feigned enthusiasm. To decline the rare invitation would have been an unthinkable slight. Art could only hope that Mrs. Nagler didn't make another attempt at moussaka.

"And bring the little woman," Nagler added.

"Uh, Marla and I aren't together anymore," Art said.

"Of course! Of course! Ahem, well, whatever you like then. Bring a date! Come alone! Whatever!"

Nagler's words stayed in Art's ears for several minutes after their conversation had ended. *Come alone! Whatever!*

He reheated his leftover pizza in the microwave, then ate it while standing over the sink. Texturally, it reminded him of Mrs. Nagler's moussaka. He was not feeling very good, and the pizza was sure to make things worse, but he continued to tear and chew until the three remaining slices were gone and his stomach was in full battle mode and his thoughts settled into a Möbius strip of self-loathing and uncertainty. His face tingled at the precise points where Hilde's raisins had struck. There could be no doubt. He was a cowardly fool, a mild-mannered number-cruncher who was destined to "come alone" for the rest of his sorry life. He had been waiting forever for a chance at Barbaraannette, but the moment had never felt right. Right? Would a guy like Bobby Quinn wait for the right moment? Now that he thought about it, there had been a lot of opportunities for him, but he'd seized up, had let those moments pass. Hilde said that Barbaraannette was like a car—a weird way to look at it but maybe she had something. All he needed was a key. Or he could hotwire her. No. That *was* too weird. Barbaraannette was not a machine. She was a person. What he had to do was to show her who he really was—show her that he was a good and worthy and interesting man—and then tell her how he felt about her. If he could do those two things, then Barbaraannette could decide what she wanted to do about it.

He turned on the tap, held his greasy hands under the stream of warm water. If only she hadn't won the lottery.

There I go again, he thought, turning off the faucet. What had he been doing before Barbaraannette had won the lottery? Nothing. Sitting and waiting for his divorce to feel real, thinking about Barbaraannette, thinking about calling her up, imagining running into her at the market but doing nothing to make it happen. If not for the lottery he might never have spoken to her at all. No, if he wanted Barbaraannette, he would have to ask for her. Now. He looked at his watch. Four minutes before midnight. Maybe it could wait till tomorrow. At the bank. She would be at the bank at nine, and that was when he would make his move. He was not sure exactly what he was going to say or do, but he would come up with something. He had nine hours to think about it.

It would have been a lot easier, Bobby thought, to move the body upstairs first, and then wrap it in plastic. But André had been worried about bloodstains, so they had used six garbage bags and the rest of the duct tape to encase Jayjay in a plastic cocoon.

"I seem to be unable to get a grip," André said as he lost hold of his end of Jayjay.

Bobby, who was halfway down the steps holding Jayjay's ankles, let go and backed out of the way. The body slid back down to the bottom.

André sat down on the top step. "Oh, dear," he said.

"Maybe we could tie a rope to him and haul him up," Bobby suggested.

"I have no rope," André sighed.

This is no good, Bobby thought as he looked down at the plastic-wrapped shape. Was there really a dead body in there? This was not what he'd had in mind when he'd left Tucson. One day he's selling cowboy boots and the next thing he knows he's partnered up with a murdering antique-collecting professor who, Bobby suspected, was more than a little crazy. Helping the guy get rid of a body. Not that he had any choice. If he went along with the plan he would get half the reward money. André had explained: "You need not worry about my giving it to you. If I refuse to pay your share, you will report me to the police and I will be charged with kidnapping and murder. And I will trust you because by helping me dispose of Jayjay you will become as culpable as I. Also, without me to turn you in, there will be no reward. It is quite simple. It is in both our best interests for us to present ourselves to your wife with neither accusation nor recrimination."

André's argument had been convincing, in part because agreeing with him had gotten Bobby untaped. Now, if he could get the body up those stairs he'd be out of the basement for good.

Bobby was no expert, but if a dead person was anything like a dead deer, this one would start to stiffen up pretty soon, and things would become more difficult. He might be stuck down there for hours. He took a deep breath, wrapped his arms around the corpse and, with a burst of effort usually reserved for removing undersized cowboy boots from swollen feet, he heaved it up onto his shoulder and carried it up the steps. André scrambled to his feet and got out of the way.

"Where you want him?" Bobby gasped.

André pointed, then ran to open the door leading into the attached garage. Bobby staggered through the doorway and dumped the body into the open trunk of André's Taurus.

"Okay," he said, heart pounding, "now what?"

André plucked a shovel from the wall of the garage and laid it in the trunk on top of the body. "Now we go for a drive." He closed the trunk.

28

In his dream, he was riding a tall horse across the big-sky country of Mon-
tana, the horse covering miles with each stride. Bobby looked back
and saw Rodney Gent bounding after him. Bobby pressed down on
the accelerator, but the horse would go no faster. He clapped a
hand to his head, suddenly afraid that his El Presidente would blow
off, then realized that the duct tape was holding it firmly in place
and something was clutching at his shoulder.

"Wake up."

Bobby swam for the surface, opened his eyes. His thoughts
moved sluggishly, reluctantly embracing consciousness. Headlights
illuminated tree trunks and naked branches. He was in a car, in the
passenger seat, in the woods. He turned his head, saw André, his
beard faintly lit by the dashboard lights. They were not moving.
The dashboard clock read 2:12. They'd been in the car for hours,
driving, the professor looking for the perfect spot for his friend to
spend eternity, talking the whole time. Bobby had finally dozed off.

"Where are we?" Bobby asked.

"A jeep trail, perhaps an old logging road, just off of Miller's
Road." André reached down and activated the trunk release. He got
out of the car, lifted the truck lid. "Well?" he said.

"Well what?"

"Start digging."

Bobby climbed out of the car, moving slowly. André handed

him the shovel. The handle felt warm, and he realized that he had no jacket or gloves, and that it was only a few degrees above freezing. Was he really standing in the woods with a shovel and a professor and a corpse? All things considered, this was not that much better than being duct-taped to a chair in a basement. Except for the half-million bucks the professor was promising.

"You just want me to dig a hole?"

"That's right."

Bobby looked around. "Where do you want him?"

André pointed to a spot several yards in front of the car. Bobby walked toward the proposed grave site, applied the point of the shovel to the earth, and stomped on it. The shovel blade penetrated three inches into the leaf-covered loam before hitting something hard. A rock? Bobby moved over a few feet and tried again with similar results. He noticed a patch of snow a few feet away. Of course. The earth was still frozen from the long winter.

"This isn't gonna work," he said.

André ordered the Trucker's Triple-X Special: three eggs, three sausage links, three pancakes, coffee, and orange juice. Bobby asked for coffee and pancakes.

"The human animal is not a collection of individuals with free will," André explained. "We are more akin to an ant colony, each of us performing a specific function, each of us contributing to the betterment of the species. You were a boot salesman, which makes you a part of the class of human elements the function of which is to protect the feet, our predominant means of locomotion. I was a teacher, a processor of information, a disseminator of knowledge.

"But that was then. Do you understand?" André chopped the air for emphasis, then waited for Bobby's nod. "So you see," he continued, "humanity can be viewed as a single organism, as the sum of its parts, without regard to individuality. We are all a part of the whole."

The waitress slid his Triple-X Special onto the Formica table. André lifted his fork and stabbed a pork link and held it up as if displaying a particularly beautiful rose. "Nevertheless, it is still possible and inevitable that certain individuals might exist outside this construct. Certain people through their own abilities or through un-avoidable circumstance might break free from the human organism to form micro-humanities of their own. And by stepping outside the organism, they might find themselves answering to different needs, different morals, and different laws." He bit into the sausage. "We stand outside," he said.

Bobby Quinn's head made a nodding motion, but André did not believe that to be a true sign of comprehension. The poor man was no mental giant.

André, by contrast, was feeling particularly brilliant. He had not felt this alive in years. Things had never been so clear to him. He had a dead body in his trunk and a million dollars sitting across the booth and he was in a truck stop twenty miles outside of Cold Rock eating pork sausage at 3:30 in the morning. It was as if he had become a different person, as if the events of the past twenty-four hours had stripped away a disguise and revealed a new André, the true André.

"You see, the moment your wife won the lottery, she triggered a series of interconnected events which led you into my cellar and led poor Jayjay to his tragic end and ultimately resulted in my being freed from my position within the organism and placed into a situation where I had to create my own laws. Do you understand?"

"Yeah. Barbaraannette won the lottery and your weird little friend hit me over the head with a wrench and now he's dead and we're eating pancakes."

"That is another way to look at it. I, however, am eating sausages."

Bobby said, "Are we going to get some sleep pretty soon?"

"Of course we are. But first we have to dispose of our friend."

"We can't bury him."

"I realize that. The earth is frozen. The river, however, is not."

Shortly after 3:00 A.M. Jon Glaus looked at the last invoice, an Escort, white. He dropped it back into the file and rolled the drawer shut. It had taken him nearly four hours to go through all the files, one invoice at a time, checking first for model, then for color, then pulling all the invoices for green Ford Tauruses. They'd sold a total of forty-six in the past five years. He hoped that Hugh—and he wouldn't forget the guy's name anytime soon—would be happy with that. He'd damn well better be.

Hugh was asleep in the back of a new Expedition in the showroom; his girlfriend had sacked out in a Crown Vic. The other guy, Rodney, was in the customer lounge reading *Motor Trend*. Jon poured himself another cup of coffee. He would take a few minutes to collect himself. The offices of Fetler Ford were cold and quiet and smelled like stale popcorn, and Jon had a pounding headache. Maybe it was the coffee, four cups in the middle of the night. He flipped through the invoices, wondering what made this pile of paper worth five hundred bucks. Green Tauruses. Why would anybody be interested in anybody who drove a green Taurus?

Two miles north of the Cold Rock city limits, County Road 12 crossed the North Rock River. The river there ran fast and deep but was no more than thirty yards wide. The banks were heavily wooded. André pulled to the side of the road just short of the bridge and popped the trunk. Four o'clock in the morning. The only conscious human they had seen since leaving the truck stop was the attendant at the Kum & Go just outside of town where they had purchased two forty-pound bags of cat litter, a box of plastic garbage bags, and a roll of duct tape.

Bobby helped André seal the bags of cat litter into the plastic garbage bags, then helped him drag the now stiffened, plastic-wrapped body out of the trunk. Bobby found that it helped him to think of the body as a dead buck. He had handled dead deer before, and it was dark enough out that the shape didn't look all that human. Bobby held up one end as André attached a bag of cat litter, wrapping several loops of duct tape around the body. The longer Bobby watched André work on the package, the more difficult it became for him to think of it in terms of deer hunting. For one thing, he would never have picked a guy like André to go hunting with. He set aside the deer imagery and tried to get interested in the half million dollars. All he had to do was get through the next few hours and he'd be rich. *He* hadn't killed the kid. *He* hadn't done anything wrong. This whole situation was, as André had said, a series of interconnected events.

He lifted the leg end of the body as André attached the second bag. As long as he couldn't see the body it wasn't so bad, but he wished he couldn't feel the shape of the boy's boots through the plastic.

André finished taping, stood up, clapped his hands together cheerfully and said, "Excellent."

Bobby lowered the weighted legs to the ground. "Now what?"

André said, "Now you carry him onto the bridge and send him on his way."

Bobby looked doubtfully at the duct-taped mass of flesh and clay. "I don't think I can. He's got kind of heavy."

André produced an exasperated sputter. "I will assist you, then."

They each grabbed opposite ends of the body and tried to lift and carry it, but the combination of the added weight, the slippery plastic, and the awkward shape of the stiffened corpse proved too much for them. After a few false starts, they found that it was easiest to drag it. Five minutes of effort brought them to the center of the bridge.

André, gasping for air, said, "Now you simply lift him up and over the railing."

Bobby, wanting nothing more than to be done with this whole business, squatted over the body and worked his hands beneath it, trying to get a good grip. As he began to lift, one of his hands slipped into a rent in the plastic and hit cold, moist flesh. A tremor went up his arm; he leapt up and away from the body, wiping his hand furiously on his jeans.

"What happened?" André asked. "Are you all right?"

Bobby shook his head, backing away, still wiping his hand. The thought of a half million dollars came and went, obliterated by the horror of the moment. He turned and ran for the car, jumped into the driver's seat, and groped for the keys.

No keys.

He jumped out, ready to head straight into the woods, but André was coming around from the back of the car with his arms high above his head. He had the shovel. Bobby raised his own arms but not in time, the flat of the shovel hit the top of his head and boomed down his spine, buckling his knees. Bobby caught himself, his hands hitting cold gravel, and lay there face down, still conscious but without the will to move. He heard a grunt of effort, but he did not feel the second blow.

29

Rolling *over, back to side, side to stomach, spinning like a chicken on a* spit, images of Bobby, Hilde, Art, and money strobing in her head. If she'd slept a wink, Barbaraannette couldn't remember it. She got up five or six times to check on Hilde, who snored peacefully through the night.

At one point, sometime around 4:00, Barbaraannette got out of bed and took a shower. It didn't help. She gave up at 5:30, threw on her robe, and made cornbread muffins.

At 6:45 she called Toagie.

"You up?"

"Not by much," Toagie said, her voice more ragged than usual. "I'm somewheres between peeing and making coffee."

"I'm getting Bobby back this morning," Barbaraannette said. "I'm meeting him at the bank."

"You're actually gonna do it? Who's getting the money? Not Hugh Hulke, I hope. I couldn't hardly stand it, he was a millionaire."

"Somebody else."

"Jeez. A million bucks."

"Listen, Toag, about your mortgage. I want to help you with that."

Barbaraannette heard the click of a lighter, the sound of her sister drawing on her first morning cigarette.

"Yeah," Toagie said wearily. "Bill said you probably would. He quit his job yesterday."

"I didn't know he was working."

"He had a gig working maintenance at the college, going on three weeks. It wasn't much money but at least he was working and not sitting around here watching TV and sucking down brewskis."

"Art said they're about to foreclose on you."

"He told you that 'cause he wants some of your money."

"I think he just doesn't want to put you out of your home."

"We might've worked it out if Bill hadn't quit. We were gonna make a payment Friday."

"Like I said, I'll help."

"You know why he quit? He quit because he figured that you'd help us out. He actually said to me—I coulda killed him—he says, 'My sister-in-law's a millionaire. Why should I be emptying garbage cans?' That's what he said."

"It's my fault he quit his job?"

"I'm not saying that. You're just his excuse this time. What time are you going to the bank? You want company?"

"I think I've got to do this one on my own, Toag. But I do need a favor. I've got Hilde here."

"Oh. You talk to the people at Crestview yet?"

"I'm leaving that to Mary Beth."

"Good idea. You want to drop Hilde by here, that's fine with me. Only let me know how it goes at the bank so I don't go nuts wondering, okay?"

Barbaraannette went to her bedroom and began to work on her outfit. She started out with a black ensemble—mid-calf skirt, silk blouse, wool jacket—but decided that would be too dragon-lady. She replaced the blouse with a camel sweater, then went to gray wool slacks. Yuk. Several permutations later, she arrived at jeans, a V-neck cashmere sweater that matched her blue eyes, and a taupe blazer. Odd, but not bad. She put on a pair of dangling red coral earrings, added a few quick strokes of lipstick and eyeliner, and stepped into a pair of oxblood moccasins. Not bad at all, she decided, striking a pose before the mirror. She heard a giggle, turned to find Hilde standing in the doorway.

"You lose those earrings, Babba, and I think you've got it."

Art Dobbleman's desk sat near the center of the carpeted area facing the foyer and front entrance of Cold Rock Savings & Loan. Sally Krone, who handled mortgages, home equity loans, and answering the phones, sat at an identical desk six feet to his left, and Buzz Nagler, the boss's twenty-six-year-old son, flanked him on the right. Nathan Nagler himself occupied the spacious glass-fronted office behind them, looking out over his "team."

Art would have preferred an office of his own. The teller cages were only twenty feet away, and on a busy Friday the line of customers sometimes spilled over from the marble foyer to intrude upon the carpeted apron in front of his desk. He had spent too many afternoons staring at the rear ends of Cold Rock's citizens. Once, Hermie Goss had actually propped a gelatinous hip on the corner of Art's desk. Art had given him a jab with a sharpened pencil, sending the severely obese Hermie hopping. Sally had nearly choked trying not to laugh, but Art had felt so bad he'd immediately apologized to Hermie and had even given him a pen and pencil set engraved with the bank logo, which were only supposed to go to commercial loan customers since they cost eight dollars each. Hermie had been pleased.

Most of the time Art blocked out his surroundings, erecting imaginary dividers, and did his work. But this morning he focused his attentions on the foyer, and on the glass doorway beyond.

Barbaraannette entered the bank at 9:12 A.M. She paused just inside the doors and took in her surroundings. Art stood up, saw her eyes find him, and remained standing until she crossed the foyer and sat down in front of his desk.

"Would you care for a cup of coffee?" he asked.

Barbaraannette shook her head. Her irises seemed bluer than usual—almost the color of the turquoise studs in her earlobes—but the whites were bloodshot, and the flesh around her eyes had a dusky, bruised look. Art thought she looked quite beautiful.

He said, "Barbaraannette, I've been thinking a lot the past few hours."

She nodded. Her pupils seemed small.

"Are you still planning to pay out all that money?"

She nodded again, still not having said a word.

"Are you okay?" Art asked.

"I'm fine," she said. "I just want to sign the papers and when Bobby comes I'm going to give his friend a check. Is there a problem?"

Art pressed his hands to his desk blotter. He had reached the point of no return. He said, "Barbaraannette, we've known each other for a long time. I feel as though I am your friend, and as your friend I have to say something."

Barbaraannette drew back in her chair and lowered her chin. "I don't really want to discuss it, Art."

Art said, "Look, Barbaraannette, I don't want to see you get hurt. Even if you get him back he won't stay."

Barbaraannette said, her voice a whisper, "He will. If I want him to."

"Even if he did stay, you'd be miserable. But I can't prove any of that to you, and I don't expect you to believe me. Barbaraannette, I was up all night trying to figure out what I could say that will convince you to give up this craziness and the more I thought about it the more sure I was that nothing I could say would change you. So I started thinking about me. And the one thing I kept coming up against was that if you wind up back with Bobby instead of with someone who deserves a woman as beautiful and intelligent as you, I really don't want to have any part of it. I can't make you do anything, but that doesn't mean I have to be a party to it. Do you understand what I'm saying?"

"You aren't going to loan me the money?" She sounded surprised, but not angry.

Art took a breath, ready to tell her that no—even though it might lose him his job—he would not, when Sally leaned their way and said, "Mrs. Quinn? I have a call for you." She smiled apologetically and said to Art, "Line two."

This is what it would feel like to have someone call time on the

second bounce of a high dive, Art thought. A surge of anger and relief and a lot of adrenaline rushing around with no place to go. Art
handed Barbaraannette his phone and pressed the illuminated button, watched her say "Hello," then listen calmly, a faint frown on
her lips. She said, "I see." She touched a hand to her breast. "All
right. I'll see what I can do. But I won't give you a dime unless I see
him. You're going to have to show him to me." She listened some
more, then said, "I understand," and put her hand over the mouthpiece.

"Things have changed," she said, her face neutral.

Art waited.

Barbaraannette said, "He wants to know how long will it take to
get the money in cash."

"It is to become the outlaw after all, to forever stand outside society's bounds. To become a pariah. No, not a pariah—an *immoraliste.*
Yes!" André leaned in close to the mirror, traced a line through his
beard with a forefinger. "I am cast out, out damned spot! Out I
say!" Waving the beard trimmer, switching it on. "And for what?
For wealth? No! For freedom!" He applied the trimmer to his
cheek and cut a swath through his beard from the edge of his right
nostril down past the corner of his mouth and over his jawline.
"The die is cast," he muttered, beginning another cut at his ear, seeing it as an unveiling, a metamorphosis. Slowly, André watched
himself emerge.

Back at the bridge he had seen himself perform remarkable
feats. When the traitorous cowboy ran, André had acted quickly
and decisively. Two well-placed blows to the head had foiled his
flight, as had André's foresight in pocketing the car keys. André
had then rushed back onto the bridge, his body buzzing with
adrenaline, and single-handedly lifted Jayjay, cat litter and all, up
over the railing and into the black water. He had never felt more
alive. It reminded him of the day he had seen the first bound copy
of his book.

He washed and toweled his face, then went down into the cellar.

•   •   •

Bobby awakened from one nightmare to find himself in a worse one. He was beginning to think that all was not as it seemed, that this entire episode had been engineered by Barbaraannette. She was capable of it. Maybe she had never won the lottery and her appearance on the TV had been a faked videotape, and maybe Phlox was in on it, too, and André was an actor working for them, and all because he'd left her to try to make a better life for himself. He'd meant to send for her once he got settled. He really had. But then he'd met Denver Dora, and then Juanita up in Casa Grande, and finally Phlox, who'd dealt him pocket aces the first time he sat down at her seven-stud table at the Desert Diamond Casino. Things had got complicated. He'd planned to pay Hugh and Rodney back their money, too. And he would've if he'd had it. Like if he'd won the lottery.

Any second now the basement wall would open. André and Barbaraannette would be sitting there laughing at him and the next thing he knew he'd be on the funny home video show with his forehead cut open and one eye swollen shut and his skin raw from that goddamn duct tape and people clapping.

The light came on and footsteps sounded on the stairs. Bobby didn't look up. He recognized the soft sound of André's Hush Puppies.

"Well? What do you think?" André asked.

Bobby did not respond.

André moved closer, squatted down and put his face right in front of Bobby's.

"Do you like it?" he asked.

There was nothing Bobby liked. He was cold and scared and angry and hungry and his head hurt and his right eye was swollen shut, and he was more than half certain that this weird little man intended to kill him.

"Well?"

Bobby said, "Well what?"

"Do you like it?" He turned his head, giving Bobby a look at his profile.

Bobby could now see that André's cheeks were smooth and

white. He had shaved off most of his facial hair and now wore only a mustache and a goatee.

"I love it," Bobby said.

André stood up, pleased, crossing his arms and inflating his chest. "Thank you!" he said.

Bobby decided that this had to be real. This was no *Candid Camera* routine. There was no way Barbaraannette could have invented André—the guy was way too weird to be anything other than real.

"What are you going to do?" Bobby asked.

André raised a hand, lightly touching his bare cheek with two fingers, his lips pursed, one eyebrow elevated. He said, "Hmmm."

"Did you talk to her?" Bobby asked.

"Yes I did. She asked about you."

"What did you tell her?"

André smirked and gave a theatrical shrug. "I told her that I would require payment in cash."

"I mean about me."

"I told her the truth. That you were alive and well." He crossed the room and picked up the chair leg he had used to kill troll-boy, grimaced at the dried blood.

Bobby waited.

"I should clean this," André said.

Bobby relaxed. "What are we going to do if she doesn't pay?"

André gave him a quizzical smile. "We?"

Bobby nodded.

André shook his head and carried the chair leg back upstairs, hitting the light switch as he reached the top.

30

"*Barbaraannette—*"

"*Just get me the money, Art.*"

"*If you'd just give me a minute . . .*"

"*I don't want to hear it, Art. Now, are you going to take care of me, or do I have to talk to Nate?*"

Barbaraannette experienced the drive home in slow motion, watching familiar landmarks. Sundstrom's drugstore, now displaying a Going Out of Business sign because the new Wal-Mart had taken all their customers. Mel Groth's '57 Chevy, which he'd planted in his front yard nearly a decade ago, declaring it to be a potting shed in order to thwart local zoning regulations. The old elm, called Spooky Tree by the neighborhood children, leaned aggressively out over Western Avenue. She had her window open. Ten o'clock and it was already up in the sixties, the gutters running with water, the last of the snow melting. The air held a rich organic odor, heavy with the promise of spring.

She felt bad about the way she'd snapped at Art. She knew what he'd been trying to do. Trying to help her make the right decision. But damn it all he should know better than to tell her—try to tell any woman not to act like a fool when she knows very well what she's acting like and the last thing she wants is to be reminded of it. He should know, just like she knew not to cut a man off at the knees while he was striking a macho pose. Sometimes people just have to do what they're going to and anyone who tries to tell them otherwise might just as well try and talk a tornado out of twisting. Had she cut Art off at the knees? No, she'd just knocked him back a step, and in any case she'd had no choice. Right now she didn't need a dose of facts and logic. But that was just Art, which was probably why he'd waited so long to get married and why his marriage hadn't lasted—although, to be fair, his marriage had outlasted hers. No, that wasn't right. She was still married, technically. If Bobby was still alive, that is. Was he? Barbaraannette shuddered, recalling what the man on the phone had told her, that if she didn't come up with the cash money he would send her an ear. She did not want to open a package and find Bobby's ear.

This whole brouhaha with Bobby was getting out of control—not that it had ever really been in control. Art was making things more complicated for her and that was too bad because she liked the way he looked at her. But she didn't want him in the middle of this thing, not Art, not the cops, not anyone who would tell her what she could or could not do. When it came right down to it, the buck stopped with her. She had to see it through to the end.

Barbaraannette turned down Third Street. Gert Pfleuger, her two-doors-down neighbor, was walking her basset hounds. Barbaraannette slowed to avoid splashing them. She pulled into her driveway, then noticed the long gray car parked by the curb. Barbaraannette muttered, "Damn you Mary Beth," but her words lacked malice and she realized that she was glad that Mary Beth was there. A time like this, she needed her family around her, no matter who they happened to be.

Toagie, Hilde, and Mary Beth were sitting in her kitchen eating Wheat Thins and pickled herring and drinking her apple cider. They stopped chewing and looked at Barbaraannette as she entered, then looked past her.

Mary Beth said, "Well? Do you have him?"

Barbaraannette dropped her purse on the counter. "No." She eyed the herring. "Did you save any for me?"

"There's a few chunks left," said Toagie, peering into the open jar.

"Tell us what happened, dear," said Mary Beth.

Barbaraannette put three crackers on a plate and topped each one with a slice of herring. Between bites, she talked.

What surprised her most was that Mary Beth let her get through the whole story from beginning to end without interrupting once, or even raising her formidable eyebrows. And when Barbaraannette had finished talking, all Mary Beth said was, "What do you want to do, hon?"

Barbaraannette said, "I want to finish it."

"Are you going to give him the money?"

Barbaraannette didn't answer right away. She looked from Mary Beth to Toagie, both of them sitting across from her, elbows on the Formica tabletop, looking as different as two sisters could while looking like sisters all the same.

"If I have to pay the money to get Bobby—to save his life—then that's what I'll do. Art says that they can have the cash here by morning, and I just want to be done with the whole stinking mess. I won't be responsible for Bobby getting hurt. I don't want his ear to get cut off."

"That's a lot of money for an ear," Hilde said.

Startled, Barbaraannette looked carefully at her mother. Did she know what she'd said?

"I've got plenty of money, Hilde."

Hilde raised her chin. "If you can get it for free, you ought to hold on to it."

Toagie said, "Mom, would you like something to drink? Some juice?"

"You should look around before you go spending that kind of money," Hilde said, one hand on Barbaraannette's forearm, squeezing.

Barbaraannette capped her mother's hand with her own. "It's okay, Hilde. We're just talking."

"You girls don't know the value of a dollar."

Mary Beth said, "Maybe she's got a point, hon. He has to be someplace nearby, and this isn't exactly New York City. If he's being held against his will, chances are it's somebody we know. Someone who knows Bobby. Maybe we should think about that before you give away that kind of money."

Barbaraannette nodded slowly, flipping through all the faces she knew. Other than Hugh and Rodney, she could think of no one capable of kidnapping Bobby, and the voice on the phone was not a Cold Rock voice at all. It was more like an Eastern voice. A self-consciously cultured voice. She shook her head. "I don't know him."

"You said there were two of them."

"Yes, the cultured one, and the first one who called, the one who said he'd gotten hurt in the Gulf War. He didn't sound familiar either, and I don't know anybody who fought over there except poor Ralphie Jorgenson and he died in a Jeep accident."

Mary Beth blinked, heavy lids slamming over gray eyes. Barbaraannette imagined she could hear the clank. "We should call the police," Mary Beth pronounced.

"Dale Gordon? I don't think so. The last time I talked to him he asked me out. I'd rather date dirt."

"He asked you out?"

Barbaraannette nodded.

Mary Beth's lips pulled back, showing her straight, square teeth. "I'll bet Sheila would like to know about *that*." Sheila Gordon and Mary Beth were both members of the City Council.

"He said they were separated."

"Not according to Sheila they aren't. Well, if you can't call Dale, maybe you should call the FBI."

"No. I made this thing happen, I'm going to take care of it myself."

Mary Beth snorted.

Barbaraannette felt Hilde's nails dig deep into her forearm. "You're a good girl, Babba. You always clean your messes."

"You sure have got a mess this time," Mary Beth said.

Hilde said, "You leave your sister alone now, dear." She grabbed Barbaraannette by the shoulders, her eyes glittering. "Babba, you listen to me. I want you to make your mother proud, dear. You put yourself out there and you give them your very best. You're a beautiful and talented girl. They're lucky to have you, what with your legs. You'll make that Lundeen girl look like an arthritic heifer."

Barbaraannette, Toagie, and Mary Beth stared wordlessly at their mother. After a few seconds Mary Beth said, "Where is she, Barbaraannette?"

Barbaraannette disengaged her arms and clasped her mother's hands. "Cheerleading tryouts," she said.

Mary Beth nodded. "I thought so." She half smiled. "She sure has Ellie Lundeen's number, though."

Hilde's bright, passionate gaze faded to embarrassed bewilderment.

Barbaraannette stood up and began massaging her mother's shoulders. "You know, I don't *want* to pay out all that money, even though I can afford it. But we're talking about Bobby's life. If I have to pay, then that's what I'm going to do. If I had an idea where to look—if I could think of one place where he might be, I'd go look."

"I still say we should call the police."

Toagie said, "Barbaraannette, what about that letter you got?"

"I got a lot of letters, Toag."

"I mean that one from the guy that wanted you to send him Powerball tickets. With the picture? Didn't he write something about getting hurt in the Gulf?"

Barbaraannette remembered the picture. A crumpled, legless man in a wheelchair. "That man didn't have a leg to stand on. I can't see him as a kidnapper."

Toagie persisted. "You said yourself there are two of them. And that guy's address was right here in Cold Rock. I remember being surprised I'd never seen him around, you know, with the wheelchair and no legs and all. Do you still have the letter?"

Barbaraannette nodded.

Mary Beth said, "Give it to the police or the FBI. That's what we should do."

"I know what we should do," Hilde said.

Conditioned to respond to their mother's voice they all gave her their attention, but Hilde was simply smiling and looking around, a puzzled expression on her face.

"You're going back to Crestview, Mother," said Mary Beth. I'm calling Dr. Cohen right this minute."

"Back to the hotel," said Hilde.

Barbaraannette was going through a stack of opened mail on the kitchen counter. "Here it is," she said.

The return address on the letter was a box number at the Post Office downtown.

Mary Beth said, "Well, that's that. You won't find Bobby in a P.O. box. I really think you should call the authorities, Barbaraannette."

Barbaraannette put on her coat.

"Where you going?" Toagie asked.

"To talk to Hermie." She was out the door in seconds.

Mary Beth looked at Toagie, puzzled. "Who is Hermie?"

Hilde said, "Hermie the window peeper."

"Oh. Herman Goss."

Toagie said, "I think he works at the Post Office. He used to have a crush on Barbaraannette."

"Who didn't?" Mary Beth went to the window and watched Barbaraannette drive away. "What does she think she's going to do?"

Of the forty-six green Taurus owners, Hugh eliminated twenty-two because the purchaser was either too old, too dead, too female, or someone Hugh knew and believed to be incapable of snatching Bobby by reason of character. Phlox had her own opinion about eliminating the women. After all, both she and Barbaraannette seemed to want the man. Maybe they weren't the only two women in Cold Rock with a thing for Bobby Steele Quinn—or a thing for money. But since they had to start someplace she'd gone along with Hugh's analysis.

With the twenty-four remaining invoices in hand, Hugh, Rodney, and Phlox began to drive from one address to the next, getting Taurus owners out of bed, catching them in the middle of breakfast, intercepting them on the way to work. In each case, Hugh began the encounter politely, then became more direct as warranted. In the first three cases, all of whom had been sleeping soundly and none of whom appreciated the 6:00 A.M. interrogation, Hugh quickly decided that the individuals were sincere in their denials. The fourth invoice, one Cory Mittendorf, was incensed enough at having his shower interrupted that he told them to go to hell and slammed the door in Hugh's face. Finding such behavior suspicious, Hugh had leaned on the doorbell until Mittendorf returned. The resulting interaction was both brief and ugly. Cory Mittendorf was eliminated as a suspect and left with a possible broken nose. Most of the other green Taurus owners they visited were more cooperative; the stack of invoices shrank, and by 11:00 A.M. they had eliminated all but three.

31

"Good Lord, Art, I thought you'd be able to handle this." Nate Nagler placed the last bite of Danish into his mouth and brushed the crumbs from his fingers onto his desk.

Art said, "I *am* handling it, Nate. She just now dropped this cash demand into our laps—"

"*Your* lap," Nagler said, using the edge of a business card to scrape the pastry crumbs into a neat pile.

"Okay, *my* lap. In any case, she says she wants the million in cash tomorrow. I think she's being blackmailed. I think that someone is threatening to harm her husband if she doesn't pay him the money."

Nagler smiled, blinking his black eyes. "The woman offered the money as a reward, didn't she?"

"Yes, but this is different."

Nagler looked down at his pile of crumbs. "I don't see the difference. Our job is to act as a lending institution."

"I'm wondering whether we should notify the police. I'm afraid she might be making a big mistake."

Nagler rearranged the crumbs with the corner of his business card, creating a star-shaped pattern. "Mrs. Quinn is a good credit risk. I don't see where we should involve ourselves in her personal life. Just get her the money, Art."

Art ground his teeth together, trying to stay calm. Just get the money? It wasn't that easy. In the first place, Cold Rock S&L was not a member of the Federal Reserve Bank, and the Fed in Minneapolis was the only bank within three hundred miles that would have that kind of money on hand. To get one million dollars in cash, they would have to go through their correspondent, Norwest Banks, and convince them to order the cash from the Fed and get it on a Brinks truck before the end of the day, or first thing tomorrow morning. Naturally, such a request would be greeted with some suspicion, and the only way it would happen would be if Nate Nagler talked to Matt McRae, his friend at Norwest, and convinced them to bypass their usual safeguards and procedures.

Art explained this to Nagler, who had abandoned his pile of crumbs and was now rolling a golf ball back and forth across his desk, a sour expression on his pasty face. Nagler loved to boast of his connections in the banking industry, but he was loathe to test them.

"So you want *me* to handle it?" Nagler said, arching his left eyebrow.

"I just need you to make one phone call. This isn't an everyday request. If I call Mr. McRae, he'll just tell me he needs to talk to you. If you'll call him, I won't have to bother you again."

Nagler sighed, shaking his head sadly. "Art, Art, Art," he said.

Art held his face rigid. Keep it together, stay calm, he told himself, and don't do or say anything you will regret later. He might have to run an extra seven or eight miles tonight, but it wouldn't kill him.

Hermie Goss had never wanted to be a postal clerk. He had wanted to be a pilot, but when that hadn't worked out due to his astigmatism, he had decided to be a fireman. He would have been a good one, but that hadn't worked out either because of a problem he had with heights, so he'd gone to Northland Business College to learn criminology, a six-month program, and had then tried to find work as a policeman, but Dale Gordon had it in for him because of the incident in his backyard when he'd noticed Hermie looking in his bedroom window. It wasn't like he'd got caught seeing anything worth seeing. He'd been passing by and saw the lit window and took a little detour into the Gordons' yard, just out of curiosity, nothing else, and he'd looked in but there'd been nothing to see but Dale's startled face, and that had pretty much ruined his chance at a career in law enforcement. Hermie thought about Dale Gordon often, and when he did he usually took the opportunity to wipe some snot on whatever letter or package happened to be in his hands.

Hermie had finally landed a job as a mail carrier, and that had gone well for a few years until Mrs. Jacobi accused him of peering into her bathroom window while he was making his rounds. Of course, that had come to nothing. But a few months later the Naglers accused him of the same thing, and even though they hadn't proved anything his super, Kevin Marney, had pulled him off his route and put him to work behind the counter. Where he could keep an eye on him, he said. Every time Hermie thought about his super he tossed a piece of first-class mail in the wastebasket to make himself feel better, and when a postal worker shot somebody someplace he always made sure Marney got an extra copy of the article.

Life had dealt Hermie Goss a sack of lemons; he was damn well going to share.

There were a few people in Cold Rock, however, who Hermie respected. His mother was one, and the guys at the bowling alley, and Rudy Samm, who owned Rudolph's Red Nose Bar and Grill, and Barbaraannette O'Gara—he could not bear to think of her as Barbaraannette *Quinn*—who he did not think about as much as he had back in high school but who still represented to him the epitome of feminine beauty. Which was why, when she suddenly showed up on the other side of the counter and asked him about Box 129, he hadn't thought twice about violating federal law.

"Fella's name is Morrow, just like you say." Hermie squinted at the photograph in Barbaraannette's hand. "Only he ain't no cripple. Kid's maybe nineteen, twenty years old. Lemme just check here—" Hermie went back to Marney's office and found the log book where they kept track of box renters. He carried it back to the counter. "He just give us a new address and phone a couple days ago," Hermie said. "You know, in case we got a package or something. Here you go."

Seeing Barbaraannette like that and being able to help her gave Hermie a good feeling inside. As soon as she left he started thinking about making a trip to the restroom to explore his good feeling, but before he could get the *Back in 5 Minutes* sign up on the door, Mary Beth Hultman marched in, paused for a moment to peruse the wanted posters, then zeroed her accusing eyes right on him. Mary Beth reminded him too much of his mother's sister aunt Aggie, who, when his mother wasn't there to hear, liked to call him Wormie instead of Hermie. The good feeling went away. He stepped back as Mary Beth pushed her cantaloupes over his counter.

"Herman," she said, "was my sister just here?" Her voice made him think of clanking cast iron skillets.

"Maybe she was," Hermie said.

"This is not a time to play games with me Herman Goss. I want you to tell me what you just told my sister."

Hermie hesitated, not sure how to handle this. He could think of no good reason not to tell her. It wasn't as if Barbaraannette had sworn him to secrecy. On the other hand, he had something Mary Beth wanted, and he hated to give up the sliver of power. As he thought about it, one of Mary Beth's hands flashed toward him and attached itself to the side of his head and he suddenly found himself with his face pressed to the top of the counter, his nose inches from Mary Beth's planetary bosom, his ear a twisted knot of pain.

"Herman? Talk to me, Herman."

The body in the river had been discovered at 7:30 that morning by Sandra Sanders and Gretchen Wolfe, charter members of the Walk for Life Club, which was sponsored by the Church of the Good Shepherd, which happened to be Police Chief Dale Gordon's church. In fact, Dale Gordon, as a member of the church board, had voted to sponsor the Walk for Life Club, and he had even encouraged his men to encourage their wives to become members. It might be argued, Gordon thought as he stared down at the elongated bundle of plastic and duct tape, one telltale arm protruding from a rent in the plastic, that he had discovered the body himself. He was glad he had been wearing his uniform when the call came.

"Let's see who we got here," he said to Fleishman, the young cop who had waded into the icy river to drag the body ashore. Fleishman removed a few feet of duct tape, then pulled away the plastic bag to uncover the head end of the corpse. It was a young man, probably one of the students at the college. Gordon did not recognize him. "You know him?" he asked Fleishman.

Fleishman shook his head. "Nope." His voice sounded weak. The Cold Rock police rarely had to deal with dead people—farm and auto accidents mostly. This was different.

Gordon looked back at Sandra and Gretchen, who were standing a few yards off. "Either of you ladies ever seen this fellow before?"

Both women took a few steps closer. "He looks like he could be a boy from the college," Gretchen offered.

"You've seen him there?"

"No, no, I wouldn't say that."

Gordon squatted down beside the body, forcing himself to stare into the dead features, driven by the same impulse that causes a man whose car has died to open the hood and look at the engine even though he knows absolutely nothing about auto repair. The boy's face was exceptionally smooth and waxy-looking. His eyes were pale brown, his hair blond, and he had a prominent violet-colored depression on one side of his head.

"Looks like we've got ourselves a homicide," Gordon said, unable to keep the pride out of his voice. In a growing community such as Cold Rock, progress was measured in strange ways. This was the first murder to occur in Cold Rock since Klaus Hopfinger gutted his wife over a bad batch of sauerkraut, and that was twelve years ago. "Blunt instrument trauma to the left temple," Gordon elaborated. "My guess is the body was dumped upstream."

Pleased with his analysis, Gordon stood up and brushed off the knees of his trousers even though they had not touched the ground, looked around with a smile on his face. He was hoping that someone from the Gazette would show up, get a shot of him standing by the river in his uniform running a homicide investigation. He was wondering what he should do next, how he could make the photo op last, when his cell phone started ringing.

Frowning—even though he loved to take calls on his mobile unit—Gordon lifted the phone from its holster.

"Talk to me," he snapped. He'd seen a cop answer a phone like that in a movie once.

"Dale? This is Mary Beth Hultman. I need you to do something for me."

Gordon licked his lips. What was she doing on his cell phone? He said, "Mary Beth? Uh, I'm kind of in the middle of something here. Got a homicide on my hands." It felt good to say it. "Got a body in the river," he added, hoping to prolong the sensation.

"Yes, well, I'm sure you do. But I need you to help me with something. Now."

"A college boy, it looks like. Hit on the head and dumped."

"Are you listening to me?" said Mary Beth.

"Like I say, I'm in the middle of something here."

"Well you'd better get out of it. I hear you and Sheila have separated."

"We—what? No."

"You told Barbaraannette you were separated. I'll bet Sheila would love to hear about that."

Gordon's thoughts exploded like a covey of quail.

"Dale? Are you there?"

"Uh-huh."

"I need a favor, Dale. Are you listening?"

32

Barbaraannette parked across the street and observed the small, mouse-colored bungalow. It was an older, well-maintained home surrounded by hydrangeas and spirea bushes. They would be beautiful come June. The attached one-car garage was probably a later addition. Several large red-clay pots topped with dead foliage crowded the front steps. The front door had been painted blue, not a color she would have chosen, but it showed that the owner cared.

She looked again at the photograph of the man in the wheelchair. Would this man paint his door blue?

When Toagie had suggested a connection between the begging letter and the threatening phone calls, Barbaraannette had been sure that if she found the source of one she would find the other. But now, looking at this unassuming little house, she feared that all she would find would be an unhappy man waiting in his wheelchair for a few free Powerball tickets. A man who had perhaps hired a blond young man to run to the Post Office for him. The poor man was probably taking a nap or sitting on the toilet. Ringing his doorbell would put him to a lot of trouble.

Of course, there was still the possibility that her original instincts would hold true, and that the house contained not only the letter writer and the phone caller, but Bobby himself. And what if it did? How would the kidnapper respond to Barbaraannette on his doorstep? Would she be in danger? Probably not, she decided, since only she could produce the money the man wanted. There was only one way to find out.

She was about to open the car door when a van rounded the corner and pulled up in front of the house and Hugh Hulke got out. Barbaraannette felt the breath leave her body. Hugh! So, Hugh was involved. Was Bobby in on it with him? No, if that were the case, Hugh would simply have claimed the reward. A second figure got out of the passenger side of the truck—Rodney Gent, followed by a third passenger. With a paranoid thrill, Barbaraannette recognized Phlox. They were all in it together, Hugh and Rodney and Phlox. But if that was true, then who had called her on the phone? And why had Phlox approached her in person? And whose house was this? As she watched the three walk up to the blue door her bewilderment coalesced into anger. Whatever they were doing, they wouldn't get away with it. She got out of her car and started toward them.

Hugh knocked on the door. Barbaraannette paused at the curb, waiting to see who would answer. He knocked again. Rodney was peering through the garage door window.

Barbaraannette saw a curtain tremble. Someone was home, but they were not answering the door. She heard Phlox say, "This is the third to last one, Hugh honey. I think we've been chasin' wild geese."

Hugh grasped the doorknob, twisted and rattled it to no effect. "You see anything in that garage, Rod Man?"

"There's a car in there," Rodney said.

Barbaraannette had come up the driveway and was standing a few feet behind him. "Whose car is it?" she asked.

Phlox, standing on the front steps, stared at Barbaraannette, her mouth open in a half smile.

Hugh said, "Whoever's name we got on the invoice, I suppose."

"What invoice would that be?"

Hugh jerked his head around. "Jesus Christ! Where the hell did you come from?" He looked for Phlox, found her still on the stoop, laughing. His brow lowered. "I don't see what's so goddamn funny."

"Neither do I," said Barbaraannette. "What are you two doing here?"

Hugh's eyes slid away. "Why? What are *you* doing here?"

Phlox, joining them, said, "Honey, we're just tryin' to find Bobby for you."

"But what are you doing *here?*" Barbaraannette asked. "Who lives here? Is Bobby here?"

Phlox rattled a piece of paper. "A man named Gideon lives here, and all we know for sure is he drives a green Taurus."

"What's that got to do with it?"

Hugh said, "If he's here, we claim the reward. We got here first."

"Now, Hugh," Phlox chided. "Don't you go getting all mercenary on poor Barbaraannette here. I'm sure she'll do the right thing once we find him. I mean, I brought the man all the way from Arizona, and she knows that."

Barbaraannette said, "Who is this Gideon? And what makes you think Bobby's here?"

"Well . . . there's the car," Phlox said. "Hugh and Rodney here saw Bobby jump into a green Taurus, so we've been looking up all the folks drive green Tauruses." She held up the handful of invoices.

"And?"

"And *you're* here," Hugh growled. "Only nobody's home."

Barbaraannette was beginning to get the picture. They were all here for the same purpose but for different reasons. And Hugh was wrong about nobody being home. She had seen the curtain move. Somebody was in there, someone who wrote peculiar letters, who drove a green car, and who refused to answer the door. Should she tell them about the curtain, or let them go check out the next green car on their list? If Bobby was inside, and if these three were present when she found him, would she be obliged to pay the reward? Barbaraannette considered what might lie inside the bungalow. A crazy kidnapper who might do anything. At the moment, the money did not seem important.

She said, "Yes there is."

"Yes there is what?" Hugh asked.

"Somebody home."

·   ·   ·

One of the best investments ever made by the people of Cold Rock had to be the new heated fully articulated Recaro seat behind the wheel of Dale Gordon's unmarked squad car. If not for that seat—a mere twelve hundred dollars installed—the supreme commander of the CRPD might have had to spend far more at the chiropractor getting his back adjusted. His performance would have suffered, and the good people of Cold Rock would not be enjoying the benefits of his one hundred percent commitment to the job. That was how Dale Gordon saw it, and if Mary Beth Hultman and those other City Council cheapskates raised a stink over the outlay, that is how he would explain it to them. Since getting the Recaro, he had been spending a lot more time in his car, getting out amongst the people, staying in touch with the community.

Gordon turned up the seat heater and adjusted the angle of the back. The salesman had described it perfectly: like floating on a warm breeze. It almost made doing this favor for Mary Beth Hultman a pleasure.

Actually, he didn't mind doing it at all. He'd left Fleishman back at the crime scene to wait for the county medical examiner. He hadn't known what to do next anyway, and the call from Mary Beth got him off the hook. He'd told Fleishman to proceed with the investigation, whatever that meant. Fleishman would figure it out, he was a bright kid.

All Mary Beth wanted him to do was drive over to this address and make sure Barbaraannette didn't get herself in trouble. "Just be there," she'd told him. "Make sure she doesn't do anything foolish." He didn't mind. He was happy to do it.

Turning up Pine Street, sure enough, there was Barbaraannette right there in the driveway with three other people. He didn't know the other woman, but he sure knew that Hugh and Rodney. Was that who Mary Beth had been worried about? Just for the hell of it, Dale whooped his siren, causing the four of them to jump. He rolled up to the curb and very slowly, for dramatic effect, climbed out of the squad car, hitched up his belt, and walked up the driveway.

·   ·   ·

André had been dreaming about bugs on his face, trying to brush them away, thousands of tiny crawling bugs. A man with a hammer, pounding, offering to smash the bugs. Malcolm Whitly with a hammer, banging and laughing.

He sat up, disoriented, fingers clawing his cheeks. He was on the sofa, his Chesterfield, his neck sore from being jammed up against the high arm, his cheeks itching. What had awakened him? He started for the phone, but it wasn't ringing.

Pounding. No, it was knocking. Someone at the door. He looked past the edge of the curtain, his heart thudding. A large man wearing a down vest. Standing in the driveway were two women and another man in a down vest. André backed away from the window, now fully awake. Who were these people? Jehovah's Witnesses? It seemed unlikely given their casual garb. Whoever or whatever they were, if he ignored them they would go away. He took a few deep breaths. Nothing to worry about. He went into the bathroom and looked at himself in the mirror, at his shaven cheeks, now covered with unattractive little bumps and red from scratching. His poor face. He splashed witchhazel onto a washcloth and held it to his cheeks, listening to the sound of his breath against wet fabric, waiting for the knocking to repeat itself. Were they gone? He dropped the washcloth into the sink and patted his face dry with a clean towel. They must have left. Probably just some neighbors collecting for some worthy cause. Of course. André always contributed money when they came calling. He did his part for cancer research and the Boy Scouts and to save the baby seals. He had always been a good man, and he would continue to be a good man, but from now on he would be a good and a rich man. He smiled at himself, at his pink cheeks, thinking about all the good causes he would soon be able to support.

The whoop of a police siren pierced the wall of the house and shattered André's moment. He ran to the front window, found a gap in the curtain, looked out to see a policeman getting out of his car. The police officer walked up his driveway. André pulled the curtain out a few inches. The two women met the policeman in the middle of the driveway, then the two men sauntered over. The four of them were talking, then all of them turned around and looked right at him. André let the curtain fall back into place, realizing as he did so that he had betrayed his presence.

"Well, there's somebody in there and that's for sure," said Dale Gordon. He looked at Barbaraannette. "You want me to go check it out?"

Hugh said, "I already tried it. He's not answering the door."

"He'll answer for me." Gordon hitched up his belt, making sure she saw all the tools of his trade: his cuffs, mace, flashlight, baton, service revolver, and pager all in their individual black leather holsters. The entire apparatus weighed close to twenty pounds and was damnably uncomfortable, but he loved to wear it. "So you think Bobby might be in there?" he asked Barbaraannette.

"It's possible," said Barbaraannette. Though she hated to admit it, she was glad that Dale Gordon had shown up.

"What makes you think so?" Gordon asked.

Barbaraannette, Hugh, and Phlox exchanged glances. "It's complicated," said Barbaraannette.

"You know whose house this is?"

"His name is André Gideon," said Phlox.

Dale frowned. "Gideon?" He knew about this André Gideon. The queer professor. He knew about this André Gideon because it was part of his job to keep track of all the perverts in this town, and André had come to his attention a couple of years ago when a runaway teenager had been found living in the professor's home. This very place, Gordon now recalled. They hadn't been able to prove anything at the time. The professor claimed that he'd just offered the kid a place to stay, that he hadn't known the boy was underage, and that no illegal behavior had taken place. The kid told them nothing to dispute that, he was returned safely to his parents, and no charges were filed, but Dale Gordon remembered.

André Gideon and Bobby Quinn? He couldn't see it.

Phlox said to Barbaraannette, "I just want you all to remember who brought him all the way from Arizona."

"And who was here first," Hugh added.

"I'm not forgetting anything," said Barbaraannette.

"You folks wait right here," Gordon said. He crossed the lawn to the front step, unholstered his baton and used it to knock on the door, five authoritative blows. After a few seconds, the door opened. Gordon looked down at the smaller man, at the gray tuft of beard and the bright pink cheeks. "André Gideon?"

Gideon placed a delicate-looking hand on his cheek, raised a thin eyebrow. "Yes?"

It was him all right, the pervert professor. Gordon remembered those little monkey hands.

"Can I help you, officer?"

Gordon leaned into the doorway. "Mind if I come in?"

"No, not at all. Please do."

Gordon stepped inside and looked around the room, his eyes adjusting. It was an ordinary-looking living room. No signs of pedophilia or other deviant behavior.

Gideon closed the door. "Would you care for a cup of coffee? Tea?" He seemed nervous, dancing around in his little suede shoes.

"No thanks. Do you have company, Mr. Gideon?"

"Me? No!" He did a little shuffle, monkey hands fluttering. "Who are those people in my driveway?"

"We've had reports that a Mr. Robert Quinn might be on the premises."

"I'm sorry. Who?"

"Mind if I take a look around?"

"As a point of fact, officer, I do."

Gordon smiled. "Tough," he said. He walked past Gideon into the hallway, opened the first door on the left. A bedroom, empty.

"Excuse me, officer, I'm going to have to ask you to leave."

Gordon opened the next door. The bathroom.

"*Excuse* me, but this is highly illegal!"

Gordon turned to tell the little perv to shut his sodomizing yap, but the guy was running at him with his arms up over his head. He had about one fourth of a second to recognize the object in Gideon's hands. It looked like a chair leg.

33

"He's sure been in there a long time," Phlox said.

"Probably got offered some food, " Hugh said. "That Dale Gordon, he's a fool for anything sweet. Eating a Pop-Tart, some damn thing."

"Honey, he's been in there long enough to eat a whole box of those."

Barbaraannette said, "She's right. I'm going to see what's keeping him." She started toward the front door. The sound of a slamming car door came from within the garage. Barbaraannette stopped. They heard an engine start, then the squeal of spinning tires and a tremendous crunching sound. The garage door bulged, glass popping from the windows and shattering on the driveway. Hugh and Phlox headed in opposite directions; Rodney dove for the bushes. More screeching, and once again the car smashed into the garage door, this time bursting through the wooden panels—Barbaraannette caught a glimpse of a red-faced, bearded man at the wheel—roaring down the driveway, cutting the corner of the lawn and scraping the side of Hugh's van. The car turned onto Fifth Street at high speed, back end sliding, and disappeared. For a moment no one said a word, then Hugh let out a howl of fury, ran to his van, followed by Rodney, and took off in pursuit. Barbaraannette and Phlox watched the van disappear, then looked at each other.

"I didn't see Bobby in that car," Phlox said. "Did you?"

"Not Dale either," Barbaraannette said, in motion now, running toward the front door.

They found Dale Gordon on the floor, senseless, his hands, feet, and mouth covered with silver tape, an enormous lump growing on his forehead. Barbaraannette pulled the tape off his face. He was breathing. Barbaraannette patted Gordon's cheeks, trying to rouse him.

"I think we better get an ambulance," she said.

Phlox, who was running from room to room searching for Bobby, didn't seem to hear her. Barbaraannette found a phone in the kitchen and called the hospital, then she called the police, then she returned to Gordon and began to untape his wrists and ankles. "You better be all right," she said. "You better be okay."

Gordon let out a groan, but showed no signs of awareness.

Barbaraannette said, "I'm sorry, Dale. I swear to God I'm sorry." She heard the clatter of boots on stairs, turned to find Phlox coming toward her with a gray object in her hands and a stricken expression on her face. "What is it?" Barbaraannette asked.

Phlox held out a lump of crumpled gray felt decorated with bits of silver tape.

"El Presidente," she said.

Barbaraannette said, "El what?"

"It's Bobby's," Phlox's voice cracked.

For the first time since leaving Tucson, Phlox felt cold, unfiltered fear. This was not an adventure anymore, it was not a game. She'd been cruising on beer and adrenaline, not allowing herself to think that Bobby might really be in danger. At least not the kind of danger that would make him dead. She'd half believed that he had disappeared willingly, that he was messing with her head, or maybe trying to figure out a way he could keep the money for himself. But finding his hat, his El Presidente sticky with duct tape and filthy from the furnace room floor, and the stain on the floor that looked a lot like dried blood—these things were truly frightening.

He's dead, she thought, forming the words in her mind, tasting them for truth, feeling her stomach drop as the concept became real.

Barbaraannette said, "But no Bobby?"

Phlox shook her head. She noticed the sleeping policeman. "Is he . . . ?"

"I think he's all right. He's breathing fine, and his pulse is strong. I called the hospital."

"Maybe Bobby's alive, too."

Barbaraannette seemed surprised. "Of course he is. The man can't get my money without Bobby."

Phlox nodded, pushing the fear down deep, gathering her forces. "You got that right, honey," she said, forcing bravado into her voice. "I wonder if this kidnapping son of a bitch keeps any beer around the house." She went into the kitchen and found a bottle of Heineken in the fridge. Sipping the beer, she walked through the house keeping her thoughts close to the surface. She could hear a siren. One of the bedrooms contained a desk with several piles of neatly stacked papers—letters, bills, and so forth. She picked up a small address book, flipped through it, put it in her pocket. She sat down and looked through the unpaid bills, paying particular attention to the one from the telephone company.

The siren was closer. She heard the growl of a male voice. She pocketed the phone bill and returned to the hallway. The policeman was on his feet, saying, "I'm all right; I'm all right. Jesus, what the hell happened to me?" Touching his forehead, wincing.

Barbaraannette said, holding his arm, "Take it easy, Dale."

"Easy, hell." His hands went to his waist. Suddenly clutching at his belt, the cop said, "Hey! My gun!" Looking down, groping at empty leather. "My cuffs!"

André drove at random, turning this way and that, heading away from Cold Rock but with no clear destination, hearing his own voice saying, "I am an outlaw now," feeling the weight of the police revolver on his lap.

"I am an outlaw now," he said again, turning onto County Road 235, cutting the corner, raising a cloud of dust. The gun slid off his lap and fell between the seat and door. André picked it up, set it back on his lap.

He was a few miles west of Rush City when he first noticed the maroon van.

Rather to his surprise, he did not experience a heart-pounding, panicky feeling. He felt peaceful, as if events to come were preordained. The moment he had clubbed the policeman, a calm had settled within him. He was a skydiver on his way down, or an astronaut on his way up. The moment of truth had come and gone, his choices were delineated, his decisions made. The incident with Jayjay had sent him along this path, but until now there had been a chance he could go back. Not anymore.

He turned at an unmarked dirt road, followed it past a small farm, then stopped the car. Twenty seconds later the van came into sight, slowed, then pulled up behind his car. He could see two men, large and angry-looking. André opened the door, got out, aimed the revolver with both hands and fired. The gun slammed into his hands, wrenching one thumb back; the sound of the explosion was much louder than he had expected. A hole appeared in the windshield, about a foot to the left of the driver's head. The man's mouth fell open. The other man ducked out of sight. Gripping the revolver more tightly this time, André aimed and fired again. A headlamp exploded. The driver's head disappeared and the van began to move rapidly backward. André pulled the trigger twice more, getting the hang of it now, but not sure where his bullets were going. On the last shot the van turned suddenly into the ditch and tipped onto its side.

André stood watching. One of the front wheels was spinning and steam rose from the grille. He got back in his car and continued down the road. Every few seconds he would lift the barrel of the gun to his nose and inhale the aroma of gunpowder. Was this the smell of freedom? His mind roamed through a European future peopled with expats and fugitives and squinty-eyed, cigarette-smoking men named Raoul and Gunther. Soon he, too, would be wearing dark shirts beneath pale jackets. He would develop a tic. When asked what he did he would make vague representations concerning import-export. He would be an art dealer, surreptitiously bringing antiquities out of the Baltic nations, dealing with the great Old World museums. He liked that.

A few minutes later he stopped the car again, got out, and opened the trunk lid.

"Get out," he said.

Bobby, staring at the gun in André's hands, said, "What are you going to do?"

"I am not going to shoot you. Just get out."

"I don't think I can." His arms were taped to his sides.

André cocked the revolver. "If you do not get out I *will* shoot you," he said, enjoying the feel of the words passing over his lips.

Bobby twisted, got one leg over the edge, and slowly dragged himself over the lip of the trunk. He fell heavily to the dirt surface of the road. André watched him writhing like a worm, trying to get his feet under him.

"Get up," André said, even though the man was clearly doing everything he could. "Hurry up," he said.

After a few abortive attempts to throw himself upright, Bobby managed to brace his shoulders against the rear bumper and push himself into a standing position.

André said, "Now get in the car."

"I can't open the door," Bobby said. His hands flapped uselessly against his thighs.

André opened the passenger door and Bobby climbed inside. Seconds later, they were driving down the road.

"What happened?" Bobby asked. "I heard shooting."

"Two men were following us. I neutralized them."

"Oh."

"Your situation has grown precarious. I thought you should know where you stand."

"Where I stand?"

"You are in desperate straits."

Bobby nodded. "Where are we going?"

"I have not yet decided. Your wife is not a trustworthy woman. She called the police. That was not a part of our agreement."

Bobby nodded. "Barbaraannette's got her own mind."

André looked at his passenger. "You know her better than I. Perhaps you could suggest a course of action?"

"Sure. I suggest you leave the state and change your name. Like I did."

"But you came back."

"Yeah, and look at me now," Bobby said. "And you know how come?"

André took a moment to think. He said, "No I do not."

"Barbaraannette. If it wasn't for her I wouldn't be here. The woman is like a jinx around my neck."

"Albatross."

"What?"

"Never mind. Let me ask you something. Do you believe that you wife intends to pay me the money?"

"Barbaraannette? You don't know what she's going to do."

"She called the police. That was foolish."

"Maybe. But I'll tell you something. You don't want to piss her off."

André laughed. "I would say it is too late for that."

"You think so? With Barbaraannette it's hard to say. She teaches second-graders, and I never once heard of her getting mad at one of them. She'd tell me stuff they did and I'd ask her how she kept from slapping the kid upside the head and she'd say to me, 'Do you shout at the rain?' "

André looked at his passenger, a little startled.

Bobby continued. "See, you just don't know about Barbaraannette. She would never get mad if she, like, hit her thumb with a hammer. But one time her mother bought her a shirt at Foreman's department store. I think it was a birthday present."

"Her mother?" This gave him an idea.

"Yeah, but the shirt's not exactly her style so she takes it back to the store to exchange it, and the saleswoman looks at it and then she sniffs the armpit and makes a face."

"How rude." André turned east on County Road 23, trying to think of what would be the best route to Diamond Bluff. He would probably have to take the interstate through the Twin Cities, or around them, and pick up Highway 61, and then cross the river at Prescott. There was simply no good way to get there from here.

Bobby said, "That's what Barbaraannette thought."

"I would take my business elsewhere. Do you know how far it is to I-35?"

"I don't even know where the hell we *are*."

"A few miles east of Mora."

"It couldn't be too far, then."

"Good." They came up behind a truck loaded with manure. Holding his breath, André pulled out to pass, then thought better of it. The driver might look down and notice that his passenger was wrapped in duct tape. He slowed down and fell in behind the truck, then slowed down more to get some fresh air between the two vehicles. As soon as he could breathe freely again André asked, "Why are you telling me this?"

"What?"

"The story about the blouse."

"You were asking about Barbaraannette. See, the woman wouldn't take the shirt back because she claimed that it had BO. So Barbaraannette drives straight over to Rolling Hills Country Club and finds out where Billy Foreman is—Billy owns the store where the shirt came from—and she finds him in the lounge with a bunch of his friends playing bridge and she goes in and pulls up a chair next to him and sits down and plops the blouse down next to his scotch-and-soda and says, 'Smell that.'

"Billy looks at the shirt and says, 'Excuse me?'

"Barbaraannette says, 'Smell the shirt.'

"The guy looks around like he can't believe his sacred country club has been invaded by this woman, and of course his friends are just dying trying not to laugh. He figures the quickest way out of this mess is to just do like Barbaraannette wants so he sort of gives the shirt a little sniff, then hands it back to her and says, 'Yes, that's very interesting. Now if you'll excuse us . . . ?'

"But Barbie, she just lifts up one arm and sticks her pit right in his face and says, 'Now smell that.'

"Well, you can imagine. The upshot was, she got him to admit that the shirt didn't smell anything like her armpit; the store took back the shirt and the saleswoman got fired and things never went right for Billy Foreman after that. I noticed the store isn't there anymore."

"Yes. Foreman's closed a few years ago," André said. He slowed and turned onto the entrance ramp, heading south. The image of the woman forcing the man to smell her armpit both excited and repelled him. "It seems a rather overly direct way to handle things," he said.

"No shit. But don't forget, this is a woman who's put out a million-dollar reward on her husband. Me."

"She does not shy away from extreme solutions."

"Like I say, you don't want to piss her off."

34

"I'm not talking to her," *Barbaraannette said.*

Toagie bit her lip, looked at Brittany, who was sitting on the floor undressing a doll. Taking her hand off the mouthpiece of the phone, Toagie said, "Mary Beth? She can't come to the phone right now." Her brow furrowed. "I'll tell her. Bye." She hung up. "She's coming over to pick up Hilde. They've agreed to let her return to Crestview. Also, she thinks you should withdraw the reward offer. She says to let the police handle things."

Barbaraannette rammed the heels of her hands into the ball of dough, compressing and spreading it. "In the first place, if I take away the reward offer, then nobody except me will care about Bobby getting kidnapped. And as for the police, why would I call them? So that idiot Dale Gordon can make a worse mess of things?" She folded the dough onto itself, flopped it, turned it ninety degrees, and leaned into it again. She had been kneading for ten minutes. The dough was elastic and smooth and ready to proof, but Barbaraannette was not finished. She was no great baker, but there was nothing like kneading bread to calm a person down.

Fold, flop, turn, press out. She could hear Hilde's snores, faintly, coming from the bedroom down the hall. Brittany had pulled the head off her doll and was attempting to reinstall it.

Toagie lit a cigarette, inhaled, blew the smoke toward the ceiling. "If it'd been you instead of Dale, you might've been the one with the bump on your head. Or worse, for cripes sake. And whose blood was that? You said there was blood."

"In the basement."

"That could have been your blood."

"He wouldn't have hurt me. I'm the one with the money."

"Crazy people don't care about money."

"The man who has Bobby cares about money."

Brittany stood up and leaned into her mother, pushing out her lower lip, holding out the decapitated doll.

Toagie shrugged. "Never the fleepin' less . . ." She took the doll from her daughter and popped the head back in place with a practiced twist. Brittany carried the doll back to her doorway and began to dress it in miniature blue jeans. ". . . you don't know what he might do."

"He wants money. I know all about men who want money."

Toagie smoked and watched her sister knead dough. "You've got strong arms," she said, looking from Barbaraannette's forearms to her own. "I got these little bird wrists."

Barbaraannette lifted the dough, slammed it down, pressed it out.

"You know what's funny?" Toagie asked.

Barbaraannette shook her head.

"You're kneading dough, and you're the only person I know that doesn't."

Barbaraannette felt herself smile. Fold, flop, turn, press out.

"So what are you gonna do?" Toagie asked.

Barbaraannette said, "Wait."

"I know. I mean, what are you gonna do when he calls?"

Barbaraannette patted the dough into a ball, slapped it with her palm, watched her hand print appear, then disappear.

News of the attack on Police Chief Dale Gordon reached Cold Rock S&L via Sally Krone, who heard about it on her lunch break from Ginny down at the Blue Plate, who got it from her sister Bette who worked at the Pinelands Medical Center where Dale got his forehead stitched back together.

Art Dobbleman caught bits and pieces of the news as Sally, sitting at her desk surrounded by a half dozen employees and customers, told what she knew. Art was stuck on the phone listening to a tinny recitation of current Norwest CD rates. Matt McRae, their lender at Norwest, had put him on hold ten minutes earlier. Probably forgot all about him. Nagler had insisted that Art handle the transaction himself, agreeing to step in only when the negotiation stalled, which was inevitable. Typical Nate Nagler behavior. He loved to be the hero.

From what Sally said, Dale Gordon had been attacked, hit over the head. That was certainly interesting news by Cold Rock standards, but Art was not listening carefully until he heard Barbaraannette's name come up. He pulled the phone away from his ear and said, "Wait, what was that?"

Sally said, "Barbaraannette was there, and Hugh Hulke, too."

"She's okay?"

"Oh sure, sure. Dale Gordon is the only one that got hurt. But here's the funny part. The man who hit him? They think it was a *college* professor. Isn't that weird? And what they were saying at the Blue Plate, they were saying that Bobby Quinn's back in town."

Art hung up the phone. To hell with Matt McRae. "Was he there, too? Bobby?"

"All I know is what Ginny told me, which was that they were there *looking* for Bobby. God, for a million dollars who wouldn't be?"

"Bobby was there?" He was leaning over her desk, gripping the edge.

"Jeez, Art, take it easy, would you? I don't know. Go ask Ginny. Better yet, ask Barbaraannette."

The only number to appear more than once on André Gideon's MCI bill was a 715 area code. Someplace called Diamond Bluff, Wisconsin. His March bill listed fourteen calls to the same number, which did not match any of the listings in Gideon's address book. At first, Phlox took this as a negative, but after thinking about it she realized that it could also be a good thing. It could be a number he knew by heart. She called up the image of the green Taurus, of the red-faced man who had nearly run her over. They said he was a college professor, but he had laid that big policeman out, no problem.

A cop-bashing, Bobby-napping college professor with a French-sounding name and a wild look in his eyes. But what about Bobby? Had he been in the car, too? Or was he hidden away in someplace like Diamond Bluff, Wisconsin?

"You ready for another?"

Phlox looked up, surprised to find herself sitting at a bar, heels hooked over the footrest of a red vinyl upholstered stool, elbows propped on a brass rail, an empty schooner holding down the phone bill. A balding, bespectacled bartender wiped his hands on a stained bar towel, smiling at her. She was his only customer.

"Thanks," she said. "Might as well." One more beer might loosen up the clogs, get her thinking clear again. At the moment, she couldn't decide whether she should go back to Barbaraannette's or try to catch a ride out to Hugh Hulke's farm to reclaim the pickup. If Hugh and Rodney had managed to catch up with Gideon, and if the professor led them to Bobby, then they'd probably haul Bobby straight to Barbaraannette, in which case it would be Phlox's best move to be there to defend her interests. On the other hand, she needed her wheels. If Hugh and Rodney failed—and she was all but certain they would—then she might have to start checking out the names in Gideon's address book, a process easily as tedious as checking out the owners of green Tauruses.

A fresh schooner of Budweiser appeared. "You ever hear of a place name of Diamond Bluff, Wisconsin?" she asked.

The bartender shook his head. "I don't know anything about Wisconsin except the Packers are from there."

Phlox nodded, then carried her beer over to the pay phone and called the 715 number. A woman answered after six rings. "Yey-ess?" She sounded old.

"Is André there, please?" Phlox asked.

"Who's calling, please?" Old and suspicious.

"My name is Fiona Anderson," said Phlox. "I'm looking for André Gideon."

"Well you're about thirty years late and besides, his name is Andrew, don't you know. You people, calling yourselves such things. What did you say your name was?"

"Fiona Anderson."

"I'm writing it down. I'm writing down your name. Fiona. Is that a Negro name?"

"Are you Mrs. Gideon?"

"Gideon? More damn foolishness! Grubb is a perfectly fine name. Who did you say this is?"

"Fiona Ander–"

"I know your Negro name, missy, what I want to know is, who are you working for?"

"I'm a friend of Andr . . . Andrew's. Are you his mother?"

"I'm not answering any more questions." Click.

Phlox finished her beer, then dropped a quarter into the phone and dialed Barbaraannette's number.

"Hi. It's me, Phlox," she said. "Any news?"

Barbaraannette had heard nothing new. She was still waiting, and she wanted her phone line to stay open. Phlox hung up, returned to the bar.

The bartender was right there. "You ready for another?"

Phlox shook her head. "You know where I can get a map of Wisconsin?"

35

Barbaraannette said, *pulling the sweater sleeve over Hilde's arm,* "Do you ever think you're a bad person?"

Toagie reached in through the cuff, grasped her mother's hand, and pulled it through. Hilde, sitting on the edge of the bed, had fallen into one of her slack-faced reveries.

"I'm not bad," Toagie said, a slight whine entering her voice. She pulled the body of the sweater up and over Hilde's head, worked it down her torso. "Do you think I'm bad?"

"That's not what I meant." Barbaraannette looked into her mother's face. "Hilde? You there?"

Hilde smiled dreamily.

Barbaraannette said, "What I mean is, do *you* ever think you're a bad person?"

"I'm *not* a bad person," Toagie said.

"But if you were? What if you were, say, a rapist. Do you think you would think that you were bad? Or would you think that you were a good person who just happens to be a rapist?"

"I would think I was the scum of the earth and I'd kill myself."

"But they don't."

"Barbaraannette, I'm a little worried about you." She grasped her mother's arm. "Come on, Hilde, let's stand you up."

Hilde rose unsteadily. "Are we going back to the hotel?"

"Mary Beth is picking you up."

Brittany, who had once again removed her doll's head, crawled out from beneath the bed. "I'm bad," she said, grinding the headless torso into the carpet. "I'm scum of the earth."

The doorbell rang.

"Are you all right?" Art heard the shaking in his voice.

"I'm fine." Barbaraannette looked past him. "I thought you were Mary Beth."

"No. I'm not."

"That's good."

They regarded one another, standing on either side of the open doorway. Why are the moments of my life so damned awkward, Art wondered. He said, "I just wanted to be sure you were okay. I heard Dale Gordon got hurt."

"He'll be all right. Do you want to come in?" She tipped her head to the side and stepped back, making room.

Art stepped inside. The house smelled of baking bread. He said, "Now that the police are involved, I suppose you won't need that loan."

Barbaraannette's mouth tightened. "Nothing has changed. The man will still want his money."

"Yes, but—"

"Listen to me, Art. I appreciate your advice, but I'm on the edge here. I just need you to do your job. Do you understand?"

Art felt a streak of ill-advised stubbornness assert itself. "No I don't," he said. "Barbaraannette, I am not going to let you do this. I'm sorry. It's wrong, and you could be hurt, and I won't be a party to it. And that's that." Art looked down, half expecting to see his words lying shattered on the floor.

"You're not going to *let* me?" Barbaraannette said.

Art heard Toagie Carlson's voice. "Who is it, Barbaraannette?"

Barbaraannette turned her head slightly and raised her voice. "It's the *banker.*"

Toagie appeared in the hall doorway with Hilde Grabo in tow and her daughter—Art couldn't remember the child's name—wrapped around her legs. "Art the forecloser," Toagie said.

"We're not foreclosing," Art said.

Barbaraannette said, "What do you mean, you won't 'let me'?"

"I won't do it. The police are involved now. Let them handle it."

"The police don't know anything, and neither do you. There was blood on the floor."

"There . . . what?"

"There was blood in the basement of that house. Bobby could be hurt. Or worse."

Art hesitated, then shook his head. "All the more reason to let the police handle it."

"It's my money."

"I won't help you buy back your marriage."

"My marriage is none of your business."

"Damn it, Barbaraannette, I want to help you!" His hands moved toward her.

Barbaraannette stepped back out of his reach; her face morphed, each feature realigning itself, searching for a new position. Art's heart lifted for a moment, seeing the change as a softening, but once the transformation was complete he knew he was in trouble. Her eyebrows dropped and came together, her nostrils flared.

"Then do as I ask."

Art raised his chin. "I won't help you hurt yourself."

Barbaraannette's voice went thick and low. "Then go away. Go back to your little desk. I'll call Nate and I'll get the money anyway."

"I'll call the police," Art said, having no other cards to play.

Barbaraannette's lip curled. "Go on, get out of my house. I don't need your kind of help. I don't even like you. And if you call the police I'll put a reward out on you, too, you self-righteous marathon-running son of a bitch!"

Toagie clapped her hands over her daughter's ears. Art brought his arms across his belly as if he'd been punched. He'd never seen Barbaraannette like this. He'd never seen the vein that popped out on her forehead, or the way her eyes became hard rectangles. Backing toward the door he said, or heard himself say, "Barbaraannette, when this is all over, whatever happens, I'd like to take you out to dinner."

"Why? So you can order for me? So you can help me eat?"

Art turned and walked out. Just before the door slammed he heard Hilde call out, "Good night, Arthur."

I am a good person, Barbaraannette thought. It's just this one little thing I have, this Bobby thing.

Toagie, still gripping Britty's head between her hands, said, "Jeez Louise. What happened?"

Barbaraannette, still shaking, sat down on the sofa.

Toagie said, "I always thought he was one of the quiet ones." Britty squirmed free.

Barbaraannette shook her head. "He's as bad as the rest of them."

"Arthur's a good boy," said Hilde.

"I hate him. Give me a cigarette."

"Uh-uh." Toagie released Britty and clamped her hand protectively over her purse. "You're not gonna start smoking again, not on me."

Barbaraannette struck her thighs with her fists and began to pace, her shoes making hissing sounds on the carpet. "I'm going to do something. I swear to God, Toag, I'm going to have to do *something*." She stopped, took her lower lip between her teeth and bit until she tasted blood. "Damn that Dale Gordon. Damn Mary Beth. Why is this happening to me? Why me? This is all that Art Dobbleman's fault."

Toagie, Britty, and Hilde were all staring at her as if she'd turned purple.

"What are you looking at?" Barbaraannette snapped.

Hilde whispered something to Toagie, then turned her V-shaped little-old-lady smile on Barbaraannette.

"What did she say," Barbaraannette demanded to know.

Toagie essayed a nervous laugh. "She wants to know if you're going to go out with him."

Barbaraannette turned an incredulous look upon her mother, then felt something give way and began to laugh. Toagie and Hilde both started laughing, too, with Brittany not far behind. When Mary Beth walked in a minute later they were still giggling, wiping their eyes.

"Well?" she asked.

Barbaraannette said, "Nothing M.B. We were just talking about boys."

Mary Beth said, "I swear, Barbaraannette, winning that lottery has made you soft in the head."

This sent Toagie and Hilde into a second fit of laughter. Mary Beth pushed her chin forward. She said, "Come along, Mother. I'm taking you back to Crestview."

Complete thoughts refused to form. Images, snatches of conversation barked at him, pestered him like biting flies. Art walked past his car, knowing it was there but unable to make his legs slow their chopping walk, hearing the sound of his wingtips on the sidewalk wet with melting snow—*thick thick thick*—and wind rasping the rough fabric of his coat. He leaned forward, let his knees flex. Walking melted into running. He should not be doing this now, not with his long wool coat and his dress shoes, not with Barbaraannette hating him and his job in jeopardy. *I don't even like you,* she had said. Hard composite heels, thin socks. Each step sent a shock wave up his spine, tiny explosions at the base of his skull. Why not just get her the money? Go back and apologize and then get back on the phone and get the cash up here and let her pay off the kidnapper or whatever he was and wait for Bobby to leave her again then move in. But now she hated him and nothing he did would matter, so why should he help? And who was he refusing to help? Barbaraannette or Bobby? Did she really not like him?

He let the thoughts go for a few seconds and sank into the rhythm of the run, coattails flapping. Had he really asked her out to dinner? A wry smile came, lasted for two strides, fell away. Desperate people do strange things. He sped up to what felt like an eight-minute pace. For the next half mile he forced himself to consider the fact that she had not, technically, said no.

36

"My mother passed on," Bobby said. "Died when I was nine."

"No!" André's eyes filled with tears. The closer they got to Diamond Bluff, the more emotional he became.

"My old man raised us, mostly. Me and my big brother, Phil. Then he, the old man, up and died a few years back. Fact, it was the year I left Cold Rock. He was a good man. Big as a damn horse. Used to beat the crap out of Phil, man, I loved it."

"You and your brother did not get along?"

"Phil's an asshole. He lives in Texas now."

"I see." André found this to be disturbing. "I never had a brother," he said, dragging a sleeve across his eyes. "I hardly remember my father."

"Where'd you grow up?"

"Diamond Bluff. We will be there in another hour." They were headed east on I-694, the Twin Cities bypass.

"Your mother still lives there?"

"Yes." André's fingers went white on the steering wheel.

Bobby said, "Do you visit her often?"

"Certainly . . . actually, it has been a few years. She seems to think I should be married."

"Oh. You never got married?"

André chuckled. "My dear boy, it was never in the cards."

"You never came close?"

"Actually, I am gay."

"Oh!" Bobby went rigid.

André said, "Does that bother you?"

" 'Course not."

André slowed and peered into Bobby's eyes. "I think it does bother you. There is nothing to be ashamed of, you know. Most straight men are homophobic to some degree. But you need not worry. You are hardly my type."

"That kid in the basement. He was your type?"

André returned his attention to the road, his eyes once again welling with tears. "Poor Jayjay," he said.

Now that Bobby realized that André was not simply going to shoot him and dump his body over some bridge, he began to think more clearly. The best way to survive would be to get André to like him, the way he would do with a woman, which was to pretend to be fascinated by him, and by all aspects of his existence. But this gay thing, that might make it difficult, since he didn't want to look too interested—but at the same time he had to let the guy know he didn't hold it against him.

"I think that's really great, you being gay," he said.

"Oh? And why is that?"

"I mean, different strokes for different folks."

André frowned, looking puzzled.

"I didn't mean that the way it sounded," Bobby said quickly, thinking, Shit, shit, shit! How are you supposed to talk to these guys? It was worse than trying to talk to a black guy, trying all the time not to say something stupid. "I just mean, I like gay guys." Damn! That definitely wasn't what he'd meant to say. "I mean, you know, to talk to, like to get a haircut or something." Shit! He kept digging the hole deeper, and André had that big old gun in his lap. He was going to get dumped over a railing yet. "That's not what I meant," he said, staring at the revolver. "None of it is."

A strange hooting sound filled the car. Bobby lifted his eyes from André's gun to his face. The man was laughing.

•   •   •

Phlox caught a ride to the Hulke place from a sixteen-year-old kid driving a twenty-year-old Camaro. At ninety-five miles per hour, the trip took only twelve minutes. Phlox gave the kid ten bucks—probably less than he'd burned up in fuel. She got her bag out of her pickup, let herself into Hugh's pigsty of a house and took a few minutes to spruce up. She changed out of her jeans into a blue suede skirt and a chambray top—the only clean articles of clothing she had left—then got in the pickup and headed back toward Cold Rock at the relatively sedate speed of eighty, still undecided as to her next move.

The first map she bought, at the Amoco on the west side of town, was a cheap fold-out that did not show a Diamond Bluff. Phlox went back into the station, demanded her money back, then drove to the Fleet Farm where she purchased a larger, more detailed map for $14.95. Diamond Bluff turned out to be a small dot on the Wisconsin side of the Mississippi River. It looked like a two- or three-hour drive, a long way to go on a hunch. She set the map on the seat and looked out over the Fleet Farm parking lot. It reminded her of Tucson—mostly pickup trucks. She raised her eyes to the horizon, looking for a mountain, but of course there were no mountains in Minnesota, only a scabby mass of leafless trees and cold buildings and billboards. The highest point in town was occupied by the Taxidermy & Cheese Shoppe. That decided her.

She started the truck and headed east toward the Interstate. She would go to Diamond Bluff and visit Mrs. Gideon or Grubb or whatever she called herself. Maybe this hunch was one of the good ones. In any case, getting the hell out of Cold Rock had to be a good thing.

A few miles south of Prescott, André slowed abruptly, then turned onto a narrow gravel road that led over a set of railroad tracks and down toward the river. He followed the road until they reached a boat ramp, got out, and opened the passenger door. He pointed the revolver at Bobby's head.

"Get out."

Bobby said, "Is this where your mother lives?" Thinking, Damn, he's going to kill me after all.

André said, "No. Get out."

"What for? You don't have to worry about me. I won't say anything. What would your mother think?"

"I do not wish to burden my mother with your existence. Get out."

"You're not going to shoot me. You can't shoot me. I can help you. You don't know Barbaraannette like I do. I can help you get the money."

"I am not going to shoot you. Get out."

Bobby swung his legs out of the car. "She's not gonna pay you, you know. You don't know her. If she thinks you're trying to make her do something, she just isn't gonna do it. Especially if I'm dead."

"I told you, I am not going to shoot you. I want you in the trunk."

Bobby shook his head, leaning forward, staring at the ground. "No." He could not get back into that trunk with its bloodstains, reeking of the dead boy, bouncing and dark. He said, "If you're not going to shoot me, I won't get in the trunk." He cringed and raised his head. "That's not what I meant."

André lowered the revolver. "All right," he said. "Tell me how I can get your wife to pay me the money."

"Are you going to make me get in the trunk?"

"No."

For a moment Bobby felt as if he was floating. "Thank you," he said, gratitude flooding his thoughts. "You won't be sorry. I'll help you."

André said, "All right. Tell me how I should approach your wife."

Bobby nodded vigorously, trying to shake his mind into action. He did not really know what Barbaraannette would do. He hadn't seen her in six years, and even when they'd been living together he hadn't understood her. She was a woman, and he was able to work her like he could work any woman, but at the same time she was working him. It had been a very confusing time for Bobby, never knowing who was in charge, but being pretty sure it wasn't him. He wished he understood why the hell she wanted him back. He wished he believed that she *did* want him back, and was not instead acting out some peculiar Barbaraannette fantasy that would end badly for him. Hell, it was *already* ending badly.

"Why do you think she called the police?" André asked. "We had an arrangement. I do not understand why she would do that."

"I don't know."

"She offered a reward for your return. Why would she not simply pay me the money as I asked?"

Bobby let images of Barbaraannette flicker through his mind. "She could have lots of reasons. Mostly stubbornness."

André produced an exasperated sputter. "It was my understanding that you had some special insights into your wife's behavior. Maybe you would think better in the trunk."

"Hold on. Let me think." *Think!* When had Barbaraannette not done something he had wanted her to do? Too many outdated memories. He stared at André's Hush Puppies, olive suede on wet gravel. "I wanted a pair of boots for my birthday one time. She was gonna buy me a pair of elk hide boots." How had that gone? Bobby groped for a clear memory. "She said she would buy me the boots and then we had a fight . . . about something. She wouldn't buy them. It was like, *bam,* one minute she's going to buy me these boots and then it was screw you, Bobby, go buy your own damn boots." He felt his face warming, getting pissed off all over again. "That was when I decided to buy the ranch in Wyoming. When I decided I'd had enough of her."

"What are you saying?"

"Only things didn't work out the way they were supposed to with the ranch, because I had to use part of the money to buy my own damn boots. And some other stuff I needed, too, and then to make it up I had to go to the casino." He had almost done it, had been up a couple thousand dollars at the blackjack table, doubling down after his losers, steadily building his stack of hundred-dollar chips. Then he'd hit a string of bad hands. Dealer blackjack. Double down. Draw to a twelve, bust, redouble. Stick on eighteen, dealer hits for a twenty. Double double. He'd lost, what? Nine, ten hands in a row? He remembered the woozy feeling as the last of his money disappeared when he hit on a seventeen—hell, the dealer had a queen up, what was he supposed to do? Hit it and busted and it turns out the dealer had a seven down. Feeling as he walked out of the casino in his elk hide boots as if he'd swallowed twenty feet of cold, greasy chain.

André said, "Are you all right?"

Bobby swallowed. "I'm fine. I was just thinking about Barbaraannette." Thinking about driving home and, careful not to wake her up, getting forty dollars and her cash card out of her purse and heading over to the bank and withdrawing her daily maximum of two hundred dollars, then waiting until after midnight and withdrawing another two hundred. Back to the casino, this time starting out conservative, betting twenty-five at a time. He was up to eight hundred when another wave of losses dragged him across the rocks. The second time wasn't as bad, since he'd been pretty much numb going in.

"The only time I ever got anything from her was when I just took it."

Home again, not saying a word as he slipped into bed. Did she know he was there? Maybe, maybe not. He'd lain awake for three hours, then finally got up and loaded his Jeep with fishing gear and threw the canoe up top and took off. He had a half gallon of mixed coins from Barbaraannette's change jar, an Amoco credit card, and his anteater boots. The note he left behind read, *Went fishing. Love, Bobby.*

"What we have to do," he said, "is take it. If you ask her for it, she won't give it to you. We have to take it. Then we get the hell out of Dodge."

André said, "We?"

"You won't get anywhere near the money without me."

"Be that as it may, your untrustworthiness has been clearly demonstrated."

"I had a bad moment. I was scared. Look, this whole thing will go a lot easier if we work together."

André pursed his lips and regarded Bobby, looking him up and down. He said, "All right, Robert, tell me what you have in mind."

Bobby rolled his shoulders, trying to loosen his neck muscles, wondering what the hell was about to come out of his mouth. "Okay then. She gets the money, cash, right?"

"Of course."

"How about you peel off some of this tape?"

"In good time. Please continue."

"Okay. She's got the money, and the problem is to get it without getting nailed by some cops coming out of the woods or in a helicopter or something, right?"

"Yes, of course."

"So here's the problem. If you ask her for the money before you release me, she won't go for it. She'll want to see me, to know I'm okay. That's Barbaraannette. She always has to know what she's getting. The other end of it, if she gets her hands on me before she gives you the money, she won't give you the money. That's Barbaraannette, too. You've pissed her off, so she's not gonna give you anything she doesn't have to. So the way I see it, the only way this can work is if I meet her someplace, and she's got the money with her, then I tell her that you've got a rifle pointed at me or something, and I take the money and run. Then we meet up someplace and whack it up." Bobby nodded vigorously, agreeing with himself. "That's what I think we should do." He smiled at André. "What do you think?"

André said, "Get in the trunk."

37

"It's not for me. It's for my sister," said Barbaraannette.

The drugstore delivery girl—she looked vaguely familiar—gave her a why-would-you-think-I-care expression and handed over the package of Nicorette gum. She looked to be about fifteen, which would have put her in the second grade seven or eight years ago.

"Were you one of my students?" Barbaraannette asked.

"I don't *think* so," the girl said.

"Did you go to elementary school here in Cold Rock?"

She shook her head. "I was in Mora, okay? It's thirty-four ninety-six with tax."

Embarrassed, Barbaraannette fumbled in her purse. They all looked the same sometimes, so innocent and full of themselves. She gave the girl two twenties and told her to keep the change. The girl stared at the bills for a second, either overcome by Barbaraannette's generosity or astonished by her stinginess, there was no way to tell. She stuffed them into the front pocket of her jeans with a muttered thank-you and rode off on her bicycle.

Barbaraannette closed the door and took her thirty-five-dollar package of gum into the kitchen. Thirty-five dollars! A carton of cigarettes would've been cheaper, but she had quit the habit ten years ago and that was that. No way was she going back on her promise to herself. When she had asked Toagie for a cigarette she'd been serious about wanting one, but she'd known that Toagie wouldn't go for it. Toagie understood. Toagie would protect her. Toagie was safe. Barbaraannette hoped that the gum was safe, too. She hoped it would make her feel better, help her pass the time. She unwrapped a piece, put it in her mouth, began to chew, slowly. The flavor reminded her of a full ashtray left out in the rain.

The telephone call came at four o'clock. Barbaraannette answered the phone, one hand on the wall to stop the room from spinning. She was on her third piece of gum.

"I am afraid you called the police," said André Gideon.

Barbaraannette pictured his face, his pink cheeks and gray tuft of beard, his small hands on the steering wheel of his green car. Her hair was alive, wriggling her scalp. "I don't expect you to believe this, Mr. Gideon, but I didn't. I just wanted to meet you, to talk." She was Medusa; she wished he could see her. The man said nothing. She could hear cars whooshing in the background. "I came alone. My sister called the police."

"You were there? Who were those other people? How did you learn my name? How did you know how to find me?"

Barbaraannette opened the top of the garbage pail and spat out the wad of gum. "It's a small town."

"It is not that small. How did you find me? Answer my questions." His voice had gone shrill.

Barbaraannette considered whether she had anything to gain by lying. It would be simpler, at least. "Your car was seen. Someone had your license number."

"Who were those people?"

"At your house? It was me and Dale Gordon—he's the police chief—and some other people. It was kind of a coincidence, all of us being there."

"I do not like coincidences. The two men who followed me now wish they had not."

"Oh." She did not like the sound of that. "Is Bobby okay?"

"In a manner of speaking. He is, in fact, in the trunk of my car. He is both unhappy and uncomfortable. Do you have the money?"

She hesitated. "I'll have it tomorrow, just like I told you before."

"I will call you."

"Wait—let me talk to him."

"That is not convenient at the moment."

"Let me hear his voice or this conversation is over." She held her breath, counting heartbeats.

"That is your choice," he said after a moment. The line went dead.

Barbaraannette hung up the phone, her hand shaking violently. She grabbed her wrist, pulled it against her abdomen and leaned against the door jamb. The nicotine in her system had gathered into a ball of fuzz filling her stomach. She sank to the floor, the hard edge of the jamb creasing her shoulder blade. What if it was Bobby's blood?

The pay phone had left a sticky deposit on the palm of his hand. André went into the service station restroom. The sink was filthy. He washed his hands, using a wad of paper towels to turn off the tap and another paper towel to insulate his hand from the doorknob. He got back in the car. A few blocks away, on High Street, his mother would be sitting in her little house, smoking cigarettes and watching the big screen television he had sent her for Christmas. André took a deep breath, wind whistling through his tight nostrils, bracing himself for reentry. He had grown up in that moist, overheated, smoky little burrow, but familiarity made the experience all the more repugnant.

But it would be safe, at least for a day. The police would not be looking for a woman named Theresa Grubb. A noise came from the trunk, a halfhearted thumping. He started the car and drove, very slowly, through the diminutive town of Diamond Bluff until he reached a small parchment-colored clapboard house, plastic stapled over the windows to keep the winter winds out, daffodils blooming on the south side.

When Bobby made love to her the first time Barbaraannette had known at once that her life would never be the same. She remembered the experience vividly. Driving into the woods in his El

Camino, the scent of summer in the air, the rough blanket, the singing of the birds in the trees. She had given herself to him eagerly, without hesitation, and he had taken her with such confidence and skill—or so it seemed to her at the time—that she had never for a moment doubted that she belonged there forever in Bobby Quinn's arms.

She remembered his smell and the hardness of his belly, and the way his big hands had held her, stripping away her clothing with practiced ease, letting the light caress her in places that had never seen the sun. She had wrapped herself around him, taken him deep into her body, satisfying seventeen years of famine in a few explosive, never to be forgotten moments.

She knew now that most women did not experience such joy upon losing their virginity. Most of them were too frightened, or experienced physical pain, or were simply overwhelmed by concerns over birth control and the state of their souls to enjoy the experience. Most women had the best sex of their lives later, after learning how to make love by trial and error and by reading articles in *Cosmopolitan*. Barbaraannette envied them. She had had the misfortune of going straight to the pinnacle of erotic satisfaction. After she and Bobby had broken up and she left Cold Rock, Barbaraannette had devoted considerable time and energy to finding a replacement. She had gone through seven or eight boyfriends and had found each of them wanting. It was not that they lacked technique, or physical attributes, or the will to please her—every one of the men she had tried to love had been attractive and capable and willing. The problem, as near as she could determine, was that they were not Bobby Quinn.

What was it about him? She had been puzzling over this for years. Bobby was clearly not the brightest or nicest guy around. He was handsome, certainly, but so were a lot of other men. Was it simply that he had been her first? Possibly, but that did not explain why so many other women found him irresistible. Could it be the size and shape of his penis, or some highly attractive pheromone, or the distribution of body hair? Barbaraannette found such notions disturbing. They suggested that she was driven by primitive impulses. If such were the case, she would prefer to remain ignorant.

The most likely answer, she decided, was that with Bobby a woman knew where she stood. When Bobby wanted her—or any other woman—he simply took her—gently, forcefully, without a hint of tentativeness or apology. Not like a rapist, although there were hints of that. Barbaraannette thought that if a woman said *no* it was probable that Bobby would back off. However, it was difficult for her to imagine. It would be like refusing a hungry child food.

38

The local GTE telephone directory was one-half-inch thick, including the Yellow Pages. It contained listings for twelve towns in that section of western Wisconsin. Phlox found four Grubbs in Diamond Bluff. One of them, a Mrs. Howard Grubb at 112 High Street, had the right phone number. She closed the book and pushed it across the lunch counter, cut the tip off the wedge of lemon meringue pie with the edge of her fork, speared it, put it in her mouth. Very sweet, with a citrus tang that hit her at the back of the tongue, just the way she liked it.

"You finding what you're looking for, hon?" the waitress asked, adding a dose of fresh coffee to Phlox's cup. She was plump and gray-haired with washed-out blue eyes and strong yellow teeth.

"I think so," said Phlox. "Do you know Mrs. Howard Grubb?"

"Which Grubb would that be, I wonder?"

"She lives on High Street."

"Oh yah, sure, I know her. Teri Grubb. She comes in here, always orders the ham steak. She still calls herself Mrs. Howard in the book? That man died nearly fifty years ago; I was just a little girl. Howie took a nap on the tracks, he did. Are you a friend of hers?"

"We've talked on the phone. Does she have a son?"

"Sure she does. Little Andy. Only I haven't seen him around here in years. He's a college professor, she says. Always talking about him, how he bought her a big TV."

"This is good pie."

"Why thank you, hon. You come back this way in June, you try our blackcap pie. It's our speciality."

"I'll do that. Can you tell me how I get to Mrs. Grubb's place?"

"You can see it from here, hon." She pointed. "All you've got to do is turn your pretty head."

Phlox looked out through the cafe window.

"Catty-corner to us, just past that white house there, you can sort of see it. That tan-color house with the plastic on the windows? That's Teri's place. She's lived there since God made the Green Bay Packers."

Phlox saw the house. She also saw the car parked in front of it. It looked like a green Ford Taurus.

"Some new people bought the Tuttle place. I believe they're Catholic. Would you get me a cup of coffee, dear?" Muttering images from the thirty-two-inch RCA danced across her spectacles. She had sunk deep into her recliner.

"Of course, Mother." André took her empty mug into the kitchen, marveling at the fact that he had spent the first seventeen years of his life in this abode. Nothing had changed, not even the refrigerator, an old Philco with a door that could be opened from either side and a rind of grease-stabilized dust on top. The blue and green tile pattern in the linoleum floor brought waves of memory. Crawling on it, being sick on it, cleaning it, seeing it in his nightmares. A shaft of late afternoon sunlight penetrated a rent in the plastic window covering, illuminating a soup of tobacco smoke and dust motes—what were they? Bits of fabric? Flakes of dry skin? He was breathing his mother. She was slowly disintegrating, floating away a few molecules at a time. He sucked her in, spewed her out. Air whistled through his nostrils.

Only the television he had bought her was new. She ran it constantly, the sound turned so low it was difficult to make out the words. From the kitchen it sounded like someone rubbing dry fingers together—*wishwishwish*. He filled the mug from the Mr. Coffee, added a tablespoon of creamer and three cubes of sugar and carried it to her, careful not to spill.

His mother, accepting the coffee in her powdery hands, said, "You heard about the Reinke boys being arrested?"

André had not heard. The Reinke brothers had done everything they could to make his adolescence a nightmare. Some evil instinct had told them that he was different long before he had admitted it to himself. Teasing him about his bookishness and the way he talked. What was wrong with the way he talked? He never knew. Calling him Dandy Andy. Writing lewd offers in restroom stalls with his name and phone number. Worst of all, mercilessly harrassing anyone who attempted to befriend him. He had left Diamond Bluff for many reasons, but the Reinke brothers were one of the big ones.

"Who did they beat up?"

"They were making drugs, dear. Meta–something, I believe."

"Methamphetamine?"

"Yes, dear, in that big old barn behind their house. The state took all their property. It just sits there empty now. Their parents will be spinning in their graves. You know, that makes seven of your classmates that have become criminals, and only twenty-nine in your class. And do you know what all seven had in common?"

"No, Mother."

"Every one of them was unmarried and childless. Children are your charm against the devil, dear."

"Yes, Mother." A newscast was showing on the television. Things happening in the Middle East. A school fire in Minneapolis. Footage of a small town: a church, a cafe, a sign that read *Taxidermy & Cheese Shoppe*–it was Cold Rock! André grabbed the remote control, turned up the sound.

". . . first murder in twenty-three years in this peaceful college community. Police Chief Dale Gordon–" A shot of the policeman standing by the river, one side of his face heavily bandaged. "–has asked for the public's help in locating the suspect, Professor André Gideon, a professor at Cold Rock College." A photo, the one from his personnel file, ten years old, showing him with longer hair and a full beard. André looked at his mother staring at the TV. Did she recognize him? She was not reacting. The newscast went to a commercial.

"Oh, look at this one, Andrew!" His mother exclaimed, sitting forward and pointing at the screen. A golden retriever wearing eyeglasses was selling bank loans. It looked to André as though the dog was trying to get a hair out of its mouth. "I love that talking dog," she said.

André sat on the wooden chair beside her. The revolver, concealed beneath his sweater, dug into his groin. The dog was still talking. How had they found out that he had killed Jayjay? One of his snoopy neighbors had perhaps seen the boy coming and going. It did not matter. André Gideon was now as irrelevant as Andrew Grubb. He would have to create a new identity. Adam something. He had always liked that name. Adam, Adam *Grappelli*. Yes, that had a ring to it. Adam Grappelli, man without a country. He would adopt his new identity as soon as he arrived overseas. They would search for André Gideon, but no one would think to look for Adam Grappelli.

He watched his mother light a fresh cigarette and wondered how the man in his trunk was doing. Was the air in there worse than this air he was breathing? André did not think so.

Diamond Bluff was a quiet town. Bobby had heard only three cars drive past, and once some distant voices which had inspired him to kick the side of the trunk several times, trying to make as much noise as possible, but to no avail. André had taken the extra precaution of attaching one of Bobby's wrists to a trunk brace with a pair of handcuffs.

"Where'd you get those?" Bobby had asked.

André had given him a perplexed look, as if a dog had spoken, then taped his mouth shut.

Bobby listened and breathed. He hoped that he would not have to stay in the trunk all night. He hoped that the professor would feel sorry for him and let him out, or at least bring him some food and let him pee. He wished he could fall asleep.

He was thinking about french fries when he heard the sound of an approaching car. The sound got louder, then remained steady, very close. He could hear clattering valves, a familiar rhythm. It had to be no more than a few feet away.

He began to kick in earnest.

•   •   •

She would knock on the door and say she had come to see Andrew, then she would see what happened. This was Phlox's plan. She was not proud of it, as a plan, but it was all she had. She got out of the truck and started up the walk, but was stopped by a peculiar thumping noise. She turned her head back and forth, searching with her ears for the source of the sound.

It was coming from the Taurus. She moved closer.

Thunk.

From the trunk? She leaned over the trunk lid.

Thunk.

She said, "That you, Pookie?"

Thinkthunkthunkthunkthunk.

It was him. Phlox shifted into emergency mode, ran to the pickup and got the tire iron from its compartment behind the seats. She had to move fast, get him out before the guy in the house looked out. She jammed the chisel end of the iron bar under the lip of the trunk lid and heaved. Metal bent. Pulling it free, she rammed it home again and pried. No good. Wait, what was she thinking? She ran to the driver's side of the car and swung the tire iron into the window, reached through crumbled glass, opened the door, triggered the trunk release, ran back and lifted the lid.

"Jesus, Bobby!" He was all taped up. She grabbed him, trying to help him out. "C'mon Bobby, we gotta move. Gotta get out of here. Jesus, what did he do to you?" He was caught on something; she couldn't get him out. Tearing at the duct tape, feeling herself lose it. A sudden, shocking pain in one hand, a broken nail. Bobby contorting his face, trying to tell her something. "Oh, shit, I'm sorry, babe!" She tore the tape away from his mouth.

"Handcuffs," he gasped.

"Shitfire, Pook." She ran back to the pickup and grabbed her purse.

Bobby said, "C'mon, Fiona, don't bail on me now."

"I'm not bailing, babe." She groped through the contents of her purse, came out with a pair of tweezers and went to work on the cuff. "Just you hold still now." Probing and turning, hearing her breathing echo from the trunk lid, trying to be methodical, poking and twisting at the invisible insides of the lock mechanism. There, she had something. A faint click, felt more than heard, and the cuff came open. She pulled it off the brace; the other end remained attached to Bobby's wrist. "Got it! C'mon, let's get you out of there."

Another click, this one louder, came from behind her. Phlox whirled. A man stood between her and the pickup. He was holding a large revolver in his two small hands, pointing it at her stomach.

"Who are you?" he asked. His hands were shaking, but not enough to make him miss, not at that range.

"I know who *you* are," said Phlox. "You're Andrew Grubb."

The man's face darkened. "Step away from the car, please."

"Why? So you can shoot me?"

"I will not shoot you. Unless you make me."

Phlox did not like the sound of that. There had to be something she could do. Were any of the neighbors looking? The waitress in the restaurant? She could not afford to wait. She had to do something. Now.

She slipped her hand into the open handcuff and locked it around her wrist.

Andrew Grubb said, "Excuse me?"

39

*—b*anking and running and running and banking and banking and running and running and banking—the words throbbed in his mind, matching his footfalls, suppressing his thoughts. Art had been running for more than two hours, and it was his second run of the day. He had run home from Barbaraannette's in his street clothes. Now he was properly dressed in his running gear, and pushing himself through a twenty-miler.

The first hour had been difficult. He had been thinking about all the things he could never be and all the things that would never happen for him. Trying to understand how Barbaraannette could love an uneducated faithless cheat like Bobby Quinn who was all wrong for her. Maybe Art Dobbleman was wrong for her, too. Thinking that if he just told her what he felt for her, what he'd always felt for her, she would have to listen. What did he have to lose?

He had Barbaraannette to lose. If he opened himself to her and she turned away, he would have nothing. So long as he held something back there would still be hope.

. . . banking and running and running and banking . . . The internal chant had arisen at mile seven, driving away thought *. . . running and banking and banking and running . . .* Art was at peace, swept up in the rhythm of footfalls and heartbeats and meaningless words. The miles melted as darkness fell.

•   •   •

Seven-forty and the sun had set. A couple more weeks it would be time to turn the clocks forward and the light would last until well after 8:00, and then summer would arrive and even at ten o'clock at night a faint light would be seen in the west. Barbaraannette stood outside her front door, testing the moist and chilly breeze. She zipped up the front of her windbreaker, pulled the woolen cap low on her forehead. The cap was a bright red, canister-shaped thing that Hilde had knit for her a few years back. Not her style, but tonight it felt right. She closed the door and walked into the dusk, into the wind. Her eyes teared, her lungs filled with cold wet air, soothing the nauseating ashtray flavor that coated her mouth. The box of gum was in her pocket. She planned to drop it off at Toagie's, but first she had some bad feelings to walk off.

Barbaraannette liked walking. She should do it more often. She wished she could run like Art Dobbleman. Would it be like walking, only better? If walking was like chewing nicotine gum, would running be like smoking Cuban cigars? She smiled, letting the rhythm of her footfalls free her thoughts. What would she look like if she were only bones, walking? Did it stay light later in Mexico? Did penguins clap their flippers, or was that seals? She could take a trip to Antarctica to see the penguins walking on the ice, diving for fish. She could find out for herself. Crazy thoughts, lasting four or five steps. At least she wasn't thinking about Bobby. She unzipped her windbreaker, letting in some air.

Following the residential streets north through town, she came to the bridge over Easton Creek. She looked down into the shadows, saw what looked like a lighter band of earth—the old path. She hadn't walked it in years. Could she get down there from here?

Moments later, one hand slightly scratched from a downhill encounter with a thorn bush, she was there. She walked slowly, feeling the sponginess of the recently thawed topsoil. Soon it would be warm enough to plant a garden. A branch dragged noisily across the arm of her windbreaker. She tried to remember where the path came out. Did it intersect Cherry Street? She couldn't remember. It was so quiet here, only the sounds of her footfalls and twigs scraping nylon. Barbaraannette stopped. She heard a car passing, the breeze rattling branches, the faint gurgling of the creek, her own breathing, then a rhythmic sound, like an echo of her heartbeat, coming from behind her. She turned, more curious than alarmed. Getting louder. Footsteps? The thought had no sooner formed than he was there, a white singlet exploding from the darkness, hitting her with the full length of his body. Barbaraannette flew back, landed hard on her back, the air driven from her lungs. Long, pale limbs clawed through the air, crashed into a bush with a wordless shout.

Barbaraannette's lungs had cemented themselves shut. She strained to inhale, got only a squeak, then felt them loosen and inflate. She sat up and turned, watched the man untangle his arms and legs, extract himself from the brush.

"Art?" Her voice sounded strangled.

He stood up, brushing twigs from his body. "Barbaraannette? Are you okay?"

"I'm feeling a little bruised." She laid a hand over her left breast, testing.

"I'm sorry. There's never anyone here at night."

"Obviously that's not true." The darkness was nearly total. Barbaraannette felt her ribs. Everything seemed to be okay.

Art said, "I'm glad I ran into you. I mean not that I actually ran into you. I was thinking . . . I was thinking that you were right."

"Oh?" She liked the sound of this.

"I ordered your money. After we talked, I went back to the bank and ordered your money. You were right. It's not up to me to judge you, or to judge your marriage. But whatever happens with Bobby—and I'm not wishing him ill—I want you to remember that I'm here."

He could never have said these things to her in the light of day, in his suit, with her eyes on him. The darkness made it possible. He was wearing his running shoes. He could see the shape of her face but not her features. He could smell her. He could hear her breathing. "On whatever terms you want. I can be your banker or your friend or your lover, or you can hate me and think I'm a jerk, but if you ever want to be appreciated for the remarkable woman you are, you don't have to look any further."

The pale orb of her face swayed, but she said nothing.

Art said, "I want you more than Bobby ever did." The sound of his breath filled his ears. "That's what I wanted to say. Also, the money is coming by Brinks truck and will be at the bank by nine-thirty tomorrow morning."

She reached out and took his hand. "You're cold."

He hadn't noticed. His skin had tightened and was covered with goosebumps. "It's a little chilly." Her hand felt like fire.

"You'd better keep running or you'll freeze." She let go of his hand.

Art turned away, came up on his toes to start running, but kept turning until he faced her again. He took her hand, saying, "Tell me something about yourself that you've never told anyone. Anything you can think of."

Barbaraannette let her grip go slack and tried to pull away, but he held on to her, his thumb trapping her hand against his palm. Big hands. She did not speak for several seconds. Art could feel her pulse. For a moment he seemed to sense what she was feeling. She wanted to answer him but she did not know what to say. She wanted him to let go and she wanted him to hold on tighter. She wanted to step into him, to press her body against his chest, but she could not. And she knew that if he moved into her, she would panic.

She said, "Sometimes I close my eyes when I'm driving. I close them and keep driving for as long as I dare. Is that what you mean?"

"A deer could run out in front of you."

"Anything could happen."

Art let out his breath. "Thank you." He let go.

"Nine-thirty?"

"Nine-thirty at the latest."

"Good. Go."

Art turned and ran, holding in his mind his moment of clarity, seeing the shape of her face, letting his feet guide him down the un-lit path.

40

"How did you find me?"

"It's a long story, Punkin. You think you could shift that elbow a bit? You're digging it into my ribs."

"I can't move."

"Me neither. This is awful uncomfortable. How long you think he's gonna leave us here?"

"I don't know. Why the hell did you cuff yourself to me?"

"It was all I could think of. I figured he wouldn't shoot me if I was attached to you."

"He's got a damn key."

"Like I said, I had to think fast. I didn't have time to think good." Phlox focused on her breathing for a few seconds. The air in the trunk was getting thick. "Sooner or later he's got to let us out, right?"

"I saw him kill this guy," Bobby said.

Phlox said nothing, considering the implications.

Bobby said, "He beat a guy to death with a club in his basement."

"I saw the blood. I was afraid it was yours."

Neither of them spoke for a few minutes.

Phlox said, "No offense, Pook, but this is one funky trunk you been living in. Is all that smell you?"

"It's not just me," he said. "The dead guy was in here, too."

Phlox took several shallow breaths. "Thanks for telling me that, Puddin. If I could kick you I would."

She would smile and nod at the advertisements, bring her cigarette to her lips and take a tiny sip of smoke, inhale, let it trickle brown from her lips, the ashtray near her elbow mounded high with butts. André stood in the doorway, the barrel of the gun pressing into his groin. He had almost shot the woman and maybe he should have.

His mother lifted her coffee mug, moistened her lips. She sipped her cigarette and smiled at a Burger King ad. Now that the sun had set, the house felt brighter inside. The smoke and dust seemed to melt away. It was a better place at night. Even the shabby old furniture took on a comfortable glow. André found himself wishing that he could stay.

His mother rotated her head and smiled at him. He imagined that she had read his thoughts and was inviting him to stay. He smiled back; she returned her eyes to the TV. Back in Cold Rock he had grown used to thinking of her as an old woman, but she was not really that old. She had given birth to him at the age of seventeen. He watched her extinguish her cigarette by drilling it deep into the overflowing pile of butts, pushing it below the surface with the tip of her little finger. When all of this was over he would hire a maid for her, a woman to come in and empty the ashtrays and clean the top of the refrigerator and make her fresh coffee. He wished he could stay with her tonight, but it was not safe. The woman had found him, which meant that others might also show up.

He had to keep moving.

He said, "Mother?"

"Yes dear?"

"The Reinke place, you said it's vacant?"

"Yes, dear. It's state property now. Up for sale, I believe. They'll auction it off. I just hope they don't sell it to someone doesn't belong here."

André smiled, thinking that the only people who really belonged in Diamond Bluff were already here.

•   •   •

The Reinke place was south of town, a mile off the highway on a twisting road that led up the bluff. A notice on the front door proclaimed the property to be under the jurisdiction of the State of Wisconsin. A second notice stated that the property would be auctioned on May 14. The house was dark. André drove around the house to the barn where, according to his mother, the Reinke boys had been caught manufacturing amphetamines. The doors were locked, still sealed with police tape. He pulled the car up to the doors until he felt the front bumper make contact, then kept going. The hasp gave way with a ripping sound. He backed up, got out, and pulled the doors open. The headlights lit up a pair of old electric stoves, some stockpots, a few wooden chairs, and a folding table. The barn otherwise appeared to be empty. André backed the car inside and closed the doors. He tried a light switch by the door. A single bulb hanging from the rafters came on, producing a ragged sphere of yellow light that turned the walls from black to umber. Good enough—he had feared that the electricity would be disconnected. André turned off the headlights, pulled the revolver from his waistband, and opened the trunk.

The first thing he saw was the woman's eyes, staring at him with such ferocity that he took a startled step back, raising the gun to ward off the intense emotion. The moment the gun came into her line of sight, her face changed. She became afraid. André relaxed.

"Are you sorry now?" he asked.

She said nothing. Bobby, half underneath her with his face against the spare tire, said something André could not quite hear.

"What did he say?"

The woman licked her lips. "He wants to get out."

André gestured with the gun. "Get out then."

"Don't shoot us."

"I will not shoot you."

Hampered by the handcuffs, it took them a while to climb out, and once they did they had to stand in an odd position. Bobby's arms were taped to his sides, and the woman's right hand was shackled to his right wrist. Only one of them could easily face him at a time and they ended up facing each other with their heads turned toward him like a pair of bedraggled, confused tango dancers.

"I will not shoot you if you cooperate," he said. "Now please tell me who you are and what you were doing."

"People call me Phlox."

André took a moment to process that. He asked, "As in the flower, or gatherings of fowl?"

"The flower, Andrew."

"My name is not Andrew. You must call me Adam. Adam Grappelli." It would help him get used to his new name.

"Adam Grappelli," Phlox repeated.

"Yes. Now, would you please tell me why you are here?"

"You brought me here!"

"I mean to say, what were you doing? How did you find me?"

"It wasn't so hard. You made a lot of phone calls to your mother."

André said, "Ah!" This business of being a wanted criminal was more complex than he had thought. "Are you a policewoman?"

"No."

"Then what is your involvement?"

"Bobby's my boyfriend."

"Oh? I understood him to be married."

Bobby said, "I'm married, but it's to Barbaraannette."

André said, "I see."

"It's sort of complicated," Bobby said.

"Relationships between people often are," said André. Keeping the gun pointed in their general direction, he dragged one of the wooden chairs to a point directly beneath the light bulb and sat down. "It is this very complexity which lends meaning to the lives of those who care to embrace it. For instance, you and I are now involved in an extraordinarily complex social interaction."

Bobby said, "No shit."

"In the end, I will have a new name and a new home in Italy, and you will perhaps be back with your wife." He regarded Phlox with a frown. "As for you, my dear, I cannot say. It is quite interesting, this little adventure we are having, is it not?"

Phlox said, "It's less interesting in that trunk than you maybe think."

André inclined his head, not conceding her point, but acknowledging its theoretical validity. "The social dynamic is not always clear to the individuals involved. In fact, many famous relationships were not entirely appreciated by those who were involved in them and, in fact, were frequently denied altogether. The affair between Eleanor Roosevelt and Amelia Earhart, for instance." André crossed his legs and rested the revolver on his lap.

"In fact, I have studied many such relationships in great depth, using analytical tools developed by Saussure and Lévi-Strauss to shed new light on certain literary alliances." He chuckled, because he always chuckled when making this joke in class. "Or rather, certain *dalliances*." He smiled, waiting for an appreciative laugh from his audience, but the shackled couple stared back at him, as uncomprehending as any pair of sophomores. André shrugged, taking it in his stride. Clearly, he had his work cut out for him.

When she closed the door behind her the echo of its slam persisted. Barbaraannette shrugged off her windbreaker, dropped it on the side chair by the front door. A faint voice in her head said, "Hang up your clothes, dear," but Barbaraannette chose to ignore it. Her body ached from the collision with Art and the house had never felt so empty. She was empty, too. She needed something. Another piece of nicotine gum? Her stomach churned at the remembered flavor. She needed something else. She raised a hand to her mouth. Was that his smell? She touched her fingers to her lips, sensing molecules of Art, letting her thoughts float free for a moment.

Abruptly, her reflections became concrete. What did he expect her to do? She was a married woman, only hours from being reunited with her husband. Why was he doing this now? For years the man doesn't say boo and now, at the most inconvenient imaginable time, he steps into her life.

Time to get serious, Barbaraannette decided. She took a pint of chocolate Häaagen-Dazs from the freezer and put an Aretha Franklin album on the stereo. Bobby had never liked Aretha. What

kind of music did Art like? She pushed the thought aside and listened to Aretha bemoan and celebrate the men in her life. All the
no good heartbreakers and Dr. Feelgoods, two sides of the same
cursed coin. She would get through this thing. The money was not
important. The money was nothing. She had done the one incredi-
bly stupid thing and she had done it on television and it was going
to cost her a few lousy bills but what of it? She had plenty more.
Even with the loan payments she would have plenty of money
coming in every year. She could still make sure that Hilde was taken
care of, and she could help Toagie keep up her house payments. She
could travel or stay put or get a job or do nothing. She could support a man. She could have a child.

Barbaraannette set the ice cream aside. Aretha was howling in
joy or pain—Barbaraannette had lost track. She let her head fall
back, stared up at the ceiling and watched it blur as her eyes filled
with tears, thinking about what might have been. How long had it
been since she had permitted herself to think about having a child?
Was she thinking about it now, or was she only thinking about
thinking about it? The album side ended, leaving only a faint hum
from the speakers. Barbaraannette closed her eyes, squeezing out
the tears. She remained still, letting her thoughts skitter over the
surfaces. In time, she found a comfortable place. She turned off the
stereo, put the ice cream away, and rinsed the coffee cup in the sink.
She hung up her windbreaker. She brushed her teeth and changed
into her nightgown and got into bed and turned out the light and
within minutes she was asleep because that was what she had decided to do.

41

At six o'clock in the morning André ordered a glassy-eyed Bobby and Phlox back into the trunk. They made no objections and, after a bit of experimenting, found a position that suited them both. André closed the trunk. He drove north in the general direction of Cold Rock, feeling melancholy. Over the past few hours he had shared a great deal with his two captives. Much of the philosophy and literary analysis had, of course, flown high over their heads. Nevertheless, his presentation was such that they would doubtless retain certain key concepts—and it was that which saddened him, for he had come to the realization, regrettably, that the man and the woman in his trunk would have to die. He had told them his new identity, and his plans for leaving the country. If they lived to tell, he might be arrested and imprisoned. He should have said nothing of his plans. He had been foolish.

Or perhaps it had not been so foolish after all. Perhaps he had been forcing his own hand, putting himself in a position where he had no choice but to do what must be done. His subconscious had created a path, and it was up to his conscious mind, now, to follow it.

André considered this new idea, and found it to be both intelligent and intriguing. He ordered breakfast at a Burger King drive-thru in Cottage Grove; bought gasoline in Forest Lake. At seven o'clock he pulled into a rest stop near Cold Rock and backed the car up to a pay phone.

•   •   •

"Mrs. Quinn?"

"Yes . . . um, Mr. Gideon?"

"Do you have the money?"

"I'll have it. At nine-thirty, like I told you before."

"Good. And let me be clear about one thing, Mrs. Quinn. If the police are involved in any way, the consequences will be grave indeed."

"You won't get the money if you hurt him."

"That is up to you. I will repeat what I have said: There must be no police. This is a simple, straightforward arrangement between two rational adults. I will be returning your husband to you, and you will be paying me one million dollars. Is this not what you wanted? I will call you at your home at ten o'clock precisely. Goodbye."

"Wait. I want to talk to him. I have to know that he's okay."

"He is fine. You may take my word for that."

Barbaraannette squeezed the phone. "If I don't talk to him now I won't get the cash. It stays in the bank until I hear Bobby's voice." She could hear air whistling through nostrils. His or hers? She could not be sure.

"You are a most vexing woman. Fortunately, I have anticipated your request. Hold the line, please."

Barbaraannette heard the sound of a trunk being opened, then Gideon's voice in the background.

"Say hello to your wife."

"Barbie?" Bobby's voice, sounding hoarse.

She heard another voice, this one female. "Let me talk to her."

Gideon came back on. "Are you satisfied?"

"No. Who was that?"

"That was your husband."

"I heard someone else. Who was it? Put her on the phone."

"She is none of your concern. I will call you again at ten o'clock."

"You hang up and you won't see a nickel. I want to talk to the woman."

More nostril whistling. "You are trying my patience, Mrs. Quinn."

"I'll try more than that if you don't let me talk to that woman. Who is she? Is she your partner?"

"Hardly."

"Put her on the phone. Do it now or I swear to God I won't pay." Barbaraannette listened, holding her breath. A few seconds later Phlox's twangy voice came over the wire.

"That you sweetie pie?" The cheerfulness had a strained sound to it.

"Phlox?"

"You got it, honey. I found him!"

André snatched the phone and banged it back onto its cradle.

Phlox said, "Hey!"

"Shut up." He pulled out the gun and pointed it at her face until he saw the fear, then slammed the trunk closed.

What should have been a simple, straightforward transaction had taken on a hostile character. First the police had become involved, then this Phlox woman had appeared, and now Mrs. Quinn was making demands. She would want to see her husband before turning over the cash, which complicated things considerably.

Nevertheless, he could see no reason not to proceed with his plan. He would have to be firm with her.

Once he had the money he could dispatch the husband and the woman and be on an airplane before they found the bodies. He would be in Italy to see the sun rise.

André started the car, imagining a luncheon of prosciutto, freshly shelled fava beans, and fine Italian cheeses.

Barbaraannette hugged her pillow and watched the telephone on her bedside table, marveling that the oddly shaped plastic device could awaken her from a sound sleep and speak to her, bringing remarkable news. Bobby was alive, and Phlox had found him. But this André Gideon seemed to be in charge. He was either in league with Phlox, or he had kidnapped her, too. He still wanted the money. In fact, he was desperately afraid that she would not give it to him. For a few moments, by threatening not to pay, Barbaraannette had been in control. She had gotten what she wanted.

She swung her feet out past the edge of the mattress, dropped them into her slippers. All this time she had been feeling like a victim, things happening around her, buffeting her like a bit of flotsam on a rough sea. But maybe there was another way to look at it. She had started it. She was the one who had won the lottery and she was the one who had offered the reward. And the money was power. Nobody wanted Bobby except her. He was a commodity with a market consisting of one person: Barbaraannette. It was a buyer's market.

She set about making coffee, feeling much better now about the way things were going. Gideon would call her in a couple hours and he would tell her where and when and what she was to do with the money, and she would listen to him and then decide what she wanted to do. She did not think that he would hurt Bobby. If he did, he would not get the money. She would tell him that. She would tell him exactly the way it was going to be.

42

he Brinks truck arrived at Cold Rock Savings & Loan at 9:10 A.M. precisely. Art Dobbleman and Moe Freidrichs, Cold Rock S&L's part-time security guard, received the shipment: two sealed canvas bags containing one million dollars in cash. Art and Moe brought the bags into the vault, where Art pried open the lead seals, loosened the tops of the bags, and emptied them onto the stainless steel counting table. The money was packaged in shrink-wrapped bricks of hundred-dollar bills, each brick labeled with a band reading $10,000.00. There were one hundred such bricks.

Art handled money every day, but he had never seen so much of it in one place. He stacked the money on one of the vault shelves, then closed the vault and went to his desk to sit and wait for Barbaraannette.

At 9:34, Barbaraannette entered the bank in black jeans, sunglasses, a black, long-billed wool cap, and a leather flight jacket. Art did not recognize her at first. Usually, Barbaraannette dressed like an elementary school teacher. She walked straight up to his desk and said, "Well?"

"You look great," Art said.

Barbaraannette smiled, tilting her head. "I mean the money, Art."

"Oh, that's here. But you still look great."

"It's just some things I had in the back of a closet. It seemed appropriate for the occasion." She seemed unnaturally calm.

"You're sure you want to do this?"

Barbaraannette shrugged. "Let's look at the money."

Art led her back to the vault, showed her the stacks of shrink-wrapped bricks.

Barbaraannette lifted her sunglasses onto her forehead. "Good lord. Are those all hundred-dollar bills?" Her quiet voice filled the tiny, metal-walled room.

"Ten thousand of them."

Barbaraannette lifted one of the ten-thousand-dollar bricks. "You could fit one of these in your pocket easy." She cut through the shrink-wrap with a fingernail, peeled it back, and riffled the bills. "When I think how hard I've worked to earn just one of these . . ."

Art said nothing, watching her as she picked up several bricks, weighed them in her hands.

"It's a lot of money," she said, her voice a whisper.

Art nodded.

Barbaraannette checked her watch. "I should probably get back home. The man is supposed to call me there." She put the money she was holding back on the stacks. "Do you have something I can carry it in?"

Art tried not to let his disappointment show. He had thought for a moment that she had changed her mind. "We've got the bags it came in. Or we could probably fit it into a briefcase."

"I don't have a briefcase."

"I could give you mine, if you want. I need a new one anyway."

"I'll buy you a new one."

"You don't have to do that. The bank will reimburse me."

Barbaraannette smiled. "I'm not destitute, Art. I can still afford to buy you a briefcase."

"I'd rather have Nate pay for it. Listen, were you planning to do this alone?"

Barbaraannette nodded, her jaw set.

"Would you like some company?"

"No thank you," she said.

Art stepped closer, took one of her hands between his palms and held it there. "If you want me to do anything, I'll be here. No matter what. Okay?"

Barbaraannette nodded, watching his mouth and eyes, pulling her hand gently from his grasp.

The briefcase was both heavier and lighter than she had expected. A million dollars. It made her feel powerful, and afraid. She paused at the front door of the bank, looked up and down the sidewalk, then walked quickly to her car. She locked the doors, something she had never before done in Cold Rock. Barbaraannette did not believe in horoscopes or UFOs or ESP, but the briefcase on the seat beside her had an aura about it, an invisible glow. She could feel it on her right elbow, a burning cold like dry ice or the way the wind feels on flesh at twenty degrees below zero. She imagined that people on the street could feel it as she passed by, radiating.

She drove slowly through town, wondering what awaited her at home. The man would call, he would tell her where to take the money. Or would he? He might be waiting for her there. She imagined herself opening the door and finding a pink-cheeked man with a gun. Maybe Phlox would be there, too, and Bobby, all of them laughing at her, taking her money.

She turned on Third Street, rolled past her house, circled the block looking for a green car, then pulled into her driveway and sat for a full minute before getting out and taking the briefcase inside. She slammed and locked the door after her, then went through the house room by room with the briefcase, locking the back door and all the windows and pulling the shades down. Once she felt secure, Barbaraannette set the case on the kitchen table and opened it and put her hands on the money. It felt cool and inert. The plastic shrink-wrap was thick and scratchy at the seams, with a faint greasiness to it. The smell reminded her of new textbooks on the first day of school.

Hugh Hulke positioned a plastic-tipped cigar in the good side of his battered mouth and lit it with a disposable lighter. "You see how she hung on to that thing, Rod Man? Like a million goddamn bucks was in there." His head disappeared in a cloud of cheap smoke.

"Yeah. But what's she gonna do with it?" Rodney asked.

"How in the goddamn hell should I know?" Hugh coughed and winced, gently touching his swollen jaw. His head had collided forcefully with Rodney's face when the van had rolled. One corner of his mouth was cut and taped together, his jaw was all purple lumps and broken veins.

Rodney Gent had also sustained damage. His nose had doubled in size and both eyes were blackened. He said, "You think you know every other goddamn thing."

"I know she came out of the bank with a briefcase, goddamnit. That's our money in there is what it is. She's gonna pay that son of a bitch off is what. I can smell it."

"I'm not saying you're wrong." Rodney clasped his hands over his orange cap. "I got one mother of a headache."

Hugh puffed on his cigar. "You bitch like a she-dog."

"My wife's gonna kill me, I bring her car back all stunk up." The tiny red Isuzu was Sue Gent's pride and joy.

"You can buy her a new one. This is a can't-miss, Rod Man. Think about it. The guy that grabbed Bobby, that Gideon guy, is a crook. He put the snatch on Bobby, clobbered ol' Dale, and took a few shots at yours . . . *ours* truly. He's fair game. All we got to do is stick with the money and as soon as she pays it over, we land on him like flies on shit. It'll be like finding money in a trash can."

"What if she doesn't have the money? What if we lose track of her? What if he starts shooting at us again?"

Hugh grinned. "There's the beauty of it. The guy attacked a cop and then shot up my van. That's how come I brought the shotgun. According to the law of the land, we get to shoot him."

"I thought that was just if they broke in your house."

Hugh shook his head. "Uh-uh. The way it works is once you get shot at, you get to shoot back. Pretty soon now, Rod Man, we're gonna be millionaires."

"Yeah, I believe that. Just like we were gonna make all that money on Montana ranch land. First I listen to Bobby, now I'm listening to you. I got a bad feeling about this whole thing. I got a headache and I don't want to get shot at. And my goddamn wife . . ."

Hugh raised an eyebrow, waiting for more.

"My wife says to me—I'm grabbing her car keys and she's yelling at me—she says to me, 'Rodney Gent, you're a goddamn moron is what you are.' " Rodney cradled his forehead in his palms.

Hugh produced a few billion more smoke particles, bringing the visibility in the car down to twelve inches. "So?"

"So I dunno. Maybe she's right."

Another thing Barbaraannette had never told anyone: She did not believe in horoscopes or UFOs or ESP, but she believed in fate. She believed that it took the unremitting application of willpower, great amounts of luck, or tremendous artfulness to alter one's predestined path in life. She believed that the day she was born she had married Bobby and lost him and won the Powerball. It was this belief that enabled her to drive with her eyes closed and teach a classroom full of seven-year-olds.

The telephone rang at ten o'clock precisely, as promised.

"Hello?"

"Do you have it?" the man asked.

Barbaraannette looked out the window to make sure he wasn't standing outside her door with a cell phone and a battering ram. "I have it," she said.

"Good. How is it packaged?"

"Packaged? It's in a briefcase."

"What will you be driving?"

"It's a Chevrolet. A little blue one. The passenger door is brown."

"Excellent. Here are your instructions. First, I want you to drive over the bridges. All six of them. Once you have done this you will take the highway north out of town approximately three miles until you reach the service station at Benson Road."

"Is that the Kum & Go?"

"I believe so. There you will fill your gasoline tank, and I will contact you."

"Is that where Bobby will be?"

"Of course not."

"You're not getting the money until I have Bobby."

"Mrs. Quinn, permit me to explain something to you. Once I have taken delivery of the reward money, I have no reason not to return your husband to you. You know my identity, and my crimes are a matter of record. By injuring your husband or the woman I would only be creating additional problems for myself."

"I'm not paying you until I see him."

"You are not listening. Allow me to explain it in another way, Mrs. Quinn. If you refuse to pay the reward, then I have absolutely nothing to lose. I will kill the woman and your husband. Admittedly, this course of action will not profit me, but I will do it to make a point. Do you understand?"

"I won't pay unless I know he's okay."

"You have your instructions. I will expect you at the Kum & Go in precisely twenty-five minutes." He hung up.

Hilde knew that she hadn't been herself lately. A simple look around her room told her as much. How could she have allowed herself to stay in a hotel without a minibar in the room? She must've had too much to drink last night—she didn't even remember checking in. She sat up on the edge of the bed and let her thoughts settle. The room was familiar. In fact, she realized after looking around, she lived here. Or someone did. But was she alone? A quick check of the sitting room and bathroom showed that she was the sole resident.

Something in her mind was refusing to engage. She decided to take a shower, do her face and nails, and get dressed up in something sharp. That would help her think. She would go with the black wig today. Dark-haired women were smarter. She would get herself fixed up, she would drive over to Barbaraannette's and pick her up and together they would go shopping.

Hilde smiled. Now that she had a plan, her thoughts began to crystallize.

43

oagie's earliest memories of her eldest sister were of Mary Beth glaring balefully at her, stuck at home babysitting her and Barbaraannette. Mary Beth had changed over the past twenty-five years. Her once athletic body had thickened, her face had broadened, and her hair had gone gray. Her baleful glare, however, had survived the decades unaltered.

Toagie, squirming under its heat, said, "Barbaraannette seems to know what she's doing, Mary Beth. Maybe we should stay out of it. She's a big girl."

Mary Beth pursed her lips, then took a sip of coffee. The hit of caffeine increased the intensity of her gaze. "You always were an irresponsible child, Antonia."

"It's her money and her husband."

"It's a million dollars and her husband is a worthless piece of garbage."

"Sure, but you know Barbaraannette. Have you ever got her to change her mind about anything?"

"She'll have to listen to reason."

"You're going to have to knock her down and sit on her."

Mary Beth's eyebrows collided in a frown. "Only if absolutely necessary," she said, standing up. "Are you coming?"

•   •   •

Barbaraannette had the briefcase in hand and the front door open when Mary Beth's silver-gray Lincoln glided up to the curb. Mary Beth was driving. Toagie sat beside her. Suppressing an urge to duck back into the house and lock the door, Barbaraannette went straight to her car, tossed the briefcase on the passenger seat, and climbed in. Mary Beth got out of the Lincoln and started toward her. Barbaraannette locked the door and started the car.

Mary Beth knocked on the window.

Barbaraannette hesitated, momentarily held in thrall by her big sister's commanding gaze.

"Barbaraannette, we have to talk. I won't let you do this," Mary Beth shouted through the glass.

"I don't have time for this," Barbaraannette muttered to herself. She set her jaw and dumped the clutch. The car shot backward out of the driveway, sending Mary Beth staggering, falling onto her rear on the wet brown grass. Barbaraannette shifted into first and took off, catching a glimpse of Toagie's wide eyes as she rocketed past the Lincoln. A glance in the rearview showed Mary Beth back on her feet, running toward her car, nearly getting hit by a little red car that had come racing around the corner.

Barbaraannette hunched her shoulders and accelerated. She would not look back again.

"Pookie?" Phlox whispered.

"What?"

"What's that I feel pressing up against me?"

"What d'you think?"

"You got a funny sense of timing, Pook."

"I guess I've been missing you."

"I got a bad feeling. He's talking to himself again."

They could hear André's voice from the front seat, muttering.

"I think he's crazy, Pook."

"No shit."

"What was that stuff he was talking last night? That was definitely crazy. I don't think he's gonna let us go, Pook."

"Barbaraannette's gonna pay him. She has to."

"I don't think that matters anymore. Do you know what I think we should do? Next time he opens this trunk we should just run. Take off fast and hope he doesn't shoot us."

"He'll shoot us."

"Better that than listen to another lecture. You know something, Punky? Ever since this whole thing started you've been acting kinda wussy. Where's Bobby Steele, that macho man I knew back in Tucson?"

"He's in a trunk half starved with a woman won't shut up."

Phlox did not reply for several seconds. André's muttering faded, but they could hear him moving around, clearing his throat.

She said, "What's he doing?"

"I dunno." Bobby sniffed. "Do you smell cheese?"

André spread a slice of Wisconsin Saga Bleu Cheese onto a cracker with a plastic knife. He set the knife on the dashboard and, balancing the cracker on his fingertips, took a delicate bite and chewed thoughtfully. He could hear the man and woman whispering in the trunk. Probably discussing some of the ideas he had introduced to them last night. He smiled, shaking his head. Those two were no more equipped to understand structural analysis than most freshmen. At best, they would retain a word or two of terminology, and the next time they heard someone using structuralism to support an argument, they would be a word or two closer to comprehension. This was his goal as a teacher. It was all one could reasonably hope to achieve.

"I do what I can," he said to his cracker.

The Taxidermy & Cheese Shoppe occupied one of Cold Rock's choicest locations, a high knoll just off the highway at the north end of town. From the parking lot, André had a commanding view of the surrounding area. Anyone leaving town would have to pass across his field of view. Turning his head in the other direction he could see downtown Cold Rock, including four of the six bridges. It was the perfect spot from which to engineer a ransom payment. He had the view and a pay phone on the outside wall, and the cheese was not bad either.

André was on his third cracker when he saw a blue car cross one of the bridges. The car followed the river road to the next bridge, then crossed the river again. The passenger side door was brown. André smiled. "Very good, Mrs. Quinn." He returned his attention to the first bridge, where he spotted a small red car and, a few moments later, a long silver car.

For two minutes, André lost sight of them, then the procession reappeared on the northernmost bridge. The blue car with one brown door. The red car a few car lengths back, and twenty seconds later the silver car. André frowned as he prepared another cracker. This was not how things were supposed to go.

Kum & Go, a convenience store and gas station chain, had opened its Cold Rock store five years ago, shortly after Bobby had disappeared. Barbaraannette had always been somewhat offended by the name. She preferred to buy her chips and fuel at the Pump-n-Munch at the other end of town, but this was no time to be persnickety. She pulled up to the pumps nearest the door and got out, lugging the briefcase. She fitted the gas nozzle into her tank and started pumping. She did not see André Gideon anywhere, but a few moments later Mary Beth pulled up in her Lincoln and parked at the next pump.

She rolled down her window. "Barbaraannette!"

"Go away. You're going to get Bobby killed."

"I doubt that. You are not being rational, Barbaraannette."

"How is that any of your business?"

"I'm your sister, dear."

"That's your problem." Barbaraannette watched the numbers roll over on the gas pump. "What are you going to do? Tie me up? Call the police again?"

Mary Beth clicked her teeth. "I'm coming with you," she said. "Toagie and I are coming with you."

Barbaraannette said, "I don't think so." She racked the pump nozzle.

"This man won't dare do anything with the three of us there."

Barbaraannette ignored her, went into the store and paid the cow-faced man behind the counter. She asked him if there were any messages for her.

"Messages?" The man mooed, blinking enormous brown eyes.

The telephone behind the counter rang.

"That might be for me," said Barbaraannette. The clerk answered, frowned, handed her the phone.

"Once again you have betrayed me," said André Gideon. "Shall I simply kill your husband now, or would you like to talk about it?"

"I haven't betrayed you. I've done everything you asked."

"You are not alone. You were followed."

"My sisters. I told them not to."

"I counted two vehicles following you. A big silver car and a very small red car."

"Oh." She had noticed the red car back in town, but had thought nothing of it. "My sisters are in the silver car. I don't know about the other one."

"You will have to get rid of them."

"I can do that. Then what?"

"Do you know where Miller's Road is?"

"Sure."

"Once you have eluded your pursuers, you will take Miller's Road west to the Sorenson Lake boat landing, where you will turn around and drive back toward Cold Rock. This will permit both of us to ascertain that you are not being followed. If all is well, we will proceed."

"Proceed how?"

"When you see a white paper bag in the middle of the road, you will throw the briefcase out of your car and continue driving. Once I have confirmed that the money is all there, I will call you at your home to tell you where to find your husband. You will do as I say, or you will not see your husband alive." The phone went dead.

Barbaraannette hung up but kept her hand on the phone. "Mind if I make a quick call?" she asked the clerk.

The cow man shrugged his assent. Barbaraannette dialed the phone, looking out the window. Toagie was pumping gas into Mary Beth's car. Mary Beth remained behind the wheel.

The phone rang. "Where do you keep the sugar?" she asked the clerk.

"We have brown and white and powdered," the man said, pointing at one of the shelves.

Barbaraannette nodded, listening to the telephone. On the third ring she got an answer.

"Cold Rock Savings & Loan."

"Sally? It's Barbaraannette. Could I talk to Art, please?"

Toagie came to a decision. She would finish doing this one last thing for Mary Beth, pumping her gas for her, and that was it. If Mary Beth wanted to keep following Barbaraannette she could do it alone. Barbaraannette could take care of herself, and so could Mary Beth, and so could she, for that matter. Mary Beth could pump her own fleeping gas from now on.

Toagie's mouth tilted in a smile, trying to picture it. No, Mary Beth would never pump her own gasoline. She would always find someone to do it for her.

The pump clicked off. Barbaraannette came out of the store carrying the briefcase in one hand and a pink box of C&H sugar in the other. She walked directly up to Toagie, her jaw set.

Toagie said, "This wasn't my idea."

Barbaraannette nodded. "I know. Excuse me." She tore open the box of sugar, and poured it into the gas tank. Most of the sugar spilled down the side of Mary Beth's car, but a fair amount went down the pipe.

"You think I got enough in?" Barbaraannette asked.

Toagie smiled. "I think so. I don't know how much it takes."

"It ought to slow you down, anyways." Barbaraannette tossed the empty carton into the trash barrel, returned to her car, and drove off. Toagie replaced the gas cap and got back into the Lincoln.

Mary Beth asked, "What did she just do?"

"She just told us to stay put."

Mary Beth wrinkled her nose. "Not likely," she said, turning the ignition key.

44

"Are you going to lunch already?" Sally asked.

"Just out," said Art. He didn't trust himself to look at her.

"When will you be back?" she asked.

"I don't know." Just go to the car, start it, get it moving. There are times to think and times to do. If he thought too hard about what he was doing he would do nothing at all.

The trees looked different in daylight. It took André ten minutes of driving back and forth on Miller's Road to find the overgrown entrance to the logging road where they had attempted to bury Jayjay. André drove up the rutted dirt path until his way was blocked by a fallen elm tree. He got out and jogged quickly back to Miller's Road, carrying the white paper bag that read *Taxidermy & Cheese Shoppe*. When he reached the road he concealed himself behind cedar bush and waited.

Barbaraannette took the highway south to Miller's Road, pulled over and parked on the shoulder just before the intersection. Miller's Road ran west from Easton Creek and continued thirty miles through a checkerboard of rocky farmland and state forest to Highway 169. Because of its many twists and turns and roller-coaster hills and wooded pullouts, it was a favorite with local teenage drivers.

The little red car zoomed past her—she recognized Hugh Hulke in the passenger seat. It disappeared over the top of a rise. Seconds later, she saw the top of the red roof peek up over the rise on the other side of the road. Barbaraannette watched her rearview mirror, waiting. Five minutes later a gray Plymouth appeared, slowing as it approached. Barbaraannette waited until she could recognize Art Dobbleman's face. She waved, put her car in gear, and turned onto Miller's Road. Art followed. A quarter mile up the road, as she topped the first hill, Barbaraannette caught a glimpse of the red car coming up behind Art.

"Who's that?"

"I dunno."

"What's he doing? Go around him!"

Rodney veered to the left, trying to pass, but the man in the Plymouth swerved in front of him.

"He won't let me by."

Hugh reached over and leaned on the horn. Rodney batted his arm away. "Jesus Christ, Hugh. Lemme drive, would you?"

"Go around him! You want to lose her?"

"I'm trying!" The Plymouth, in the middle of the road, had slowed to a crawl.

"Now! Punch it!"

Rodney punched it. The Isuzu groaned and slowly began to pick up speed. Rodney faked a move to the left, then, as the Plymouth moved left to intercept, wrenched the wheel to the right. They were suddenly abreast, both cars accelerating, the undersized four-cylinder engines clattering and moaning.

Hugh leaned across Rodney's lap and gave the guy the finger. "Up yours, asshole!" he shouted.

Rodney flailed at Hugh with his elbow, swerving onto the shoulder, then back onto the roadway. "F'Chrissakes, what are you—" He swerved again, this time to avoid hitting the guy in the Plymouth. "—Jesus! You trying to get us killed? I—shit!" He steered the car toward the shoulder again. "—The guy's a maniac. What's he think he's—" The Plymouth slowly pulled ahead, then cut in front of him and abruptly slowed. Rodney stood on the brake pedal; Hugh slid forward, his knee smashing into the glovebox. Rodney grappled with the wheel, tromped on the accelerator, managed to pass the maniac on the left. Hugh was gasping in pain. Rodney said, "Look what you did to the car, man!"

The door of the glovebox was crushed. Hugh, agonized and gripping one knee, looked back. "You better hit it, Rod Man, he's right behind us."

"I'm going! I'm going! This thing don't go all that fast, man. Jesus Christ. My wife is gonna kill me."

"Here he comes again." Hugh leaned over the back of his seat.

"What are you doing?"

"I'm getting my goddamn shotgun. I–oh, shit."

"What?"

The Plymouth slammed into the rear bumper. Hugh's seatback collapsed, sending him sprawling into the back; the Isuzu careened across the opposite lane and onto the far shoulder. Rodney wrenched the wheel to the right. The Isuzu spun three hundred sixty degrees and came to rest on the right shoulder.

The Plymouth pulled over ten yards ahead, the reverse lights came on, dust exploded from beneath its front wheels and it headed toward them, picking up speed. Rodney covered his face with his arms. The Plymouth smashed into them, sending the Isuzu lurching back a few yards. Hugh, still tangled up in the back seat, let out a howl of rage. The Plymouth drove forward a few yards, then stopped. Rodney pressed on the gas pedal and tried to turn the steering wheel, but his efforts produced only a metallic shriek, and then the engine died.

André remained hidden as Barbaraannette Quinn drove by in her blue car. He waited, watching, but no other cars appeared. Good. Everything was going according to plan once again. She would drive to the landing, another couple miles, then drive back. She would throw out the money, he would retrieve it, get rid of the couple in his trunk, and head for the airport. He would be rich and free, and he would be Adam Grappelli. He walked out to the center of the road, placed the weighted *Taxidermy & Cheese Shoppe* bag on the centerline, then returned to his hiding place.

Art stared into his rearview mirror at the mangled front end of the Isuzu, his hands dancing on the steering wheel. He'd done it! He'd stopped them. This was better than winning a race. Better than bumper cars at the fair. He wanted to do it again. Maybe he should, just for the hell of it. The back end of his car was ruined anyway. Had he hit them hard enough? They weren't moving. His heart rate had to be up over two hundred. He felt great.

Someone in the Isuzu was moving around. The door opened. Was that Hugh Hulke? Art turned his head. It was Hugh all right, with something in his hands—a shotgun! Art dropped the gearshift into drive and stomped on the accelerator, ducking his head as low as he could. He heard a shot, then a second shot and suddenly his car was traveling in a slightly different direction, one tire blown. He cranked the wheel to the left, trying to stay on the road, but he overcompensated and the car spun into the ditch. A third shot shattered the rear window. Art scrambled out the passenger door and, keeping his head low, took off running.

"She's gonna kill me," Rodney moaned.

Hugh pumped a fresh shell into the shotgun and aimed, but the guy had disappeared over the top of the hill.

Rodney climbed slowly out of the car. "You might just as well shoot me, Hugh. Just shoot me now."

"Don't tempt me," Hugh growled.

"Look at her car, man. Would you look what he done to it?"

"Yeah, yeah, it's history. Big fucking deal." He started toward the Plymouth. "C'mon, Rod Man, we got work to do. Lets just hope the guy's got a spare in his trunk."

Rodney didn't move. "Just shoot me now."

"Shut up."

"I'm dead."

Hugh raised the shotgun and aimed it at Rodney's belt buckle. "Okay then."

"Wait!" Rodney screeched, crossing his hands over his groin. "I was kidding."

"All right then. C'mon, let's get this thing on the road."

Following instructions, Barbaraannette drove to the landing at Sorenson Lake, turned around, and headed back, looking for a white paper bag.

She had really started something. The strange thing was that even now she did not really regret it, at least not yet. An important and not altogether pleasant chapter of her life was about to come to a close. No matter how it ended, her life would go on. She hoped that several lives would go on. She hoped Art was okay. She hoped that Bobby was okay, and Phlox, and that nobody would die on account of her one foolish moment in front of the TV cameras. Except maybe this André Gideon.

Barbaraannette drove slowly, watching the road. A white plastic bag in some bushes caught her eye; she stopped. The bag was in shreds. The man had specified a paper bag on the road, not a plastic bag in the brush. She continued on. Less than one mile farther down the road she came upon a white bag, bright with menace, standing upright in the precise center of the roadway.

45

"*Where do you think we are, Pook?*"

"In the woods someplace. It sounded like we were driving slow over leaves and sticks. I can hear birds."

"He's been gone a long time."

"You miss him?"

"Not much . . . what are you doing, Pookie?"

"What do you think?"

"Seems to me you're tugging at my belt buckle."

"I got one free hand, I figured I'd use it."

"I don't have any raincoats, honey."

"We're probably dead anyways."

"You've got a point there. Let me just shift around here. Oh! You really do have a point!"

"I just couldn't resist you no longer."

"You really think we can do this?"

"Why not? I did it once in the back seat of a VW bug, wasn't even this much room."

The woman rolled to a stop on the opposite shoulder. André clenched his teeth. She was not supposed to stop, she was supposed to simply throw the money out and continue on her way. He thought he had been quite clear.

For a few seconds she sat in the car, then got out carrying the briefcase. She walked over to the paper bag and looked inside. André, twenty yards away, considered shooting her, but he was not entirely sure he could hit her at that distance.

She straightened up and looked around, looking straight at him for a moment but not seeing him in the brush. She returned to her car, rested the briefcase on the hood and stood there waiting.

After a minute she shouted, "I have your money here!" She lifted the briefcase and thumped it on the side. "You want it, you bring Bobby to me."

André cleared his throat and raised his voice. "I am pointing a gun at you, Mrs. Quinn. Leave the briefcase by the side of the road and drive away."

She turned toward him, peered into the brush. "No. You show me Bobby."

"If you do not do as I say, I will shoot you."

"No Bobby, no money."

André cocked the gun and took careful aim, placing the sights dead center on the woman's midriff. He stroked the trigger with his forefinger, wondering whether he could hit her. If he missed, she might panic and flee with the money. She must have felt the danger, because she brought the briefcase in front of her and hugged it. André considered his options. A new, even more brilliant plan asserted itself. Perhaps this could work out to his advantage. He could lure her up to his car, take the money, and leave her there with her precious husband. André's mouth tightened in a grim smile. Beware your desires, Mrs. Quinn. Of course, he would have to kill them all. He would simply take the woman's car to the airport. It might be days before they were found. The solution struck him as elegant, efficient, and inevitable.

He stepped out where she could see him.

"Mrs. Quinn?" He pointed up the overgrown logging road. "Your husband is up there, in my car. If you will accompany me, I will take you to him."

André Gideon was smaller than she had imagined him. Barbaraannette kept the briefcase in front of her and her eyes on the gun.

"Are you coming?" he asked.

"You bring Bobby here, to me." She did not want to follow this man into the woods.

André scowled and walked toward her. When he was a few feet away he raised the revolver and pointed it at her face.

"If you do not come with me, I will kill you here and now and take the money and take your car and your husband and his friend will likely die of thirst in the trunk of my car."

Barbaraannette looked at the gun, at his small white hands. "How far is it?"

"Not far."

Barbaraannette took a breath. "All right. I'll come with you, but you go first."

"We will go together." André gestured with the revolver.

Barbaraannette crossed Miller's Road, walking sideways, keeping her eyes on André, holding the briefcase between them. They entered the logging road side by side, watching each other, walking like a pair of mating sand crabs.

"I know who you are," Barbaraannette said.

"No you do not."

"Everybody knows who you are. You're André Gideon. You teach at the college."

"You are wrong on both counts. I am no longer with the college, and my name is now Adam Grappelli." He stopped. "Mrs. Quinn, why have you created all this trouble for me?"

"Me? I'm not making any trouble."

"I disagree. You made a perfectly straightforward offer to pay one million dollars for your husband's safe return, is that not true? Yet you refused to pay me."

"That's not true. I was ready to write you a check."

"You involved the police."

"No. That wasn't me. My sister did that."

"Even now you refuse to give me the money."

"I have it right here. I just want to make sure about Bobby."

"Yes. You want your precious husband." He began walking again. "May I make an observation? The man is no great prize."

"I know what he is." They continued up the road. Barbaraannette saw the reflection of sunlight on glass. The green Taurus. They both stopped. "What's that noise?" Barbaraannette asked. The car was squeaking. They moved closer. It was visibly shaking. Barbaraannette turned to André, or Adam, or whoever he was, and found herself once again staring into the barrel of his revolver.

"Your husband and his little friend are in the trunk, Mrs. Quinn." He laughed. "I believe they may be trying to escape."

Barbaraannette edged forward, getting herself between André and the car, still holding up the briefcase.

André said, "Put the briefcase down, please."

Barbaraannette shook her head. "You let him out first."

"You can let him out yourself."

Barbaraannette backed up until her hip touched the car, felt it shaking. She banged her palm on the trunk lid and raised her voice. "Bobby? Is that you?"

The shaking stopped.

"Barbie?"

André was smiling, a weird light in his eyes. "You see? Now set the briefcase down, please."

Barbaraannette did not like the look on the man's face. Something was wrong with him. He was a man about to do a terrible thing. She sidled to her left, holding the briefcase out as a shield.

"Mrs. Quinn, you are trying my patience. Put it down, please."

Barbaraannette shook her head, her eyes locked on the gun. She saw his finger tighten an instant before the flash and boom reached her senses.

All Art knew to do was to run. First, to run away from Hugh Hulke and his shotgun; second, to find Barbaraannette. She was somewhere ahead of him. She was supposed to meet the man on this road, but Art did not know whether it would be a hundred yards or ten miles, or farther. All he knew was to run. If he came upon her, then perhaps he would know to do something else.

The sound of leather soles slapping tarmac, the chuffing of his breath, the shockwaves traveling up through his skeleton. Faster, he commanded. The tempo increased. How far had he run? Two miles? Three? He could run harder, but without knowing how long he would have to continue, he settled into a seven-minute pace, six strides per breathing cycle, stretching out on the downhills, shortening his stride on the uphills, coming up over each rise with new hope. He had been running for twenty minutes when he rounded a bend and saw Barbaraannette's car parked on the shoulder a quarter of a mile ahead.

Art slowed, his head swiveling left and right, looking for Barbaraannette. He tried to run silently, his senses keyed to any sound or movement. Other than the car, all he saw was a white paper bag in the middle of the road. He kept moving. Where was she? He heard a muffled explosion—a gunshot? He stopped, trying to locate its source. A second shot came to his ears, ahead and to the right. Art picked up his pace, running flat out now, refusing to let his mind form an image.

The first shot hit the briefcase dead center, knocking it out of her hands into her chest; she bounced off the side of the car and fell to the ground. The second slug cut a trough across her left thigh, ripping through denim and flesh. Barbaraannette howled, grabbed the briefcase by the handle and hurled it at André. The corner struck his forehead; he staggered back, recovered, aimed the revolver at her again and pulled the trigger.

The hammer came down, but the gun did not fire. André pulled the trigger again with the same result. He threw the gun aside, and started toward Barbaraannette, his face a mask of rage. He hadn't needed a gun to deal with young Jayjay, he would not need one for this woman.

Barbaraannette scrambled to her feet, feeling the pain in her thigh as from a distance.

"You shot me," she said. She spread her arms and took a step toward him. "Do you know what I'm going to do to you?"

André stopped. He could see all of her teeth and nails and—he suddenly realized—he had no weapon at all, not even a chair leg. He glanced down at the briefcase, grabbed it by the handle and fled back toward Miller's Road.

• • •

Art spotted an opening in the trees, an old logging road, fresh tracks in the soft earth. He veered toward it, had just stepped off the shoulder when he came face-to-face with a man running in the opposite direction. Art took in the man's face, and the familiar briefcase. Without slowing he closed his hand and dropped his shoulder and brought all of his momentum into a single roundhouse blow. He aimed for the chin, but the man ducked and Art's fist caught him directly on the nose.

It was good enough. The guy went down, flat on his back, and lay there without moving. The briefcase continued on without him, tumbling end over end, coming to a rest in a clump of bramble.

Art kept running, air ripping through his lungs. He heard something farther up the trail—voices?

He saw the car first, then Barbaraannette standing behind it, looking into the trunk making a peculiar gasping sound. Was she sobbing? Art slowed and tried to control his breathing. Scanning the surrounding woods. The man might have an accomplice. He saw no one else. As he approached, he realized that Barbaraannette was not exactly crying. She was laughing.

He called out her name.

She looked up. "Art?" Her face displayed a collision of emotions—laughter, fear, relief, and agony. One leg of her jeans was stained dark with blood.

"You okay?" he said, stupidly.

Barbaraannette nodded, pointing into the trunk of the Taurus. Art came up beside her, swung an arm around her shoulders, looked where she was pointing. Wedged into the trunk was Bobby Quinn, his pants pulled down to his knees, his very white, slightly pimpled ass pointing directly at them. Attached to Bobby's front side was a blond woman, her blue leather skirt hiked up around her waist.

"I do believe they're stuck in there," said Barbaraannette.

"You damn right we're stuck. Are you gonna help us out or not?" Bobby said.

"Who is she?" Art asked Barbaraannette.

"My name's Phlox," said Phlox. "And I claim the reward. I found him and I brought him and I found him again."

Art frowned. He couldn't help asking, "How on earth did you get into that position?"

"It's a long story," Bobby growled.

Art shook his head in bewilderment. He took a closer look at Barbaraannette's wound. "He shot you?"

"It's just a flesh wound." Barbaraannette winced at his touch. "I always wanted to say that."

Bobby said, "Hey! How about a hand here?"

Barbaraannette's mouth twitched. She put one hand on the trunk lid, winked at Art, and slammed it shut.

"Hey! Hey!" Bobby's muffled pleas were barely intelligible.

"Let's go," she said. "Is my car still out there?"

"It was last I saw."

"I thought maybe he had taken it."

"If he's a smallish man with a beard, I don't think so. Can you walk?"

"I can limp if you'll give me a hand."

Art put his arm around her and they started down the road.

"Thanks for coming," Barbaraannette said.

"It's all part of Cold Rock Savings & Loan's customer appreciation program."

"I'll have to throw more business your way."

"We appreciate that. By the way, not that it's any of my concern, but how long are you going to leave them like that?"

Barbaraannette laughed. "I don't know. What do you think? Another couple hours? I'll call Dale Gordon, tell him where they—" She gasped; her leg collapsed but Art held her up. "Just a twinge," she said.

Art bent over and put one arm behind her knees and picked her up.

Barbaraannette said, "You can't carry me."

"The hell I can't." He moved down the logging road at a brisk walk.

"I guess maybe you can."

The road and the unconscious André Gideon came into view at the same time. Barbaraannette asked, "What happened to him?"

"I ran into him. I—hey!"

"What?"

"I—oh, damn, damn, damn. My briefcase, Barbaraannette . . . your money, it's gone!"

46

"*Open it up! Open it up! I wanna look. C'mon, Rod Man!*"

They were traveling west in Art Dobbleman's Plymouth, Hugh behind the wheel. Rodney was trying to figure out the latches on the briefcase. His hands were shaking so hard he couldn't work them.

"Push the end," Hugh said. "Push in on the end."

"I'm trying! The damn thing's locked."

The right wheel dropped onto the shoulder, Hugh muscled the car back onto the roadway. Rodney said, "Why don't you pull over, man, you're bouncing me all over the place."

"I'm not slowing down till we hit Montana."

"Montana?" This was the first Rodney had heard about Montana. "What are you talking about, Montana?"

"We buy ourselves a ranch, Rod Man. That son of a bitch Bobby's gonna buy us a ranch after all. It's what you call justice."

Rodney grunted. He had his pocketknife out and was hacking at the leather around the clasp.

Hugh said, "And you want to be as far away from your old lady as possible when she finds her car, right?"

"You got that right."

They had traveled seventy-three miles in the general direction of Montana when Rodney finally cut through enough leather and pressed wood to rip the top off the briefcase. He looked inside, blinked rapidly, and produced a sound that fell somewhere between a whimper and a moan. Hugh glanced over, then looking equally stunned took his foot off the accelerator and let the car drift to a stop. He did not even bother to pull off the road.

Using several bungee cords from Barbaraannette's trunk, Art attached the unconscious André Gideon to a nearby poplar tree. "This won't hold him long, but it should keep him until the police get here."

Barbaraannette said, "You think Hugh and Rodney took the briefcase?"

"I don't know who else it could've been." They crossed the road to the car, Barbaraannette limping. Art said, "Want me to drive?"

Barbaraannette handed him the keys. Art opened the door for her and helped her in. She could not remember ever having been a passenger in her own car. She watched him get in the other side and adjust the seat and put on his seatbelt. His big hands made the steering wheel look tiny.

"I'm taking you to the Medical Center," he said, starting the car.

"No, you're taking me home."

"I am?"

"I mean, I'd rather go home."

Art looked over at Barbaraannette's leg, frowning. "I know it's just a flesh wound, but don't you want to have it looked at?"

"I'm looking at it. It's just a bruise with a little furrow cut through. When I was a Crockette I hurt myself worse sliding into second base."

Art was about to argue, but caught himself. It was enough that she was letting him drive her car.

A couple miles down the road they came upon an abandoned red Isuzu with a mangled front end. "There's the car they were in. My car's not where I left it. They must've changed the tire and got it started. I bet they stopped when they saw your car, and found the briefcase." He slowed as they passed the Isuzu.

Barbaraannette said, "What did you do? Smash into them?"

"They didn't want to stop," Art said with a note of pride.

"I wonder if they've looked in the briefcase yet."

"I'd like to see that." He turned onto the highway. When they passed the Kum & Go, Art let up on the gas and said, "Isn't that your sister?"

Barbaraannette slunk down in her seat. "Keep driving." She giggled. Art wasn't sure what was so funny, but he laughed, too.

Rodney fished out another paper. "Listen to this. 'My Dad, by Adam Berg.' It says, 'My Dad is big. My Dad is strong and he can beat up other kids Dads and he can drink a whole case of beer. That is what Dad can do. My Dad.' You think that's about George Berg?"

Hugh scowled. "How the fuck should I know?" They were still heading west in Art Dobbleman's Plymouth, destination unknown.

"George has a kid, doesn't he?"

"Would you just throw that shit out the window?"

"And he's always getting in fights."

"Christ, Rod Man, just toss it, would you? There's no money in there. We been scammed. All we got's two wrecked cars."

"We got this car."

"Yeah, and it's not ours."

Rodney shrugged and began reading another paper. There were hundreds of them. Essays and worksheets and old tests. Thousands, all written by little kids. "You ever think of having kids?"

"How am I s'posed to have a kid? My wife divorced me."

"I think about it a lot."

"You're a goddamn idiot."

"Yeah, I know. Hey, listen to this one."

Hugh grabbed the paper out of Rodney's hand and threw it out the window. He pulled over, got out, grabbed the open briefcase and threw it on the road. He got back in the car and resumed driving.

Rodney said, "Well now, that was pretty childish."

"Screw you," said Hugh.

While Barbaraannette was in the bathroom cleaning and bandaging her flesh wound, Art called the police and told them where to find

André Gideon. At Barbaraannette's request, he neglected to mention the location of the Ford Taurus. He had just hung up when Barbaraannette limped back into the kitchen. She had changed into a pair of soft khaki slacks and a white cotton sweater.

Art said, "They want us to come down to the police station."

"Now?"

"I'm sure it can wait. You look nice. No one would guess you'd just been shot."

Barbaraannette smiled. "You want a cup of coffee?"

Art nodded, then shook his head. "You wouldn't have a beer in the house, would you?"

"I might just have two." Barbaraannette found two cans of Budweiser in the refrigerator—Phlox's leftovers. They sat at the kitchen table holding their cold cans of beer and looking at each other.

Art said, "So."

"So?"

"All that trouble to get Bobby back here and you're just going to leave him in that trunk?"

Barbaraannette shrugged. "I'll let the police know. Later. Right now I'm kind of enjoying thinking about him being stuck in there. If it wasn't for poor Phlox being in there with him, I might leave it go till morning."

Art grinned. "You're a cold, hard woman, Barbaraannette."

"I'm an ice queen." She tasted her beer. "It was pretty weird, seeing him again. I don't know what I expected." She took a long swallow, feeling the icy liquid tumble down her throat. "I didn't know what I would do, what I would feel. I couldn't even imagine why I wanted him, but I did want him. And then there he was, stuck in that trunk with his pimply ass in the air and I just wasn't interested. He's losing his hair now, did you notice?"

"I didn't look that close." In fact, he had hardly been able to look at all.

"I saw him and all the want just disappeared." Her eyes lost focus for a moment, then she smiled and slowly shook her head. "I wonder if I knew that would happen?"

Art was watching the little things happening on her face: the way the remarkable blue in her eyes intensified for a split second every time she blinked; the faint quiver of her upper lip that preceded each string of words; the flash of her tongue between her teeth. Her hand was only ten or twelve inches away from his. He could reach across the table and take it and she wouldn't pull away. Sometime soon he would do that. There was no hurry now.

She said, "Did you ever want something for such a long time that when you finally got it you'd used up all your want of it?"

Art nodded—not because he had ever experienced such a thing, but just to keep her talking. He had wanted Barbaraannette forever, it seemed, and his feelings were in no way diminished now. He could not imagine not wanting her. But now, for the first time, he could imagine having her.

She said, "I remember once when I was a little girl I spent a whole summer thinking about going to the Isanti County Fair so I could get a corndog because I'd had one the year before and I thought it was the best thing I'd ever tasted. Then when the fair finally came I went to the corndog place and the man selling them was really old and ugly and the skin on his arms was flaky and the smell of the hot grease was so strong that I bought the corndog but I couldn't take a bite so I gave it to Toagie. Then we went on the Tilt-a-Whirl and she puked it up."

Art could see she was being serious, but he couldn't help asking, "Bobby is the corndog?"

Barbaraannette gave him a startled look, then started laughing. They were still laughing when the phone began to ring. They watched it for five or six rings.

"I suppose I'd better," Barbaraannette said. She picked up the handset and said, "Hello?"

"Barbaraannette? This is your sister."

Barbaraannette flinched. "Oh. Mary Beth, I'm sorry about your car!"

"Yes, well, you should be. Antonia and I are still where you abandoned us, waiting for the tow truck. But that's not why I'm calling. I just this moment spoke with Dr. Cohen at Crestview. To say that he was apoplectic would be to understate the case by several orders of magnitude, dear. The poor man could hardly get a word out."

"What happened?"

"Apparently mother has stolen another car."

"The Porsche again?"

"Dr. Cohen's Porsche is in the shop as a result of Hilde's last adventure. No, this time she borrowed a Mercedes-Benz, which, unfortunately, also belongs to Dr. Cohen. The poor man is beside himself."

Holding back laughter, Barbaraannette said, "I suppose we'd better go find her."

"Yes you should. Your sister and I are otherwise occupied, no thanks to you."

"Don't you want to know what happened with Bobby?"

"Since you did not want our help, I thought it better not to ask. You are alive, presumably?"

"I'm fine, and so is Bobby, more or less."

"And are you one million dollars poorer?"

Barbaraannette smiled. "No Mary Beth, I'm not. And I'm finished with Bobby Quinn."

"That's good, dear. Here comes the tow truck."

Barbaraannette hung up the phone. "Hilde's taken another joyride," she said to Art. "I have to go find her."

"Would you like some company?"

"You know what I'd really like? Would you take the money back to the bank? It makes me nervous to have it here in the house."

"I don't blame you. Where is it?"

Barbaraannette stood up. "In a grocery bag in the closet in the spare bedroom."

Art followed, watching the way her body moved inside her clothes. Barbaraannette opened the bedroom door and went rigid. Clothing and shoes were strewn on the floor and on the bed. Dresser drawers hung open. She ran to the closet, looked inside, turned an anguished face to Art.

"Are you sure, Mrs. Grabo?"

"Yes I'm sure."

"That's eighteen cashmere sweaters, Mrs. Grabo. You want them *all*?"

"They're twenty percent off, right?"

The saleswoman nodded helplessly.

"Then I want them all." Hilde's attention was captured by a display of scarves. The sign on the rack read *Spring Clearance*. She grabbed the woman's sleeve and pointed. "Are all those on sale?"

The saleswoman winced.

"I'll take them all," Hilde said. "They'll make great stocking stuffers. Let's see, I'm going to want them all gift-wrapped."

The saleswoman swallowed, then caught sight of Mr. Himmelman, the manager of Harold's Fashions, watching from the far side of the aisle, half concealed behind a rack of spring coats, motioning to her. He held up a hand and rubbed his thumb and forefinger together, raised his eyebrows.

The saleswoman said, "Mrs. Grabo, excuse me but, how will you be paying?"

Hilde Grabo smiled broadly. "That's not a problem, dear." She reached into her bag and brought out a plastic-wrapped brick of hundred dollar bills, plunked it down on the counter.

47

"Is she still mad?" *Barbaraannette pushed the cap back onto the lipstick* tube. "It's been two days."

Toagie, sitting on Barbaraannette's bed chewing furiously on a piece of Nicorette, shrugged. "You know Mary Beth. She'll get over it. Right now I think she's busy keeping Hilde out of trouble."

"What do you think of these?" Barbaraannette held a pair of dangly earrings up to her ears.

Toagie squinted and pushed out her lower lip. "Not with that necklace."

"I was going to change the necklace."

"The necklace is perfect with that dress."

"I'm not changing the dress." The dress was new, bought specifically for tonight. The saleswoman at Harold's had promised that it would render her date speechless. The plunging neckline alone would probably do it.

"The dress is fleeping awesome." Toagie removed the gum from her mouth and gave it a frowning inspection. "This stuff is awful."

"It'll grow on you." Barbaraannette displayed a set of pearl studs.

"Much better." Toagie stuck the used gum to the instep of her left boot and dug a crumpled pack of Salems out of her purse.

Barbaraannette frowned, shrugged, installed the studs in her earlobes, regarded her reflection. "How does Hilde like living at Mary Beth's?"

"She calls it 'jail,' but I think she's doing fine. Wears a different cashmere sweater every day. That was sweet of you to let her keep them."

Barbaraannette shrugged. "I did it mostly for Harold's, to make up for all the stuff she shoplifted over the last thirty years. Nine thousand dollars' worth of sweaters, scarves, and shoes ought to even the score."

"You've been doing a lot of that." Toagie lit a cigarette. "Evening up the score."

"I can afford to."

"Only I still don't get why you gave that Phlox woman ten grand."

"It just felt right. I figure I'm nine hundred ninety thousand dollars ahead." Barbaraannette smoothed the dress over her hips, turned to check out her backside in the mirror. She liked what she saw. The stress of the past week had caused her to drop a few pounds.

Toagie said, "I haven't seen you looking this hot since you and Bobby got married." She blew smoke toward the ceiling. "You're amazing, B.A. Look at all that leg."

Barbaraannette grinned. "I do look pretty damn good, don't I?"

The doorbell rang.

"It's like in one of those books, Pookie."

"What books are those?" Bobby growled. He had one foot on the dashboard and was picking bits of duct tape adhesive off his boot. He'd been working on his left boot since Des Moines.

"You know. The man goes off to seek his fortune, and all these terrible things happen to him, and in the end he finds out that all he really wanted was what he had to start off with."

"What's that?"

"His true love." Phlox smiled and knocked out shave-and-a-hair-cut on the steering wheel.

"I don't think I ever read that one." Bobby lifted his other foot onto the dashboard and examined both boots. He'd gotten most of the gunk off, but they still looked like hell. He might have to go over them with some turpentine or something.

"It's like, 'You can go home again.' "

"I thought it was 'You can't go home again.' "

Phlox shook her head. "Nope. It's just like in *The Wizard of Oz*. You can go home again, Punkin, and the proof is that that's what we're doing. Going home."

"I think you got something backward." Bobby reached behind Phlox's seat and fished a beer out of the cooler. "You want one?"

"Sure, Pook."

Bobby and Phlox popped open their beers and drove for a while without talking.

"It was nice of her, all things considered, to give me the that money."

"You mean give it to us."

"Actually, Pook, she gave it to me." Phlox giggled. "With conditions attached."

"What conditions are those?"

"We made a deal. She gave me the ten thousand and made me promise to make sure you never ever go back to Cold Rock again. Ever."

"So I'm right, you *can't* go home again."

Phlox shrugged. "What ever." A few miles later she asked, "You think you still got a job?"

"I dunno. What about you?"

"I can deal cards; they'll take me back at the casino."

"*You* can go home again."

"That's right, Punky."

Barbaraannette felt his eyes on her body. The dress was working. The poor man could hardly breathe. He thrust a bouquet of roses at her.

Art had bought some new clothes too: a natural silk sport coat and a pair of tasseled loafers. For a small-town banker this was some wild and crazy stuff. The tie was new, too, she guessed: yellow explosions on a navy blue background. And the haircut. Art had good hair, nice and thick.

Barbaraannette puttered around for a few minutes, putting the flowers in a vase, chatting about the weather, telling him how handsome he looked in his tasseled loafers and his new tie, letting him stand there and watch her, wondering what to do with his hands. She hadn't felt this way since the night she'd convinced Bobby Quinn to propose to her. No, that wasn't quite right. With Bobby she had been making a point. This time, this was something entirely different.

Dear Mr. Keillor,

I recently had the great pleasure of reading your superb book *Lake Wobegon Days.* I, too, am a published author. Perhaps you are familiar with my most recent work, *F. Scott and Papa: Homoeroticism in the Roaring Twenties—A Structuralist Perspective.* I also grew up in a small Midwestern community much like Lake Wobegon, so I feel that you and I have a great deal in common.

As you can see from the return address, I am currently a resident of Stillwater State Prison, where I have been incarcerated after being falsely accused of a crime of which, needless to say (though I feel compelled to say it now), I am not guilty. Prior to reading *Lake Wobegon Days,* I was profoundly depressed. Life in prison is difficult for an educated man such as myself. The inmates here are crude, violent, and unrepentant. My only solace, and the only thing that now keeps me from utter despair, is great books such as yours.

Unfortunately, I am on a very limited budget, as all of my worldly possessions were sold to pay for my unsuccessful defense, and the small amount of money which I receive upon occasion from my ailing mother is as a rule confiscated by my cellmate, Frank Reinke, who refers to it as "rent."

Do you have any copies of any of your other books with which you might be willing to part? I would be most grateful if you could help me through these long, dreary days.

Respectfully,
Your most sincere admirer and
fellow author,
André Edmund Gideon

ACKNOWLEDGMENTS

Thanks to Kate McCarthy of the Minnesota State Lottery for providing me with accurate information, much of which I corrupted to serve Barbaraannette's cause, and thanks to H.B. for helping me move the money.